Praise for Kathryn Walker's

A STOPOVER IN VENICE

"Thoughtful, sympathetic. . . . Walker . . . beautifully describes the bitter decline of the marriage . . . and just as eloquently [the] sweet salvation." —*The Boston Globe*

"Unashamedly romantic . . . but the book's themes are profound and unforgiving." —*San Francisco Chronicle*

"Kathryn Walker's beautifully written story of parallel discovery and restoration is powered by searing insights into the costs of love and loss. Longing leads to the recognition of the 'mysterious gifts concealed in the dark folds of pain.' The results are joyous." —Amy Hempel, author of *Reasons to Live* and *The Dog of the Marriage*

"Tender. . . . Venice is lovely any time of year." —*New York Daily News*

"[Walker] writes with a graceful fluidity that elevates this novel and makes it an immensely enjoyable read." —*Planet*

Kathryn Walker

A STOPOVER IN VENICE

Kathryn Walker attended Harvard University and was the recipient of a Fulbright Fellowship. She has appeared in leading roles on and off Broadway and has received an Emmy Award for her performance in the PBS series *The Adams Chronicles*. She adapted and directed a series of classical Greek productions for the Verse Drama program at the 92nd Street Y and has been an artist in residence at Harvard. She lives in Tesuque, New Mexico, and Washington, Connecticut.

A STOPOVER IN VENICE

A STOPOVER IN VENICE

A novel

KATHRYN WALKER

ANCHOR BOOKS
A Division of Random House, Inc.
New York

FIRST ANCHOR BOOKS EDITION, OCTOBER 2009

Copyright © 2008 by Kathryn Walker

Grateful acknowledgment is made to Alfred A. Knopf for permission to reprint an excerpt from "The Glass of Water" from *The Collected Poems of Wallace Stevens*; copyright © 1954 by Wallace Stevens and renewed 1982 by Holly Stevens. Reprinted by permission of Alfred A. Knopf, a division of Random House, Inc.

The Library of Congress has cataloged the Knopf edition as follows:
Walker, Kathryn.
A stopover in Venice : a novel / by Kathryn Walker.—1st ed.
p. cm.
1. Americans—Italy—Fiction. 2. Women travelers—Fiction. 3. Married women—Fiction. 4. Marital conflict—Fiction. 5. Separation (Psychology)—Fiction. 6. Dogs—Fiction. 7. Dog owners—Fiction. 8. Countesses—Fiction. 9. Venice (Italy)—Fiction. I. Title.
PS3623.A35947 S76 2008
813'.6—dc22   2008012792

Anchor ISBN: 978-0-307-38650-2

Book design by Iris Weinstein

www.anchorbooks.com

Printed in the United States of America
10 9 8 7 6 5 4 3 2 1

Here in the centre stands the glass. Light
Is the lion that comes down to drink. There
And in that state, the glass is a pool.
Ruddy are his eyes and ruddy are his claws
When light comes down to wet his frothy jaws.

— WALLACE STEVENS, "The Glass of Water"

Ah, Giorgione! there are those who mongrelize
And those who heighten anything they touch . . .

— MARIANNE MOORE, "Blessed Is the Man"

A STOPOVER IN VENICE

CHAPTER ONE

Watching the train roll out of the station, picking up speed, it occurred to me that I had been impetuous. Disappearing down the track, within that train, were the only human beings of my acquaintance in northern Italy—in all of Italy, for that matter, if you didn't count Guido, the ingratiating concierge briefly known at our hotel. My husband and his band of not entirely merry men were speeding away to Verona, to Milano, to Bologna, on and on until they would arrive in Roma, the Eternal City, in several weeks' time.

And where was I?

There was no sign that I could see on the narrow platform. It was, I think, the second stop the train had made since leaving Venice. Venezia the beautiful, the sinister, the enchanting city of water and light. Venice, the place I had not remotely experienced in the days I had just spent there. That's how the argu-

ment must have started. My regrets. My regrets dismissed and
so on, until I found myself there, outside the train.

And the argument? I couldn't remember. It hardly mattered; whatever it was, it was the same thing. It's true, isn't it,
that the long dispute that is marriage, for the unlucky anyway,
loses its energy after a few years of failing to reveal much to
anyone? It loses its optimism, its hope of revelation; the whole
thing dissolves into a miasmic pall, a kind of weather. A miserable way to live. The damp penetrates the spaces between, then
gathers and rains down the usual resentments, barely spoken,
of no particular interest to anyone. Neither party seems to
retain much apparent hope or regret, and that in itself is
unbearable. So I couldn't remember how it started, the blank
amnesia of low-level numb despair brought on by these events.
We spoke probably; few words are necessary. I did remember
the familiar sensation of gloom rising and the awful visceral
sense of entrapment that I feel in that sullen climate, as if my
body was trying to conceal itself in back of itself. Also the certain
knowledge that there would be no help found in the present
company. Encircling doom. I would sit in a bitter fog for however long it took to get to Verona. Lovely Verona, no doubt.
Encountered in misery. One more unexperienced destination.

Then something unusual happened. I stood up, stepped over
my husband's long legs, not particularly carefully, dragged
down whatever piece of my luggage was stashed above our
seats, and got off the train.

That, after eight years of marriage, had taken a mere five
minutes, the time required for the train to pull in, halt briefly,
and pull out of the station. How? What desperate, gagged
Ariel in my beleaguered soul had struggled free in this lunge
for the air? And what did Antony think? That I was still on the
train? Sulking in the club car?

The train was gone. The track and the platform were empty; I was standing next to an unoccupied green bench. I was aware of being marooned in every sort of emptiness. My suitcase looked unfamiliar. I felt light-headed and disoriented. The afternoon was blustery and threatening. Lightning actually cracked.

I did not speak Italian.

I pictured myself sitting in the now vanished train and felt like a ghost.

These regrets of mine, the previously mentioned problem with these trips, these tours, rather, was that we went to wonderful places, wonderful cities all over the world. We went, just as we went to Chicago and Cincinnati, and it made not a bit of difference wherever we might happen to be. It would always be a late arrival at an upscale corporate hotel, a five-star something that could be anywhere, room service, sleep, room service, sound check, performance, exhaustion, and moving on—or doing the same thing the next day, with a possible brief interval of shopping or lunch. I was not exhausted because I had nothing to do. Nor did I seem to have the courage to find transportation from a venue miles from the city to explore alone a place I'd never seen. Though I longed to. The being-aloneness of the effort tended to overwhelm the impulse. Or had.

I am not well suited to be a solitary traveler. I'm not gregarious, too cautious, too shy in a way, and had not usually, not ever, done the research necessary to enable me to move swiftly in determined pursuit of places of interest in a huge unfamiliar city. Also, I couldn't see where the pleasure would be. That was what companions were for, no? The whole day before us and what shall we do? Companionship made all things possible, delightful, if I remembered. That was my fantasy anyway, time spent traveling to rise every day like a little cake, a treat to be savored. Companionship. That was the real issue, of course, disguising itself as another sort of deprivation, the deprivation of a glorious city unseen, a city passing by like a smear on the windshield, which had often, in fact, been literally the case. Oh, that was Brussels? I wish it weren't dark.

I wish we could see it together.

Of course that wasn't what we were there to do and I had no right to this self-indulgent resentment. I was free to do whatever I liked but other people were working. If I was so miserable, I could always stay at home and do whatever it is I do there. Or go home, for that matter. Life would go on; I had a credit card.

I had a credit card.

It had begun to rain. I couldn't just stand there for the rest of the day. Alone and palely loitering.

I didn't know the geography of Venice but felt sure I could locate the Gritti Palace Hotel, or someone could do it for me. A Doge's palace. Truly, anciently Venetian. A dream. I would check in; later I would have room service, compose myself for whatever would happen tomorrow, and go to sleep. I did not miss the irony. I crossed the track and hailed the inbound train.

Not much could be viewed of the Grand Canal from the cabin of the water taxi; the windows were curtained and opaque with steam. Outside the cabin door, water was everywhere, the only thing to see, above, below, huge sheets of spray to each side. A high-speed shipwreck, I thought. And then we were there.

The lobby of the Gritti Palace Hotel is neither palatial nor even particularly opulent; it is, as it happens, cozy, small, and wood-paneled. Still, I sensed that one should sweep in here with an excess of expensive luggage and a retainer or two; one should not be alone, apprehensive, and without a reservation. Nevertheless, the desk clerk was charming and welcoming. My single suitcase was not embarrassing and I was dressed in black, the all-purpose disguise. Disguising what?

He was sorry to tell me but the hotel was full, except for one or two small rooms on the side of the building undergoing some renovation. Would that be all right for tonight? He might be able to move me later. So relieved was I by his friend-liness that I thanked him effusively and offered my credit card, saying it would be fine for me and how grateful I was to be able to stay.

It crossed my mind briefly to wonder what this might cost, even the small room. Antony would be disapproving. He would assume one of those disdainful, sour expressions that make even *his* face ugly. To indulge myself in this way! If indulging myself was, in fact, what I was doing. On his money. Unspoken naturally.

And so I was shown to my accommodation. I had to laugh. The room was a cell. Tiny, a narrow bed, pretty furniture apparently, although it was hard to know since the single win-dow was shuttered tight and only a dim lamp illuminated the gloom. The window opened an inch or two, but any attempt to move the shutters was frustrated by scaffolding pressing from the outside. A little five-star cave. No wonder the desk clerk was amused and accommodating. Or perhaps he was sincere about the move, but really, what did it matter? The room had all the features of a hideout, and wasn't that what I was doing, what I'd done? All I seemed to have achieved so far was an extemporaneous flight to a sumptuous little grotto like some decadent eremite on the run. I had no idea what I was doing.

The bed was hard, for which I was grateful. I wanted to wash away the travel film and think. The afternoon was getting on; the rain had stopped. Having come this far, I felt I should at least set foot on the pavements of Venice, glimpse the famous light, but that would require going outside and I lacked the will. I had spent so many hours in hotel rooms, so many hours by myself, laying down my Russian novel and thinking, yes, I am alone, but my enviable husband is out there somewhere and will come back. If only to get his clothes, as had sometimes crossed my mind. The shocking idleness of that life, the waiting, the emptiness, the pointlessness. As if I had been partially paralyzed. There is some sort of wasp, I think, who, already having enough to eat, paralyzes his victims to keep them fresh and immobile, ready and waiting, should his appetite return. A harem must be a similar event.

Antony was in Verona by now. I had his itinerary but he didn't have mine. Was he alarmed? Annoyed? Postponing a reaction until he checked in, worked out, and had dinner? Until he found himself alone in his room, something he can hardly bear? All performers, I suppose, have a double personality, but Antony's seemed extreme. He was so glamorous and engaging onstage, so generous and embracing, boyish in some way but passionate, like a human searchlight throwing its golden beam across the adoring crowd. I myself was still subject to that seduction when I watched from the wings. Here in Italy, a famous writer visiting backstage during a show only last week could hardly be restrained from flinging himself into what he called the "Dionysian heat" of the occasion.

Offstage Antony was another man. By offstage I mean in a place where there was no one left to seduce, no stranger, no reporter, no plumber for that matter, just what I'm tempted to call the trusted few who actually knew him. They were neither trusted nor, I think, did they—we—actually know him. The offstage man shut down like a folded tent. Occasionally his impulse to perform was briefly aroused and he was suddenly, adorably, funny and delightful for no apparent reason, for no one's particular benefit. Otherwise, once the seduction was accomplished, established, indifference set in pretty thoroughly. He was preoccupied, withdrawn, annoyed by attempts at what I have called companionship, and more often than not pretty cranky. Solitary, focused, gathering his energy for the next performance, the next album, the next workout. Those had been my observations, anyway, and I did observe, having not much else to do.

Antony is a star, a big star. He is Antony and never, never, Tony. He is a talented composer, a superb musician; his instrument is the piano, although he can play almost anything and sings very well too. A capacious gift. He has the charisma of the especially endowed as well as the unusually handsome. He set out to have a classical career but his extreme good looks and charm—in addition to his first marriage to a popular although somewhat insane film star—pushed him into crossover mode. Through her connections, he composed several film scores, arty but successful independents, mostly foreign. He appeared briefly in one at last and became—a what? A matinee idol, I suppose. The Richard Burton syndrome, you might say, a great gift diluted but hardly extinguished. His popular career was substantial and international; he played large venues, not concert halls; he was considered hip and a bit edgy, but his classical career was essentially over.

For all of his emotional unavailability, Antony hated to be alone. What he liked was to have someone, me, waiting for him somewhere so he could call from the road or from backstage to complain about other people or, in happier moments, make plans for us that would probably never take place. Antony preferred plans to outcomes. Outcomes tended to bore him. They made him feel trapped.

My growing loneliness in our own particular outcome led me to speculate that our marriage was based on two established principles: familiarity breeds contempt, and absence makes the heart grow fonder. He was nicer when not there. But it had not always been so.

Antony is blond with dark eyes, a fetching combination, while I am dark with pale eyes, not blue but hazel. Reverse in some way, like a photograph and a negative. One of the many ways in which we were opposite. Part of my appeal for Antony, I think, was a return to the idea of his splendid patrimony.

His father, Frederick Casson, handsome and alluring, was a distinguished civil rights attorney of some renown, first in his class at Harvard Law. Although I never knew him, he was also reportedly a narcissist and womanizer; he certainly produced a bevy of ill-adjusted children, left mostly in the care of his several neurotic and neglected wives. Antony's mother, the first wife, was a midwestern beauty of Italian descent, the daughter of a wealthy industrialist, whose nurturing, passionate nature turned venomous and controlling in her isolation. Nevertheless, Cristina believed she had married a prince and her children were royalty, most particularly the gifted Antony. Antony was volatile as a boy, missed much of his schooling, indulged in drugs on and off, and only finally made it through Juilliard, years later, on his native gifts.

Antony had been taught to worship his father and did. He wanted to be him, to have at least the same glorious aura that surrounded him in the family myth. The Harvard part eluded him, until—voilà! There was I, a Harvard graduate with a complement of successful, clever, amusing Harvard friends ready-made to redeem the misstep of that first marriage. All he had to do was devour me. Not such a mistake, that first marriage; it enhanced his celebrity and gave him a daughter. More than I did.

And I? Also a family of progressing alcoholics but from farther down the coast in Baltimore. Also bright, also talented, but with an unfortunate reclusive side residing with deep skepticism next to the brighter false self. Youthful ambitions to be a stage actress, hours spent enacting *Oklahoma* and *Carousel* and every other musical I could find in my parents' collection, although I couldn't sing, was a stage actress, had success, found the exposure strangely embarrassing and could never quite adjust to the gregarious community of players due, no doubt, to the recluse. The recluse had already earned a degree in English literature. These two suspiciously cohabiting personae had both loved a brilliant, kind, witty, self-destructive genius of a man, a writer of startling innovation, another Harvard star, who wrote one greatly acclaimed novel and died at thirty-three in a hiking accident.

Antony and I first met at a party in New York when Nils was still alive but not present, a party of writers and actors, major and minor celebrities. Antony was a bit drunk or high or something and flirted with me. He asked me to leave the party with him, but I declined. I was nevertheless flattered and, like everyone, charmed.

We met again in the Hamptons after Nils's accident and Antony's separation from Natalie. Both more or less at a loss, we fell into each other's arms. We went back to his cottage and built a druidic fire, a sacrificial fire to commemorate the beginning of the new life. We spent the night together, very well, and every night thereafter. We both felt, as people do in the first throes of passion, of love, that we were destined for each other; we had achieved salvation. We married six months later and I disappeared into his life.

The road, the road, the road. City after city, suitcases, passports, trains, planes, buses, limos, hotels, venues, screaming crowds. We had no real home except my small apartment in New York. We didn't need one; every hotel room was perfection, an enchanted zone of privacy. It was exotic and blissful; we floated above the banality of ordinary life; nothing could touch us.

Except time. Time could touch us and did, with the usual icy finger. Ecstasy fades, but one hopes that companionship, that word again, replaces it. Antony was now forty-two and became obsessed with maintaining his beauty. He began to work out compulsively, gave up drinking, gave up eating, gave up fun. He became a new man. A remote man. I was more and more alone, at home or on the road, while he pursued his new obsession. Loneliness and the humiliating sense that my life was being wasted began to gnaw at me. Natalie was with us ceaselessly, worldwide, on the phone, accusing Antony of neglecting Liddie. Neglecting Natalie, I think she meant. I became sullen, feeling neglected myself, and gradually found any discussion of my problem futile since Antony felt beset with obligations. Five years of this. My attempts to talk about our situation, to save this marriage, as they used to say, left me feeling like a beggar. Or a fan. No one of importance.

I had no idea how long I'd been lying on the bed. I knew I'd ordered a bottle of white wine from room service and taken off my clothes. There was still some light, narrow slots of light, dimmer, from the window. But from somewhere outside, just beneath my cave, someone was playing an accordion! The music crept by me upon the waters. How picturesque, Venice after all!

I forced the window open another half inch but the shutters would not relent; I could see nothing. But how delightful, a serenade! And what was that song? So familiar, what was it? In a rush it came back to me. The phantom minstrel under my window was playing, especially for me, the haunting strains of *Perfidia,* a Xavier Cugat favorite, the scratchy records I listened to compulsively as a child. So lush, so melancholy, *To you, my heart cries out perfidia, my heart cries out perfidia, perfidia's won, goodbye!* I could remember myself at seven or eight singing it with fervent passion. This had to be a joke, it was too ridiculous. Just the sort of joke that Nils with his perfect sense of the absurd might invent. Was he down there fingering his celestial accordion?

I sat down on the hard little bed, laughing. If this was not being left in the dark, I didn't know what was. Then the strange day, my strange life—the wine, the song, everything, the dimness of the strange unnerving room—overcame me, and I was suddenly weeping with the desolation of a terrified child.

Striations of light shifted and changed. Resisting, I began to surface; the mysteries of the deep were slipping away as intrusive awareness drew my mind and body back to reclaim our presence on a narrow bed in a strange dark room. Whatever I'd been dreaming fled away, eluding scrutiny like a fish flashing into deep water. I'm always bereft to lose a dream. The dissolving aura lingers, but I come loose from some deep comfort, a sense of being orphaned. I feel abandoned into a diminished world. What it is about that other place that's so consoling?

I don't have much confidence in what's called reality. It seems barren to me in comparison to the riches of the unconscious. Daytime purges the loss, of course; the tribulations of the ego resume unchallenged. One forgets and soldiers along with plans and obligations. But I'm one of those who craves sleep, an oblivion seeker. To lie down and close my eyes is erotic and irresistible. It's fortunate for me that opiates, opiates I'd tried with Antony, made me ill.

The room, the little dim room in Venice. I had to reconnoiter, run through the series of events that had deposited me here: Antony, the train, the station alone, the boat, the Gritti, the song. The song. The tears. No food, just wine. Falling into an exhausted, anxious but uninterrupted sleep. For how long? My watch said seven-thirty. Could I have slept twelve hours? I felt drugged.

Slivers of light from the window looked dim and diffuse this morning. Probably another rainy day. September in the Rain. April in Paris. Where was the accordionist? Silence from the street. No mocking wit out there today. Disoriented and a bit depressed, I determined to arise and go. I would not spend the day in eternal twilight or things could become quite grim.

The desk clerk, the same one, young, good-looking, Guido redux, was expansive again today and seemed thrilled to see me.

Signorina, *buona sera*!

It was after noon.

I don't know how long the signorina will be staying, but tomorrow I am able to move her to a very nice room. On the *canale*. Windows! *Sì?*

Oh, thank you. I don't know how long I'll be staying either, but that would be lovely. I can let you know, perhaps, tomorrow?

Of course, of course. Everything is satisfactory?

Yes, I replied, smiling, liking the slightly ironic tone of this exchange. I like my room very much, very restful.

Yes, yes, of course. Very restful here. Many centuries of rest.

Can you send this fax for me?

Yes, yes, of course. To Verona? You know Verona?

Not at all.

A lovely place.

No doubt.

You are going out?

I thought I would.

The weather is difficult today. May I fetch you an *ombrello*?

That's very kind, thank you.

Tonio! *Un ombrello* for the signorina! Have you a map, Signorina?

Yes, thank you. I had no map but did not wish to appear entirely hopeless.

The *ombrello* arrived, offered by the entrancing Tonio with a dazzling smile. Where did these Italian men come from? I couldn't help wondering how I would be rated by Tonio and the chivalrous desk clerk after my departure. Nevertheless, their attentions improved my spirits. I offered them a little wave and stepped out of the hotel into pelting rain.

I found a guidebook at a nearby bookstore for tourists. One couldn't, however, stand there reading in a monsoon, so I made my way to the Piazza San Marco, head down against the onslaught. I went into one of the ancient cafés, took a table, and tried to concentrate on my book. It was getting late in the season but it was still the season, even in the rain. Florian's was full of what must have been upscale tourists—the prices were amazing—but how awful most of them looked. American style seemed to me like a stigma here, yet they all seemed confident. Confident, but aware somehow in their noisy conviviality that they were exposed.

My own hair was dry, I had Tonio's *ombrello,* but I could feel it rising into a halo of unappealing ringlets from the ubiquitous damp. Hunched over my coffee and book, I tied it back with a hair band. I hoped no one would speak to me. I was wearing black, the same black, and tried to appear unapproachable to any sociably inclined compatriots. I needn't have worried; I went entirely unnoticed. So different from being in the company of a famous person when everyone about is trying covertly to determine if it's really him. Once on a transatlantic flight, when Antony had gone to the bathroom, a flight attendant approached me and asked if I knew *him.* No, I replied, not really.

I couldn't take in the vast store of culture the guidebook offered me; I still felt too dazed and muddled and alone. I didn't wish to encounter this same company in the Accademia or the Doge's Palace and had to resist the impulse to return to my room too soon. I decided to take Tonio's *ombrello* and walk. Walk as far away as I could.

I headed back out of the square the same way I had come, through a narrow passage. It wasn't raining as hard and I could look around. I was on the shopping street I knew from my recent visit; here were the Venetian glass shops, the better ones; here was Prada, and here was the hotel where Antony and I had shared a room the night before last. I cast a furtive glance into the lobby and kept moving. Was Guido there?

The streets became emptier, fewer people but still a tourist area. I saw dogs, serious and businesslike, wearing important collars, fulfilling what appeared to be demanding schedules.

Free dogs. I passed through plazas, crossed bridges, maneuvered narrow passages, and kept walking; the rain was diminishing; I began to feel that I had emerged from the zone of itineraries into what might actually be domestic Venice. I followed the sound of a ravishing countertenor aria into a CD store on a narrow side street and spent half an hour perusing the collection. After experiencing a fair amount of confusion regarding the pretty money, I bought the Vivaldi I had heard on the street.

Back outside I headed farther away, beginning to feel heartened and courageous. By now the rain had stopped. The sky was still gray—no, a faded lavender. Venetian light! I was nearly exhilarated. More plazas—they don't call them that—more tiny passageways, until I saw an impressive large building across a *campo*—I believe that's what they call them—that seemed to be at the edge of the water, the Grand Canal, perhaps not, but as far as I could go in that direction.

A huge banner hung from the façade: THE WORLD OF CASANOVA, it said.

A stately renovated old structure, a palace, probably, but in the gallery itself more like a warehouse, uncluttered space artfully divided with panels and fabric screens, the universal twentieth-century exhibition space.

Having purchased a ticket, I began to make my way through the exhibit. Clearly they had gathered everything, everything imaginable bearing on the time of our hero. Fans and playing cards, hair combs, small paintings of Venice of the period, clothing that might have been his, shoes, laces, bathtubs, portraits of women, a gondola, snuffboxes, watercolors of his cell, maps of his prison escape route, samples of his writing, early editions, letters that mentioned him, and surely every known portrait of himself—in all of which he looked remarkably dissimilar and not particularly irresistible. The escape route was interesting. Virtually impossible, it seemed.

I summoned an unprecedented interest in the life of Casanova and closely observed everything. I forgot myself for an hour trying to imagine eighteenth-century Venice, wearing these clothes, bathing in these tubs, knowing, perhaps loving—desperately, of course—Giacomo Casanova. Escaping from a horrifying prison. Finally there was nothing more to see. Above the exit was a card quoting the man himself:

Life, be it happy or unhappy, fortunate or unfortunate, is the only good man possesses, and he who does not love life is unworthy of life.

A few rooms back he had also advised us not to be cheated, being a cheat himself.

In the inevitable gift shop I found a small, plain blue book, the product of an elegant press, Stefan Zweig's *Casanova,* something to read in my cave. It was after six; there were signs of closing, so I took my package and emerged into the *campo* under a dry yellowish-pink sky, wondering how I would get back to the hotel. I tried to remember which passageway I had used to come into that place, but there were several at close intervals and they all looked the same. There was nothing to do but choose one, so I did.

Nothing looked familiar, but nothing would. I walked and walked. Not so many *campos,* not so many bridges. I thought if I kept turning right I might regain my old route. A mistake. I entered a maze. Turns, dead ends, turns, no sign of open space. The light was beginning to fade, not panic yet but concern.

Then, down a side street, I saw a group of boys, young boys, shouting and leaping in a circle. Something about their energy alarmed me; my instinct was that these were boys being boys in the worst way. What was the object of this aggressive little dance? I was lost anyway and couldn't control an impulse to disrupt them, stop the fun or torture or whatever it was; everything about their behavior suggested a victim in their midst. I turned into the street.

I approached the frenzied group and saw that something small was, in fact, trapped in the center of the circle. Whatever it was, was itself running in circles as the boys jumped and flapped around it. Was it a rat? Getting closer I glimpsed a creature larger than a rat, brown, making little noises and leaping at the boys in a terrified attempt to escape them but driven back into the tormenting circle by their stamping feet and waving arms.

I shouted, *Stop it!*

The imperative got their attention. The boys, five of them I think, stopped and looked at me. The creature in the middle fell down panting. It was a tiny dog.

What are you doing? I screamed, rushing toward them.

They looked at one another and a chagrined, contemptuous laughter began among them. Boys giving boys courage. Also courageous in my outrage, I broke into the circle and picked up the dog.

How dare you torment this poor thing? I demanded.

They shouted back at me, incomprehensibly.

These boys weren't shy; they frightened me. They couldn't have been more than eight years old and didn't look particularly criminal, just neighborhood boys, but their mob energy was aroused and there was no one in the street but us. They exchanged knowing smiles, a woman, a tourist, what were the possibilities? The dog pressed against my chest, panting.

I reached into the pocket of my jacket and pulled out change for the large bill I'd used to pay for my book. Paper and coins. I had no idea how much it was.

Take this and get lost! I threw the money on the ground.

There was an immediate scramble; it must have been serious cash. I ran back out of the street, clinging to the dog, the free-for-all behind me fading as I turned in random directions, trying to disappear, up one tiny alley and down another until I couldn't hear their shouts.

At last I emerged into a *campo*. From an adjacent passageway I could hear the countertenor still intoning Vivaldi. Bless you, Vivaldi, now and forever. Yes, yes, that was my street; turn left and be free. I pushed the tiny collapsed dog under my jacket and hurried ahead.

There was Prada, there was our old hotel, I could relax now. I'd already passed the Gritti without stopping. I could relax, but I was carrying a dog and had no idea if that would be acceptable to the management. Particularly a collarless stray, if stray he was. I headed instead back to San Marco.

Twilight was gathering in the piazza, but the crowds were unabated. Florian's was crowded as well, only a few tables were open. I needed to pull myself together. I found as distant a seat as I could and turned away from the others enjoying their drinks and conversation. When the waiter came, another beauty, I ordered coffee and white wine although I still hadn't actually had a meal. As he turned his back, I reached into my jacket, lifted out the little sufferer, and set him on my lap. Yes, it was a him.

He was no longer panting but looked exhausted in the way that dogs do. I knew so well from Dora when she was ill. He was a tiny boy, no more than six or seven pounds, brown with black markings on a lovely face, a full-bred Chihuahua and a handsome one. I laid the corner of my jacket over his body and stroked his head.

Poor little boy, I said. Poor little boy.

He curled up against the inside of the jacket and gave my hand a weak kiss. I could see a collar mark in the fur of his neck. This was not a street dog, this was a dog used to love. Surreptitiously I lowered the glass of water the waiter had brought. He took a long drink, then settled back and fell asleep almost immediately; his head just dropped. A pretty awful day for this fellow.

Over the wine and coffee I wondered what I would do about the hotel. I had to smile. This was just the sort of thing that would drive Antony mad, picking up a dog in a foreign city. But he wasn't here to argue or stop me. The thought gave me my first frisson of freedom and also a pang. I hadn't spoken to Antony in more than twenty-four hours. That was unprecedented.

I remembered when I found Dora. Another brown dog, bigger than this one but by not much, one of those generic small mongrels called "Chihuahua mix" in animal shelters. Antony called her a "rat dog" and said the characteristic of the breed was to be abandoned. He grew to love her but had been apoplectic when I discovered her outside a diner, collarless and cadging food. I bought her a sandwich, holding us up, then insisted on taking her with us. We had stopped for lunch in a tawdry little tourist town on our way to a big venue in Colorado. He and I had been hiking for a few days at a spa and had rented a car to drive to the venue and hook up with the rest of the band. Dora was still a baby, less than a year old. Certainly not housebroken.

Back in the car Antony didn't know where to start with his annoyance. What an enormous inconvenience it would be. We had not agreed to have a dog; if we had agreed, he should have some input into what sort of dog. He preferred big dogs. Who would take it out at night? The hotel would probably not allow it (hotels allowed Antony anything); he had work to do and didn't have time for this; if the dog kept him awake the dog was going; the dog was probably sick. I just held her, my beloved Dora, our first day. He hated that this had been my decision. We had a lovely trip.

Later in our room, it was better and then worse. Antony could see, after all, that she was adorable and he truly liked animals. As she sat on my lap in bed, he made an attempt to play with her. He leaned over her and growled. Dora, safe in my lap, growled back and showed her perfect white teeth. She didn't grow up on the street for nothing. Dora was clearly going to be mine more than his, and Antony did not take well to being the less preferred anything. It was a godsend for me. With Natalie, Liddie, the Casson family, the band, the managers, the agents, and the fans focused relentlessly on Antony and vying for his favor, I, I personally, now had a staunch friend and ally.

And a brilliant companion she was. She had her own backstage pass with her picture on it, worn on her collar. She was widely admired but did not tolerate fools. Nor did she hesitate to show the lovely teeth when irritated. But she was charming and witty in her responses, her preferences. She had a passionate commitment to private property, myself and everything else that she thought of as hers, including Antony, who grew to love and admire her. He used to say that Dora's mother had told her, "Dora, nothing is really yours until you eat it." So funny, sometimes, old A. But why would he think of that? Perhaps his mother had told him the same thing.

When Dora and I would check into one of the endlessly recurring hotels on the tour circuit, arriving to meet Antony, the girls at the desk would cry "Dora's back!" as we crossed the lobby. Treats would arrive at the hotel room door. Once a miniature hamburger arrived on a tray, a rose next to the napkin, with a note saying, *To the divine Dora from a secret admirer.* She was a star in her own right.

She died of a heart defect nearly two years ago, much too young. But remarkable beings move swiftly through this world, as Nils had taught me. Golden lads and girls all must. Those two, so dear to me, so gone. I felt a bright twist of grief in the center of my body. My eyes stung. I looked up.

It was dark now. I had to face the hotel. I paid my bill, lifted the small sleepy body, and lowered him into my bag with Stefan Zweig and the rest of the chaos.

You be a good boy. Very, very quiet. Not a word. Good boy, yes? *Sì?* And then we'll have some dinner.

He blinked up at me and obediently lay down in the jumbled bag.

We entered the lobby of the Gritti trying to appear nonchalant. There were people around, so I thought we could pass unnoticed. I retrieved my key without incident and was heading for the elevators when a voice called *Signorina! Signorina!* Did they have dog detectors? I kept moving but just behind me a voice repeated Signorina, quieter now, less imperative. It was my desk clerk.

Yes? Hello! Yes? I said.

Sorry to bother, Signorina. You have received a fax. With an eager smile he extended a envelope toward me.

Thank you very much. *Please don't move, please don't bark.*

Did you enjoy your day in the rain?

Very much, thank you. Venice is so beautiful. *Where was the ombrello?*

Yes, very, very beautiful.

We paused awkwardly.

Will I be able to have room service?

Oh, yes. Yes, of course. At all hours. Lovely smile.

What have I said? Thank you so much. I will see you tomorrow?

Oh, yes, Signorina. At your service at all times.

Thanks very much, good night. An elevator arrived. I stepped in.

Buona sera, Signorina. The door closed.

I pressed the button and the elevator rose.

What a good boy you are.

The single dim light, curtains closed, the bed turned down, a chocolate on the pillow. We made it. A radiant sense of relief and the bliss of privacy. No little boys here.

I took off my jacket, put the bag on the bed, and opened it. My own little boy was wide awake, sitting in the detritus of the appalling mess of the bag. He looked up at me with such bewilderment in his enormous, slightly protruding, soulful eyes that I swept him up into my arms and kissed his brown head.

You are an excellent conspirator, young man. You have done very well.

I kissed him again and again and put him on the floor. His feet had not touched the ground since his ordeal. He stood still and looked around, sniffing into this new space. I brought him another glass of water, which he drank with enthusiasm. He was going to have to do something with all of that water, so I spread the morning's newspaper in the corner of the room and hoped he understood the gesture. He walked around tentatively. He looked at me.

I assure you, Signore, you are safe now. A bite to eat?

Later, after room service had come and gone, my young man waiting in the bathroom while the waiter laid out our table, we shared a steak. I do not often eat steak. I rolled the table into the hall, locked the door, and lifted him onto the bed.

So, how did you get into this mess? I asked.

With more energy and confidence after his dinner, the boy hopped around the edge of the bed looking down at the precipitous three-foot drop, then came back and plopped down next to me with the first real expression I had seen on his face. You could call it a smile.

Oh, I see, not telling. Not telling your name either, I suppose?

All ears.

Well, we have to use something. How about Giacomo? He was an escape artist. Is that what you are?

Head cocked, ears.

Perhaps you don't speak English? Well, I think you are an angel sent from heaven to keep me company. I think you're my new best friend.

My best friend. Good heavens. I hadn't even looked at the fax, which could only be from Antony. I leaped up and searched for the envelope. Giacomo watching, I tore it open and read a single line: *Hope you're enjoying yourself.*

Well, yes. As a matter of fact.

In the morning, after a tender night spent with Giacomo curled next to me under the covers—who cared about hygiene—I lay in the expansive bathtub, hot water perfumed with aromatic oils offered gratis to the lucky guests of the Gritti Palace. Every fixture in the bathroom was an art object, every sense indulged; the bathroom was as big as the room. Fragrant steam condensed on the sealed window. I sighed in bliss. Giacomo had extended his body full length on the voluptuous bath mat, having a nap. He didn't realize that he was next in the tub.

That's the price you pay for life in the fast lane, I said to him.

Without opening his eyes, he thumped his tail at the sound of my voice. I felt so restored by his company.

Hope you're enjoying yourself.

I tried to imagine what it would be like if that sentiment were offered with sincere good wishes: Hope you're enjoying yourself! Have a wonderful time, sweetheart, wish I were with you. Hope the Gritti is terrific. Take your time, enjoy it. We'll meet in Rome; I'll arrange a few days at the end of the tour so we can be together and see the city in this beautiful weather. Where would you like to stay? Never mind, I'll surprise you. Can't wait. Miss you so much. Love you. If you find any little dogs, be sure to bring them along!

Is anyone's life like that? I'd often wondered. Once, early in our courtship when Antony actually took my suggestions, I bought him a copy of *War and Peace,* which he perseveringly read. Enjoyed it too, thrilled to it. I felt then that I could bring him armfuls of riches, books that had meant so much to me, books he had missed in his disrupted education. We'd have those worlds to share. We would read to each other. We'd have a private life. That phase didn't last long.

One phrase he retained from *War and Peace* was "marriage is a covered dish." He was delighted with it. He understood this from his own experience, what his marriage had seemed to be to the public and what it had actually been. At the time he imagined that our relationship could never become that. While he was reading Tolstoy he used to make the sign of the cross over my head before we went to sleep, blessing and protecting me, as was the custom of nineteenth-century Russians. "We're so lucky, Nel. You must take care of yourself and live to be a very old girl," he once said. He wanted me to stop smoking because it annoyed him, but he loved me too. He seemed to. I couldn't swear to it. I adored him.

A friend of mine says that life is nothing but phases; we never arrive anywhere. I was familiar with this idea but liked the way he put it. I remember the pain and shock I felt when Antony first brought out "marriage is a covered dish" in company, the implication not being a happy one for us. Another phase. Sadly, each one took us farther from each other, and somehow Antony was always the one, I felt, setting those demarcations, withdrawing, and I couldn't understand what was happening. It was as if he had some concealed schedule or had only a limited amount of energy allotted to each phase; once that was exhausted, we took another step away from each other. Another block of cold air between us, another permanent stain. I tried to think if I was complicit, but all I remember is panic. I also began to realize then how little I knew him. I desperately wanted the previous man back.

I began an obsessive ongoing analysis of his secret self that might help me to reach him. On this project I wasted a world of my time. So many theories, some quite elaborate, all pointless. Useless, anyway. I knew him very well; I could predict what he would do in any given situation; I was usually right, and yet I knew him not at all. He took his heart away and marooned me in the desolation of behavior. He turned out the lights, one by one. I sometimes felt that one day he would step over my dead body without noticing or feeling implicated. Whistling. To the world he remained charming, but I was no longer given access. Why? He was turning me into something I was not; what good did that do him? What was the secret I didn't know?

The phone was ringing. Giacomo sat up, ears erect, looked toward the phone, looked at me. Splashing, I scrambled into the luxurious Gritti bathrobe conveniently at hand and hurried into the bedroom. How many phone calls, how many hotels?

Hello?

Buon giorno, Signorina! It is Carlo at the front desk.

Oh. Good morning, Carlo.

If you will be staying with us, Signorina, I can offer you today a very nice room. Several windows. A view of the *canale*. The small *canale*. *Sì?*

Ah, *sì*.

My plans for the day had been to bathe Giacomo, smuggle him out of the hotel, somehow find a pet store and buy him one of the chic collars I had seen on other Venetian dogs, also a leash, then return to the hotel with an important-looking animal and pretend I had decided to buy a dog. I came to Venice to buy a dog. I'd already read in the Gritti brochure tucked in the desk drawer that small animals were allowed. I had had no plan to change my room.

Oh, *grazie,* Carlo. Thank you very much.

I would miss my cave but how nice it would be to see the sky and the *canale.* The small *canale.*

I have an appointment today, Carlo, but I believe I would like the new room.

How much did the new room cost? I was piling up violations.

Is it terribly expensive this room, Carlo?

No, no, Signorina, the same. We wish you to enjoy the hotel.

That's very kind. I'll try to get my things together.

No need, the staff will do that.

Well, thank you very much. I'll speak to you when I come down. Within an hour, is that all right?

Of course, Signorina.

Thank you, Carlo, thanks very much. I hung up.

Giacomo would be with me, in my bag, when I spoke to him. But Giacomo was a good boy.

It all went smoothly. The now sweet-smelling Giacomo was perfection, not the smallest murmur. Our new room would be ready at two and the day was spectacular, a cloudless Giotto-blue sky. San Marco was swarming with dry and happy tourists. We would go in search of a pet shop, a very good one. Giacomo was allowed to stick his face out of the side of the bag to enjoy the air. A promising day.

There is no need to speak Italian in Venice. The city is accommodating to tourists, to put it nicely, but there is a mild sense of disdain detectable in even the friendliest shopkeepers. I wished I knew Italian to surprise them and put myself on better terms. I would seem one of *them*. I immediately regretted the snobbery and accepted my circumstances. But having lived with a celebrity, I had a keen awareness of the inside and the outside. For that matter, I had a keen awareness of the inside and the outside of myself. I disliked, or rather, mistrusted celebrity and all that it represented at home, perhaps everywhere, but nevertheless I would have liked a key, a password, something that would offer me a more interesting access to this very concealed city.

Giacomo and I inquired in several shops but no one knew, or cared to know, about a pet store. Finally I saw a handsome fat boy, an English bulldog, well-collared, sleeping outside an Asian art shop that would have been a terrible temptation to me if I had not been on a mission. A refined, middle-aged blond woman greeted me when I entered. *Buon giorno,* she said, with a lovely smile and the reserved Venetian manner. I knew I must not even look at the bronzes of dancing Sivas that I saw artfully displayed on two or three solitary pedestals, enlightenment annihilating time in the most ecstatic way. I needed less transcendent information.

So sorry, I said, but I wonder if you can tell me where I can find a good pet shop? My dog—indicating Giacomo's little head peering from my bag—his collar is broken.

Che angelo! Guarda com'é carino! É femmina o maschio? A little *tesoro.* Come here, *tesoro,* she said, reaching her hands toward Giacomo.

I left it up to him. Giacomo didn't seem disturbed so I lifted him out of the bag, and the lovely blond woman took his head in her hands and kissed him four or five times.

Giacomo was the key.

Articoli per Cani! she exclaimed.

I'm sorry?

By now the fat bulldog was dancing, if you could call it that, a sort of plodding jig around our feet, looking up with unmalicious, grinning curiosity, a string of drool dangling from the corner of his mouth. Giacomo again seemed unfazed, although he glanced at me.

Articoli per Cani. All of Enrico's things come from there. A wonderful shop! Enrico has a mask and a cape, a Christmas collar with bells, many things. You see how manly he looks today.

Enrico was wearing black, with studs.

I will give you the address, she said, going to the desk for paper and pencil. You know Venice? Well, not hard to find, she said, writing.

I pictured a dead end. A circle of boys.

Somehow, after much confusion—wrong turns, inquiries, crossing the canal—we found Articoli per Cani, a tiny fanciful shop catering to the Venetian passion for dogs. In a city without other animal companions readily available, no horses to ride, no cows to graze, no pigs to slop, the dog reigns supreme. Cats have a more difficult but not terrible time. Many strays, I was told, when I asked the proprietress about cats, but all fed punctually at fixed locations—monuments and street corners—by a band of devotees. Venetians clearly cared for Venetians of all species. Excepting possibly pigeons.

Every sort of dog costume was available. I tried to picture Enrico's closet. He must have a Sherlock Holmes rat-catcher hat; he was, after all, British. I knew he had a mask and a cape; which mask? I wondered. Was he the beaked plague doctor at Carnavale? That would be very silly on Enrico. A leather motorcycle jacket to go with his studs? A raincoat, certainly. Angel wings. Antlers. Anything was possible.

I mentioned Enrico and the owner was instantly more hospitable. She too kissed Giacomo's head repeatedly.

We settled finally on a distinguished braided, brown leather leash and a Black Watch plaid collar in which he looked enchanting. Suited up, Giacomo stood at last on the ground at the end of his leash, clearly no stranger to the device.

We left the shop and for the first time walked together down the street. We had no particular destination. What I felt was joy.

As we walked, Giacomo turned his head and looked up at me as if we were in this together and the fun could now begin. He trotted rather than walked; he was jaunty, confident. Restored to his authority, he was proud. I felt that he could show me Venice, the insider's Venice, but remembered that he too, after all, had been lost himself.

Museums and churches were not possible for us so we walked. For hours it seemed. I began finally to register the splendors and intimacies, the façades, of this odd, gorgeous city. Venice felt a very secret place. The public spaces were abandoned to tourists and strangers while real life went on behind those alluring, often decaying, exteriors. Seeing Venice would never be knowing it. The lives of the native Venetians seemed more shrouded than in other cities. Perhaps it was different in winter.

We crossed bridges, wandering away from the water and back again; when Giacomo appeared to flag, I carried him. We had lunch in the sunshine outside a café on a remote *campo*. I had a salad and he the roast beef sandwich. The waiter brought us a dog biscuit and another glass of wine, gifts from the man-

agement. We were attractive. I smiled to think that my traveling fantasy was being so unexpectedly fulfilled. There we were,
two happy companions, spending a congenial day in a glorious
place. By three we were both thinking of a nap. The new room
would be ready, our sanctuary with views of the small *canale*.
We headed home. I began preparing my speech for Carlo.

Heading home in Venice is just that, hoping that you're at
least moving in the right direction, more or less retracing your
steps. We made a few wrong guesses but finally found the
Rialto Bridge; after that the arrows to San Marco were rela-
tively easy to follow, although the crowds became oppressive.
Giacomo as a native was undaunted. I'd been told that every
confusion in Venice is resolved by San Marco. It's the center of
gravity; you can't avoid it. We emerged finally into that huge
space, which felt like the Great Plains after the welter of tiny
streets. Once we'd crossed the piazza, we'd only be a few blocks
from home and then alone at last. I wondered if a more forthcoming message might be waiting for me.

Signorina! Signorina! A man's voice was calling.

If this was not Carlo's afternoon off it could not be me he
meant. Unless, perhaps, Antony had arranged to have me
apprehended and my credit card seized.

Giacomo and I continued on our way, but the calling voice
was closer and grew more insistent.

Signorina! Signorina! Aspettami! Aspettami, per favore!

I stopped and saw a young man, thirtyish, blond, anything
but a tourist from his looks, rushing toward me from the other
side of the square. Oh, God, what was this? The last thing I
wanted was an encounter with someone else's agenda. What

could he want? I felt a wave of irritation and wondered how I could escape. It was too late; he was there in front of me, looking slightly distraught.

Scusi, scusi, he said, panting a bit from his efforts to reach me.

I looked at him and said nothing.

Il cane, Signorina, questo cane, é il suo?

I'm sorry? I replied, not attempting to conceal my annoyance.

Oh, you are English?

Oh dear. A Venetian took me for an Italian? Not likely that, but meant, no doubt, to be flattering. I may not look like all of the Americans here, but I do not look Italian.

No, I replied tersely, I'm an American.

American, he said.

Did I catch a hint of disdain? I thought that now he might go away, not wishing for the association. Unlike Carlo, he didn't have to be nice to us.

He collected himself, coughed. His English was accented but good, more British than American.

Forgive me, he said, for disturbing you. I wanted to ask about this dog. This is your dog?

My dog?

Yes, I said, this is my dog.

I don't mean to be rude, he went on, forgive me. This dog, you have had this dog many years?

What was he after? Could he be from animal control? He hardly looked or sounded it, but Giacomo had no tags. Perhaps they were relentless in the enforcement of civic requirements here.

Not many years, no.

Ah. Perhaps you found this dog recently?

Why do you ask? Quite annoyed now and becoming uncomfortable.

I will explain, he said. A friend, a good friend, an older woman, has recently lost a dog very much like this one and she has been frantic. We have looked everywhere but without luck. When I saw you walking, I could not help remarking the similarity of these dogs. I hoped that perhaps you had recently found this dog and then our search would be over.

We looked at Giacomo. He went over to sniff the stranger's shoes, looked up at the man and wagged his tail. Not overt enthusiasm, I noticed, but possibly some recognition.

When did you lose the dog? I inquired.

Two days ago. We could not find him anywhere. Although we are very careful with the door, we feared a workman had left it ajar. It was in the afternoon. He is so small, we were afraid for him in the streets. It has been terrible for the signora.

The dog's name? I asked.

Leo, Leonardo, the beloved child of my employer.

I looked at Giacomo. Even as I said it I knew the game was up. Leo?

Giacomo stretched his legs on my calf, wagged his tail, and smiled at me in the way that he did. There was no help for this. I hated this man.

And what is your name? I asked.

Matteo, he replied, extending his hand, Matteo Clemente. I am working at Signora da Isola's home at this time.

I shook his hand. Cornelia Everett, I said.

The first faint wave of grief began to flutter and rise.

Again we were out on the streets, crossing bridges, making turns. The peaceful room with windows was slipping away behind us as we hurried along. We were walking much too quickly for Giacomo—Leo—so I carried him and felt his small weight against me. My dread was growing. I felt that I was carrying my hopes in my arms and would soon have to surrender them to a stranger. My confidant, my companion. How did I love him so much, so soon? Like Dora, we were delivered to each other in distress. It seemed fated, an unexpected grace, a gift of the gods. Some part of me must have imagined that he was sent to ransom my sorrows, that together we would step away from disappointment and be free. Such an encounter does not happen often. Life is not filled with miraculous redemptions.

Matteo Clemente was practically bounding by the time we crossed a narrow bridge that led to an equally narrow street. We seemed to be in a remote part of the city, quiet and empty. The first house on the right, palazzo, I supposed, faced canals on two sides and on this side faced the street. I could see four stories of windows on the façade, Gothic, all dim and obscured. There were steps leading down to a landing platform, but the door to the house on that side looked permanently sealed.

The exterior facing the street was less ornamented. A huge, ancient, water-stained door was the central feature. Matteo stopped there, and although there was a heavy brass lion's-head door knocker, he pushed an anachronistic white plastic buzzer that had been jimmied into the wall next to the door.

Here we are, he said smiling, very pleased.

I wanted to kill him. I wanted to clasp Giacomo to my heart and run away. He had no idea where we were staying, how could he find us? I would hide and then leave town. Why had I not run away sooner?

An old woman opened the door. Cronelike, wizened, all in black. Expressionless, she looked at Matteo Clemente and impassively stood aside. I noticed her eyes fall on Giacomo and then on me. Her look suggested that the culprit had been apprehended. Centuries of public hangings flashed before me, transmitted in the warmth of her regard.

È lei? Dov'è? he said.

Su.

The large interior courtyard was open to the sky, unadorned, with a carved wellhead in the center and walls the color of winter squash patterned with a delicate green filigree that looked disturbingly like mold. One or two doors stood at ground level and to our left a stone staircase rose to a landing, also with a door and interior windows. The three of us started up the steps. I looked back. The gate was closed, the crone gone.

We arrived on the landing, a hall to the left and right and, in front of us, a painted door. Although the paint was faded, I could make out a religious motif, angels leading and carrying children, something like that. Matteo knocked.

Entra, said a soft voice.

Matteo opened the door and suddenly, after the stark courtyard, we were in a space full of windows; light refracting off red walls cast a pink glow around a large elegant room. A dazzlingly backlit figure rose from a low white chair by a window and extended its arms in a gesture so passionate and embracing it might have been an operatic moment. All in white, like an angel descended.

Caro, my darling, my darling, it sang out.

I felt as if I had waited all my life for such a greeting, but it was not for me.

Giacomo squirmed in my arms and struggled to be released. He raced across the room, flew into her embrace—it was a woman—and covered her face with kisses. Kisses I had known.

Oh, Leo, Leo, the woman cried, I was close to death! You're home, you're home, my darling. *Grazie a Dio! Grazie, grazie.* My boy, my son! More kisses, passionately exchanged.

I began to feel embarrassed to be present at this scene, the guilt of the interloper. Uncomfortable and upset, I wanted to be gone now, gone from all of this belonging. I didn't feel in control of myself. I was afraid I would begin to sob. The part I had to play was over. I had no place in this reunion, this meeting of souls. I longed to escape.

And here is the hero, Matteo said at last, smiling at me. The heroine, I mean. Leo's angel of mercy.

At this the woman, a not-young but distinguished and somewhat intimidating woman, looked up at me with unmistakable animosity, instantly checked.

We cannot thank you enough, she said.

I'm very fond of dogs, I replied inanely. Then, fighting tears, my voice choking, How was Leo lost?

She could see I was in distress and answered more kindly. We don't know. It must have been a stupid man. These men are so careless. They kill you and don't notice.

Her voice was charming, a soft lilting accent, a refined voice. She must have been nearly eighty but still lovely. A halo of fine white hair lifted from her face, pinned in back with large tortoiseshell combs. She wore a white silk gown that looked not unlike a choir robe and embroidered slippers.

Cornelia, said Matteo, this is Signora Lucrezia da Isola. Signora, Cornelia. . . . He glanced at me, chagrined.

Everett, I whispered.

Still holding Leo, she extended her hand. Forgive me, she said, I have had a most terrible time. We have all been mad with despair. Dear Matteo has been our salvation. Will you have a cup of tea? A glass of wine?

Outside the day was fading and becoming overcast. I felt helpless and completely passive. My eyes kept returning to Giacomo, who smiled at me from the signora's close embrace. I thought of trying to find my way back to the hotel alone. I thought of the room on the *canale,* the happiness it had promised and the night that would be waiting for me there. I had lost track of what world I inhabited. I had no idea where I was. I felt the floor rising and then nothing.

An insistent sensation penetrated the blackness and pressing lethargy that held me in place. I concentrated on my eyes until slowly, very slowly, they began to drift open. Far away I could see Giacomo in his plaid collar lying next to me, licking my hand. I smiled to see him. Had we gone back to our room? How did we get there? What a big room. Gradually, awareness began to reassemble itself; I recalled a place like this but couldn't grasp my relationship to it since I seemed to be horizontal. Then in a swift shift I was conscious again. My eyes snapped open and my body pitched forward.

No, no, you must lie back, said a soft voice. I did as I was told.

Oh, yes, the signora. I gazed at her in bewilderment. I was struggling to recapture the events that had placed us in this new arrangement, myself recumbent against pillows on a long couch, the signora seated on a stool next to my face, watching me with concern. Something had happened. Was this another life? What had I missed?

Everything is fine, Cornelia, you are not hurt.

Nel, I'm called Nel.

Very well. Have a sip of this.

The sharp tang of brandy filled my nose and throat. I felt

warmer instantly. In spite of the soft gray blanket that I saw thrown across me, I realized I had been cold. Another sip and the question arrived.

What happened?

I think you were overcome; you swooned.

For a moment I couldn't comprehend what she was saying. I swooned? Oh, I see, I must have fainted. I had fainted before. Having a bandage pulled off by a nurse in grammar school, I watched her recede and disappear. Choir practice for a Christmas concert at my Quaker girls' school at sixteen, when I tumbled onto the chorister in the row in front of me just at *who mourns in lonely exile here.* In the Boston airport, bringing Nils's body home from Mexico, waiting for the coffin to be unloaded from the plane. My first impulse, of course, was to apologize.

Forgive me, I said.

Forgive you? But you are Leo's guardian angel. See how he loves you.

Giacomo was curled next to me on the blanket, his head resting on my stomach. His eyes were heavy; he was nodding, now that his ministrations had returned me from the void. Leo. Giacomo. Two such dissimilar allusions to characterize the spirit of this charming dog. I suppose we all contain an abundance of identities and seem to others what they imagine or wish us to be, what we imagine or wish ourselves to be. Romance does that, showering one with attractive new attributes, the charms of projected desire. And who we are depends so much on whom we're trying to please. Unless they refuse to be pleased, and then what happens? I suppose it's possible to run out of identities and become a speechless blank. That's what estrangement is, losing the signal, becoming unknown, a non-being, lost. Giacomo, Leo, was no longer estranged, he was rich in projected desire. The signora and I exchanged glances and gazed at him in complicit devotion as he dropped off to sleep. How nice it felt.

I must leave, I said, handing back the brandy glass. I'm very grateful for your kindness and sorry to have caused such a commotion. I hope you'll forgive me. I should get back to my hotel.

Had we known which hotel, Matteo would have phoned. You must stay here and rest tonight; it is no time to be alone in a tourist place. Annunziata will bring us a little supper. You see it is already dark out there. Then you will rest until tomorrow. This is truly the best.

Matteo, who had been standing by the windows, crossed the room and stood next to the signora.

I felt suddenly exposed and slightly ridiculous, languishing there like a Pre-Raphaelite heroine in affliction. I struggled to sit up, rousing Giacomo—Leo—both of us fumbling in the blanket.

No, I've put you to too much trouble already, I said. I'm certain that I'm fine now.

Which hotel? said the signora.

The Gritti.

The Gritti, Matteo. Miss Everett is visiting friends and will return in the morning.

My bedroom, as it happened, overlooked a small canal. But I was alone. Giacomo in his manifestation as Leo had retired with his relieved and adoring mother. The room was wonderful. Spare, not large, soft white plaster on empty walls, except for a small section marked off with a sort of wooden frame. Inside the frame was a square of much older plaster with something apparently frescoed within it. When I went to bed, it was too dark to examine it closely. Annunziata, who had been a new woman while serving us supper, nodding repeatedly, smiling an alarmingly wrinkled smile, all approval, had shown me up another flight of interior stairs to this room, flapping her hand behind her and muttering *Avanti! Avanti!* as I followed her up the narrow steps. She brought me a lovely linen nightdress and took my clothes, presumably to clean them, all done with more nods and smiles. I had passed through some invisible barrier.

Lying in smooth worn linen sheets, propped with pillows against a bedstead painted with a profusion of roses, a bed of roses, I looked out at the dim building opposite, also Gothic, I thought, and contemplated the day, which seemed to me like a waking dream. To have arrived in this house, this room, didn't feel plausible in the usual way.

We had drinks first and then supper at a round table by the windows, roasted chicken with grilled asparagus and a superb bottle of white wine. The conversation, at first polite and a little awkward, warmed up under the benign inducements of good food and wine. I had the feeling that they did not entertain often. The signora had lived in this palazzo for fifty-five years. It belonged to her husband, the Count da Isola, now dead, had been for much of that time. She was not Venetian but Roman—Roman only because her British parents removed themselves to Italy in the early twenties and she was born there. Educated in convents, she appeared entirely Italian to me. Although she was gracious and seemed kind, there was a trace of preoccupied melancholy about her, nothing palpable but rather absorbed, you might say, into her being.

Matteo had been staying in the house for six months. Apparently this palazzo was a convent at one time, during a plague in the fifteenth century, when it was used as a hospital. In a large room above the one in which we were dining, now unused, some plaster had peeled off a wall and what seemed to be a fresco began to appear. Experts were invited to look at it, and it aroused some interest, since it was atypical in a way that I couldn't understand when Matteo explained, subtleties of technique. Matteo was an authority on conservation and had been sent here by a foundation to oversee the uncovering of the fresco and determine its potential importance.

Matteo seemed an interesting man. He was fascinating on the subject of conservation, yet he struck me as withdrawn, a little unavailable, being polite. Not seductive. I may have been wrong. He might have been a type I wasn't used to. And he was European. When I looked at him more closely, I guessed that he was at least thirty-five, handsome in a wavy-blond, blue-eyed, northern Italian way. A noble face. He also was not Venetian. His mother also was British and had married a Milanese architect who fled to England during the war. Like the signora, he had been educated in Italy, since his father had taken a strong aversion to the Brits—excepting only his wife—during his sojourn there. No wonder he and the signora, having so many antecedents in common, seemed to be such good friends. I sensed that they had been living a quiet secluded life here and were a little unnerved to have an unanticipated guest.

Still, the atmosphere at supper was gracious and animated. All the stories were for me, stories about themselves and Leo's escape, the project going on in the house. I told them about the awful boys, the details of the rescue, our night in the hotel, the bath. We stayed up until nearly midnight. I had miraculously arrived in a charming and welcoming haven after what had seemed to me, I realized then, an almost criminal escapade. I'd encountered generosity and hospitality and by what unimaginable fluke? I had acted spontaneously. Twice. How long had it been since that was an option in my life? Of course it would be over tomorrow, this magical sanctuary, Giacomo, these interesting people, the palazzo, all of it. Venice. Our revels now are ended. I would go back to the Gritti and then find Antony, wherever he might be. It felt so drab. Only Carlo would seem to care. Antony perhaps briefly. Or not.

Antony. I thought of my vacant room at the hotel. The chocolate on the pillow, the curtains drawn, outside the small *canale*. Emptiness. Had the phone been ringing in that expensive abandoned hideaway? I couldn't even guess. And if it had been, what did he think? Was he angry? I dismissed the thought. There would be plenty of time tomorrow to trudge around that track for the thousandth time. For now I was elsewhere, pleased, and in the most improbable place. I was inside Venice.

CHAPTER TWO

In the morning, Annunziata came to my door with a cup of coffee and my freshly cleaned clothes. She indicated the same bathroom down the hall that she had shown me to last night and then, in elaborate pantomime, that I was to dress and go downstairs. *Colazione! Signora! Colazione!* she repeated, pushing imaginary food into her mouth and pointing downward.

Thank you, Annunziata.

I found myself eating the same imaginary breakfast and pointing in the same direction. Convinced that her message had been grasped, nodding and smiling the wrinkled smile, she backed out of the room and closed the door.

It was still early. Outside the window a broad stripe of pale blue was gathering light. I could see the house across the canal clearly now, a decrepit old beauty with Gothic windows not unlike the ones I remembered on this building. This was a secluded neighborhood; it had not much of the spruced-up reconverted look of more stylish areas through which Giacomo and I had passed yesterday on our walk. I could see pots of geraniums sitting on various sills, white curtains in open windows moving slightly in the morning breeze, a maid very much like Annunziata shaking a tablecloth out an upper-story window. No sound but the water in the canal lapping quietly, responding to traffic much farther off, and the muffled knocks and bangs of housekeeping getting under way. I heard two tiny robust barks. Giacomo having his *colazione.* If so, this was the first time I had heard him bark since his ordeal. He was home.

I carried my coffee back to the bed to enjoy the quiet for a few more minutes and noticed again the wooden frame on the wall. It seemed to contain a kneeling figure. I went closer and saw it was a draped woman; strangely, she was turned away from the viewer, a small portion of her profile showing where her scarf had fallen back. There was nothing else: no room, no altar, no context of any kind. Underneath, in faded script, were the words ORO PRO NOBIS. Pray for us. Could this be the Virgin? What an odd way of depicting her.

There was something captivating about the figure; it felt suffused with strong emotion. The curve of the body seemed wrenched by some urgent appeal. One felt there was a missing element, another person, a crucifix, something addressed, but there was nothing, just the figure. Whatever was going on didn't feel particularly contemplative or holy; it felt, if anything, tormented.

The plaster around the image had yellowed with time. It must have been very old; the surface within the frame was layers deeper than the plaster on the walls of the room, yet the colors of the painted draperies were still rich. Under the purple robe was an edge of crimson, not noticeable at first glance but showing where the body turned and reached upward. I couldn't think this was the Virgin Mary; I had never seen her portrayed in such a distraught state. Maybe this was a petitioner to the Virgin, a woman in some kind of pressing need. What was it doing here? I'd been told this palazzo was once a convent, but this fragment didn't seem the work of a chastened soul. I'd ask the signora.

I showered in a bathroom full of chains and brass pipes, a facility clearly not renovated for decades, and dressed in my now sunny room, brushing my hair by the open window. Finally I collected my things to go downstairs and find my hostess. I was reluctant to leave such a consoling haven. I also felt uncomfortable abandoning this woman in so much apparent distress, although it was hard to imagine what I could do for her.

Signora da Isola was seated at the same round table where we had supper. She was alone, having coffee and reading a folded newspaper. The room was filled with pink light. Giacomo— Leo—was curled on a velvet pillow next to the window; he jumped up when he saw me, frisked across the room, and stretched his paws on my leg. I knelt down and we exchanged kisses.

Buon giorno, the signora said. You rested well? Today she was wearing a beige silk dress and a soft, intricately embroidered shawl. She looked lovely. You feel much better?

I'm very well, thank you. I appreciate your kindness. What a nice room that is.

Come and have a bit of breakfast. I have just been reading about the terrible world. Reading also about poor Venice and the desperate efforts our government hopes to take with other people's money to save us. What will happen, I do not know, but they will certainly enjoy the money.

She smiled and rolled her eyes. Come and sit. She indicated the chair next to her.

As if she had been loitering in the hall, Annunziata entered at once with a tray. Fresh coffee, rolls, a wonderful-smelling frittata that she divided and served to us—potatoes, herbs, and onions. I hadn't really had a meal in Venice until I came here.

I think you were sad to find that Leo has a home, no? Signora da Isola began, delicately slicing her food. Last evening Matteo and I were so busy telling you about ourselves and this work, we learned not very much at all about you. I think you have a great heart for dogs? There are not many visitors here in Venice who would stop and help a small dog in trouble, who would not think instead, What can I do? I do not live here. Yet you confronted the bullies and gave Leo a night in the grand Gritti Palace, something he has never imagined, also new clothes and a luxurious bath. Perhaps you were thinking of purchasing a palazzo and settling down for several years? It would take that long, probably, to collect the necessary papers for his departure, I'm afraid. And yet you acted on his behalf, for which I am more grateful than I can say. Now you must tell me why you are visiting Venice before this great adventure.

I felt at a complete loss for words. I was a tourist? I ran away from my husband? My life is a shambles and I'm desperate? I have no idea why I'm in Venice, I came here to find out? Any of these would bring me close to breakdown.

No, I said.

No?

No, I don't know. I don't know why I'm here.

I see. You are here on an impulse? You were passing by?

Yes, in a way. I was passing by with friends. Well, friends and my husband.

Mmm.

He's working here in Italy and I decided that—well, I thought, since I myself am not working here, I thought perhaps I'd have a little time on my own. I thought, in fact, that I would get off the train and leave him on it.

What an interesting idea! She laughed.

I had been refolding my napkin and gazing into the remains of my breakfast. I looked up at her. She was watching me with curious, kind irony.

What did I say yesterday? Careless men. Perhaps you have observed that?

I was able then to speak. I had intended to tell her a condensed and edited version of my history with Antony, to make a joke of it, the absurdity of life. Instead, to my surprise, I began with Nils's death, something I never speak of, as if the story could not make sense without that preface—which, of course, it couldn't. Nothing in my life now makes sense without including that transforming event. Still, I was surprised to hear myself speaking so candidly, going on and on, becoming anecdotal, as if I had never before been allowed to tell these things, as if in telling them I was trying for the first time to understand them myself. How humiliating the story of my marriage seemed to me. It made me feel ashamed to recount the cliché of failed marriage and utter confusion. I told her so.

No, no, my dear, I understand far better than you imagine. And what will you do now?

I don't know. He'll be in Rome soon. Perhaps I'll go there and wait for him. Face the music. I had to smile. Anyway, I

went on, now that I will not be eloping with Giacomo—
Leo—I can't really begin life anew at the Gritti Palace, can I?
Pleasant as that might be.

Not so pleasant, I think, after a while.

We sat in silence for a few moments. We'd been at the table
for more than an hour I saw, glancing at my watch. I was
freshly ashamed to have taken up so much of her time with my
tiresome story. I was becoming unhappy with myself and felt
again the impulse to escape and be alone.

Why don't we go upstairs and visit Matteo in the museum,
as we call it, the signora said at last.

Really, I said, I don't want to disrupt your day.

But you must see the museum, she replied, rising.

The room above was not as spacious as the salon but had its
own wall of arched windows and was full of light. At the far
end, the floor was covered with rumpled tarpaulins on which
sat an assortment of buckets, rags, and cans. Matteo and two
men in overalls were huddled together at one side examining a
portion of the wall. On the wall itself there was a great deal of
peeling plaster. Here and there I could make out colors and
fragments of shapes and what might have been a large figure;
the rest was in a dilapidated condition, as were all the walls in
the room. But only on the far wall was there something clearly
painted beneath the general decay.

Buon giorno! the signora sang out as we entered.

Matteo looked up, engrossed, and then smiled. *Buon giorno!*
Good morning, Signora, he said. You have come to show Miss
Everett the mystery. How are you, Miss Everett? Better, I
hope.

Her name is Nel, the signora replied.

And these are Fabio and Alberto, my coworkers.

Fabio and Alberto smiled and nodded.

So, I suppose this doesn't look like much after six months' work?

It looks like more than six months before, said the signora. This work is a great challenge for Matteo, Nel. It was the first time she had called me by my name. Matteo had not.

Many frescoes fade and many are damaged, she went on, but this one has been covered over entirely with plaster. No one suspected its existence until the walls began their collapse. Now we are trying to discover what may be here. Very difficult. Very interesting.

We must be careful not to remove everything as we remove the plaster, Matteo said, or we will have nothing but colorful dust. We begin to see outlines and a few details but have no previous photograph, nothing to compare it to, so we are faced with an unknown. Still, what we have uncovered is remarkably intact. I will show you.

We approached the wall. Through a thick veneer, I could make out pale green draperies, perhaps a bit of an arm, the top portion of a headless body that looked feminine. Lower, a golden fragment with a single green eye. What might be leaves, what might be circles.

This is beautifully painted, Matteo said, indicating the drapery, full of energy, even this small piece; one can almost feel the figure coming forward. Look, Signora, this eye, so strong, gazing up; it may be a lion. See how bright the eye is, and the light on this area, probably his mane.

Do you have any idea who painted it? I asked.

Not yet; there are provocative hints. What has interested the experts is the subject. A woman and a lion, if that's what it is. Also the painting style, unusual in such an old casa. It can't be earlier than the sixteenth century, we think. A rarity, whatever it may be. A few more layers and we'll know more. We hope.

Don't you feel that she, such as she is, is trying to reach us? the signora remarked. She comes forward so.

I did feel she was trying to reach us and thought at once of the figure in my room, who was also reaching for something.

She makes me think of the praying figure, Signora, I said.

The praying figure?

Yes, in my room, in the wooden frame. She has great energy as well.

What is that? Matteo asked.

How clever you are, Nel, and how stupid am I, the signora said, putting both hands to her mouth. Oh dear. There is a room, Matteo, the room where Nel stayed; it is used so rarely I never think of it. A small painting is on the wall, very old; at some point a wooden frame was put around it. The room has been plastered many times but never the painting. Alvise believed it had something to do with the convent. It did not interest him. His family had not lived here for—well, centuries, actually. Their great collection was in the Canal house, but this figure was not removable, so it was a forgotten thing. I have not thought of it in years.

Alvise was the count?

We headed back upstairs to the room I thought I would never see again, Leo bounding ahead of us, taking each stone step with a mighty leap. The room had been cleaned; the embroidered bedspread was back in place. And there she was, unchanged, still supplicating.

The signora pointed and Matteo went to the frame and examined the picture in silence.

How extraordinary, he finally said.

What is it? the signora asked.

I don't know. Certainly very nearly the same period as the fresco. The line is not dissimilar. Very strange. Only nuns lived here?

Nuns! said the signora. Who knows what they were up to. Although I believe these were good nuns for the most part. They nursed the sick during the plague, I was told; beyond that I know nothing.

Doesn't she seem distraught? I remarked. She doesn't seem like a nun. I thought at first that she was the Virgin because of the inscription, but it would be hard to pray to such a disturbed person.

They both turned and looked at me.

Of course I don't know; I went to Quaker schools. Signora, are there records from the time of the convent? There might be a mention of some person or event, a painter who decorated his room before succumbing to the plague? I laughed. I'm sorry, but you feel in the presence of a story; I felt it this morning. She's strong, isn't she, in spite of the fact that you can't see her. Why is she here?

Why, indeed? said the signora. Who saw her?

More to the point, who painted her? Matteo remarked.

We stood contemplating, enthralled for the moment by her manifest crisis. She continued motionless, but I could imagine her turning slowly and revealing a tearful, tormented face, confronting us as if we had arrived at last, too late, to answer some long-abandoned hope.

Back in the salon, over fresh coffee and rolls, we regarded one another like conspirators.

I'm bewildered, Matteo said. Something has been revealed, but I can't possibly say what it is. What an odd piece of work.

I feel an idiot, said the signora. All these months I have sat here a complete dullard making no connections. If, indeed, there are connections. But it feels so, doesn't it?

The same period, a similar hand, Matteo answered. It suggests a lead, a clue. Also a piece of work not utterly obscured, something to look at.

It's probably sentimental, I said, but doesn't she seem to be pleading for help?

I felt it too, the signora replied, putting her hand on her heart. As if she's been waiting. I've never really looked at her before.

Has your family always owned this house? I asked.

Oh, no, no, not my family. It was the casa of my husband's family, one of several. Now it is mine. They are all gone, all of their great houses and fortunes gone with them. My husband and I were given this place when we married. She laughed. We were put aside here.

I wonder, Matteo said, not listening, are there records? We've never really discussed it. I assumed you knew what existed. I assumed there was nothing left.

I am not a student of my husband's family, the signora replied, a little coldly, nor am I a scholar. It may be that there are records; I would not know how to find them. Those houses emptied many years ago. I am not equipped to search out such documents. There must be people who do that sort of thing; I can't imagine how.

Scholars know how to do that sort of thing, I said. Matteo, you must know.

I don't do historical research in that sense. I know something about art, but I'm not really a historian. And I don't have the time.

I have an idea, the signora said, with a curious smile and then began to laugh. Someone who could be quite useful if we can put up with it.

Who? Matteo asked.

Let me see first if he is available, she replied.

Well, this is awfully exciting, I said. It will be fascinating to find out whatever there is to know. I should leave you now and let everyone get back to work. I've had a marvelous time, really; thank you so much. I stood up and bent down to kiss Leo.

Leave us? the signora replied. So soon?

I rose and said nothing.

But you have discovered this grand clue; you have been so helpful. Won't you be disappointed not to find out more?

I'd love to know how it turns out, I said, but I won't be staying long.

No? You yourself have said you have no responsibilities for several weeks. You have delivered Leo, and Leo has delivered you, has he not? We must pay attention to such portents. We must always listen to what dogs say. No, I think you must stay with us for this little time and keep us company; it certainly seems so. A very good idea. We've been rather dull, haven't we, Matteo? It's just getting lively; you'd be a great help. Much better than the Gritti, which is so formal and expensive, a better way to know Venice. You can keep our friend upstairs company; perhaps she'll tell you her secrets. What do you think, Matteo? Wouldn't it be nice to have Nel here?

Matteo managed a weak smile.

I don't know, I said, I wouldn't want to impose. I doubt I could be terribly useful.

You are a scholar, a Harvard person, very useful. You were the first to make the connection with our discovery. No, you must think of it as a little experiment, a little research project. Matteo is too busy and I am unable; you will help me. Also an occasion for you to employ your wits and not worry about the same old things all the time. You must be careful of that, you know; your brain will go soft. I would like you to stay; it would make a change. Leo also would enjoy it. We will have this investigation together, you and I and Matteo; you will have a good reason to visit Venice for this while. Why else have you come here? I see so few people, it would be pleasant to have a visit. Yes, I think so, why not?

I didn't know what to say. Matteo looked stricken.

I don't know what to say, I said. It's an extremely kind offer, but I don't want to interfere. Perhaps it would be a distraction, glancing at Matteo. It would be wonderful to be here with you, but I think—

Good, that's settled then. The signora smiled and patted her lap, Leo made a great leap, sat down, and smiled too.

I looked at Matteo. He was frowning and gazing down at his hands.

Again I was wandering through the streets. I couldn't organize my thoughts. I felt dizzy. What was I doing? Was this real? Presumably I was on my way back to the Gritti Palace Hotel to check out and remove my things to the Ca da Isola. I hadn't spoken to Antony for two days, going on three. There was a quality of hallucination about my circumstances. I had been completely dislocated from more than one reality in this brief time. I was also being frustrated by the infuriating streets that were enjoying their game of leading nowhere, and I was desperately longing to be alone in my as yet unseen room for an hour of solitude to pull myself together. I should at least attempt to reach Antony. And what would I say? I found a dog who took me to a palazzo where I fainted, and I will now be staying there until I come to Rome? I have consented to engage in a research project involving unknown sixteenth-century painters, unexpected, of course, but how could I refuse? Antony, these things happen.

There at last was a familiar sight. Enrico the bulldog was asleep at the entrance to the Asian art shop, a place visited it now seemed weeks ago; it was, in fact, yesterday. Enrico was wearing a Black Watch collar, a large one. This was absurd. I vowed then to surrender to the enchanted island, do anything asked of me, if only I could find San Marco and my hotel, escape to my room and close my eyes.

Carlo was not at the desk. He never heard my interesting story about purchasing a dog, never got to warn me about how difficult it would be to get the proper papers. Someone else, less forthcoming, offered me my key and two envelopes. I didn't mention that I would be checking out; I was afraid they'd take the room away and I'd be marooned on the streets.

Nevertheless, Carlo had outdone himself. The new room was a dream: tucked away at the end of a hall; pale peach walls; poison green and white striped upholstery on two miniature wingback chairs, the curtains, and the bed; an antique desk; and windows that did indeed look out on the small *canale*. It was quiet and sunlit. The room I had imagined in my flight here. I felt happy to inhabit it and sorry to leave it so soon. Perhaps, I thought, I can telephone the signora and move tomorrow. I had had all the human contact that I could bear for one day; I wasn't used to it. A night alone would restore me to my right mind. And there would be room service.

The envelopes. I opened both, a fax and a phone message. The phone message first, although it came later. *Antony called,* it said, a phone number. The fax was more expansive, his big, familiar, boyish handwriting. *Assume you're okay. The show was good in Verona but I sprained my ankle. Fell off a bike. Not too serious but edemic, Ace bandages, ice. Three days until the next show. Kinda blue. And you?*

I? Why was I not carrying the bucket of ice? I was not carrying the bucket of ice because there must be thirteen other people available to do so and because your ankle is more important than my disappearance. That is why I would not be rewrapping the Ace bandage and carrying the bucket of ice. My brain is going soft, you know, and therefore I am undertaking an investigation into sixteenth-century painters during the plague years. Any other questions?

Edemic, indeed. He called to talk about his symptoms.

This was the way all our conversations were framed; Antony was the entrée and I was the condiment. I imagined for as long as I was able, and it did seem so at first, that we were equally entitled to a point of view. I later realized that every conversation had, in fact, a weighty ballast that shifted us entirely to his concerns and his opinions — if only his opinion of my tone. This came up often and was useful since it swung things back to him. "Can you hear yourself?" he would say, when I tried to explain my frustration. It took a long cold time to realize it was a trick. For years I earnestly examined my tone. We never discussed his tone. This tactic saved Antony time and effort. Once, while he changed into his gym clothes, I sat on the bed and asked if we could have dinner, take a walk, talk to each other sometime. "We're talking now," he replied, tying his running shoes.

Recently I no longer pursued understanding. I didn't know if he'd noticed. I might make the odd, what he would call provocative, remark but was no longer trying for anything. I had come to feel a little spectral but doubted he could tell the difference. Asked about me, he would imply in a genial, elliptical way that the going was rough. He was up against it. I'd watched him in conversation give people permission to ignore me. They picked up on the cue because the association with him was what they craved and I appeared to be a mute.

I don't remember the first time I was able to see Antony objectively, the first moment I registered a gesture of his that could only be called paltry, something I would dislike in another person. Come to think of it, there was a time early on when he let a door slam in my face. "Antony!" I objected. He replied, smiling, "I'm not responsible for your ego." I was willing then, because I wanted him and would not believe him capable, to take it as a joke.

I would have to call him.

Antony has an alias. Every star has one. Unless you know the alias you will never be connected to the room; only a fool would try the famous name. A dear friend from the theater calls himself Albert Hall. Antony's alias is Clarence Darrow. One can guess why.

The phone rang in an empty room. In which city? Yes, I'll leave a message. *Nel called.*

I spoke to Signora da Isola. Matteo would meet me at the hotel at ten o'clock the next day to carry my bag to the palazzo. How easy it was to live without taxis. It was five; the evening was now mine.

I pulled a green striped chair to the open window. I wanted to make a feast of the light, which was beginning to slip from the saturation of summer into the crystalline transparency of early autumn. I would watch the pale blue shimmer of the September afternoon fade into twilight. I would think my thoughts.

I wanted to think about Signora da Isola and the extraordinary events of the last day. Instead I found myself still thinking about Antony. Old habit. How different the space around me felt than in all the hours alone in hotel rooms or at home, hours organized around the expectation of his arrival or call. *Free* was the word that occurred to me, but I knew I was not free. How had I let it happen? Why hadn't I done things I wanted to do? Why hadn't I thought of things I wanted to do? Why was I forever thinking about him? What happened to me? Why, as the signora said, did my brain go soft? I was never a meek or particularly dependent person, although I became one in my own mind. Why? Was he really able to change me so entirely? Antony is clever at having his own way, but I complied, gradually, I complied. Like the frog in water heating up on the stove, I never noticed the change, but instead of slowly coming to a boil, I had slowly gone blank. In these few days I had felt more vital than I had for years. Did I think he was more important than I was? I was sure he did.

My mother had been like that; our relationship was a competition. Any success of mine was seen as a betrayal of her, and she, being my mother, had the upper hand. I was allowed to be successful only if I promised not to be happy. I was meant to remain a passive and feeling witness to her grandeur, her suffering, but never quite an adequate witness, never passive or feeling enough. Never quite right. My analyst told me I needed to put my focus on other people in order to feel close to my mother, not to lose her, lose the maternal dynamic. Passive and feeling, self-obliterating. Was that right? It sounded right with Antony but it hadn't been that way with Nils. Nils had been proud of me, loved every success I had, doted, made me feel admired. More like my father. Could we never escape these parental paradigms? It was sad to think that every attempt at release became nothing more than fitting dysfunctional pieces together. Was there no escape? Had I chosen my mother to punish myself for the betrayal of loving my father? Who knew? What a way to go through life, soldered to the past, endlessly rehashing limited options, naming and blaming. It had to be more mysterious than that. What about souls?

And what about people who were truly not so nice? Antony had triumphed over his siblings; it was painful to watch. Was that the paradigm for our relationship, to win? Another family affair. He told me once that he enjoyed it when people chatted him up and had no idea what he was thinking about them. We all do that, but I don't know if we enjoy it. Smile and smile. People were not quite real to him. He would regard the notion of *otherness* as something the weak are forced to do. He assumed deference and mostly got it. I once naively imagined that companionship without deference might be a relief, a chance to be himself. It turned out that he *was* himself and didn't really care for cozy alternative realities. Antony is perceived as a romantic, shy, self-effacing, sensitive, waiting to be embraced by the supremely sympathetic soul who has yet to show up. A besotted acquaintance once called him a saint. One doesn't get to be a star by being a saint, obviously, but his persona is persuasive and irresistible. Sometimes he seemed to me like an underwater creature, watchful, menacing eyes in the dark deep. I would have loved to be privy to the thoughts that went on in those depths but was not invited to drop down. I might have been sympathetic myself. But why should he change? If it works don't fix it, one is told. He could always rid himself of a meddlesome nuisance. If someone has a problem with him the world will imagine it is that someone's fault. That was the luxury of being a star. One of them.

It was also true that I had loved him. He was adorable and elated with me, with us; we were joyful. He was ardent and amusing. Also beautiful. Who would not love him? We had wonderful times. When the chip first reappeared on his shoulder, I ignored it. Once I had the temerity to ask him why it was there, what was bothering him? Lessons learned. The adorable person seemed entirely gone from me now, but the chip remained. The mighty chip.

I had become so tired of thinking about these things. My longing for something else was visceral. This project of the signora's was like a cartoon version of my desires rising up in front of me waving their arms, and I sensed that she knew it.

And where were the children Nils and I should have had? Where was that life? How strange it was to live a phantom existence running always parallel to the actual one. But he was never meant for domesticity. He was a meteor that shot through this sorry world. Gifts. He was the great giver of gifts, the most obvious presented at unexpected moments with a courtly little bow and contained pleasure. Nils, full of grace. His terrible death held gifts as well. Blown to pieces as I was, somehow the universe seemed to open around me, a stream of radiant attentiveness flowed into me, a connection I could not have imagined. What it was or what it meant I never questioned. I assumed it was him.

After, I was a different person, shards of a person, not collected. That's when I met Antony. In fairness, he never knew me. I was improvising a self. His attentions were healing, exciting, they offered a way back to life, a life I wouldn't have envisioned. We were lost, we rejoiced. We knew nothing of each other. It was probably too soon but I needed to survive. Perhaps he felt deceived when I gave up idolizing him. He'd never known me when I felt powerful myself. He might not have liked it. He never asked. I never said.

Evening was falling; the sky was dissolving into deep pink and lavender. I was hungry. I wanted a glass of wine. Time for room service. Memories of Giacomo, our shared dinner. I went to the phone and it rang in my hand. Carlo, no doubt, wanting to know how pleased I was with his arrangements.

Hello?

It's Antony.

Hi.

Hi.

Silence.

You hurt your ankle?

Boris and I rented mountain bikes. Got nabbed by a tree root.

Not too bad?

Not too great. Tendon might be torn.

It hurts?

I'm taking painkillers and prednisone. Still pretty swollen. I have to ice it and they gave me crutches. They say I should be able to do the show on Thursday if I stay off it and don't move around too much onstage. May have to do steroids if it isn't better. Can't get any exercise, which is driving me crazy.

Silence.

I'm sorry.

Yeah, well.

Where are you?

Milan.

Is Milan nice?

Hotel's okay. Town's pretty industrial.

Silence.

It's nice here.

Good.

So, Antony, shall I meet you in Rome?

Rome?

Yes.

You're not coming here?

Well, it's been interesting here. I'd like to stay for a while.

Interesting in what way?

Lots of things. Do you want to hear?

Silence.

I found a dog and I met a countess. She's offered me a sort of job.

A job?

Well, it's ridiculous, I guess, not really a job. It involves this fresco in her house, who painted it. She thought I might be able to help her to research it.

Since yesterday?

The day before.

Nel, what are you doing?

I don't know. I want to do this.

Silence.

Everyone thinks it's strange that you're not here.

Well, can you put up with it?

Put up with what?

My staying here until Rome.

Silence.

Sure, I can put up with anything. Yvonne can help me.

Yvonne is his trainer. Yvonne worships him. He confides in Yvonne.

Then I'll stay.

What kind of dog?

A Chihuahua. A rat dog. A boy.

Brown?

Yes.

Give him my regards.

Antony?

Yes?

Please understand and let me do this.

Listen, Nel—oh, whatever. Well, I guess I'll see you in Rome then. Assuming I get there.

Silence.

Thank you.

It was strange what you did.

I know.

Okay, I'll talk to you.

Yes. I'll call you. I'll be staying at her house. Do you want the number?

What is it?

I told him.

I hope your ankle feels better.

Me too.

Take care of yourself.

Okay.

I miss you.

Miss you too.

Silence.

All right. I'll call.

Okay.

Bye.

Bye.

We hung up.

The ghostly sensation these exchanges induced afflicted me briefly. How could anything so empty be so painful? I went to the window. The sky was now deep violet; a crescent moon was rising. The air smelled of the sea. How much in the past I would have wished for him to be here, to say, Look at the moon, stand with him in the presence of so much beauty and mystery, feel close to him, connected, married. I had wished for it too long. The evening breeze was cool on my face; a tremor passed through my body. I found myself suddenly conscious of all the others who had stood at this window, on nights as beautiful as this one, generations of watchers, with how much expectation, joy or despair in every gaze? My heart expanded in sympathy. *I dream in my heart the dreams of other dreamers* did Whitman say? I shivered again. Were we assembled here, centuries of us, conjured by the softly darkening sky, the pale moon? It felt uncanny; the reel of time seemed to spin away. By a simple coincidence of proximity, I was among the unknown many. Another would come, tomorrow night probably. I would be gone then, among the invisible. This was my night to watch. A wave of longing surged through me. *I become the other dreamers.*

I came down in the morning with my suitcase; these were not enough clothes for three weeks. Matteo was lounging in a chair in the lobby with a wry smile on his handsome face. Did he find it pretentious and absurd? I suppose there is something vulgar about this level of luxury, but the place was at least old and real once, not the inert, marble-veneered excess of American hotels, so many of which I had seen. It had been a privilege for me to stay here. He saw me, got up, crossed the lobby, and took my bag.

Good morning, he said. Not bad here, is it?

I had been justifying myself to Matteo, who couldn't care in the least.

No, I had a sweet room on the small canal. I tried to imagine who might have lived in it when the great Gritti was here.

There was no Gritti here until the nineteenth century and not a great one then.

No doge?

No doge. They like to pretend that Giorgione frescoed the exterior walls, but that isn't true either.

How disappointing.

It is old. You can imagine, if you want to, that some poor conservator lived in your room, making his way through university touching up the Giorgiones that weren't here.

Cheerful, I thought.

We proceeded to the front desk. No Carlo. I left him a note thanking him for his efforts, how much I had liked the room. I paid the bill with my credit card, and Matteo and I set out across the little *campo* I would miss.

Were you a poor conservator making your way through university touching up frescoes? I inquired.

No, I was more fortunate. You are also lucky? You stay in such places often?

Sometimes.

And when you are not doing that?

I live in New York.

Ah, New York.

He waited for me to go on but I did not.

When I saw you with Leo I didn't imagine you were American. American tourists don't often bring their dogs. But Leo is small enough to be a world traveler, no? Half a ticket.

Did you think I was Italian?

Not Italian, possibly French.

I had no idea what that meant or if it was complimentary, but I smiled at him. He didn't notice.

You looked self-absorbed. European travelers don't look around so much as Americans. They are not so surprised to be on this side of the ocean. They're more used to things being old. At least the Americans one sees on the street. There have been American families who lived in Venice, famous Americans in Venice. Someone should show you Palazzo Barbaro, which belonged to Americans. Henry James stayed there and wrote one of his books. It's about a search for documents. Just what you will be doing. He smiled without looking at me.

Are you making fun of me?

Why would I do that?

You think this idea of the signora's to have me here is a bit foolish? I'm not what you'd call an expert in the field, am I? Is she being kind? Offering me this—what did she call it— investigation—because I found Leo? And fainted, I wanted to say.

I don't know what she has in mind. You reminded her of the painting in that room. That pleased her. She doesn't often have guests. Perhaps it was Leo's idea; he usually has his way. He glanced at me briefly, with another wry smile.

I wasn't able to interpret his tone. We didn't seem to know what to make of each other; it didn't feel encouraging.

We arrived at the signora's house. The door opened as if by magic; Annunziata was there, loitering again, it appeared. She wrested my suitcase from Matteo's hand, smiling at me all the while. Our successful communication regarding breakfast yesterday morning had put me further in her favor apparently. A series of nods in my direction told me that we were confidantes. She would see to me.

Matteo and I climbed the staircase; I heard two voices in the salon. The signora had a guest. We entered. She was seated at the table having coffee with an odd-looking gentleman. Tall and heavy, in the tweedy ensemble of an English squire, complete with a knobby, rustic-looking walking stick, he appeared an unreconstructed expatriate from another era; a wild mane of shoulder-length white hair exploded around his surprisingly narrow, aristocratic face. He and the beautiful white-haired signora made an impressive pair. Henry James could have made a third.

Oh good, Matteo, you have brought Nel, she said, extending her arm to me.

Now I want you both to meet my very old friend—my very dear friend, I should say—Professore Renzo Adolphus. Renzo, these are the young inquisitors who require your advice, Matteo Clemente and Cornelia Everett.

The professore, with the help of his walking stick, rose to a towering height and shook our hands with a cordial smile. Annunziata was instantly present with more cups and fresh coffee. Making polite remarks, we gathered around the table and sat down in the light of the arched windows, filtered now by nearly transparent linen curtains billowing to the floor. Leo, who had been prancing around my feet, resumed his position on his scarlet velvet pillow; we exchanged smiles.

Renzo and I have known each other since we were children, have we not, my dear? The professore nodded, half closing his eyes. We were the little English children, although we had never, either of us at that time, seen another country but Italy, our families being friends in the expatriate community. So long ago, those ribbons and sailor suits, no, my friend? And Giuseppe, the pony, who bit us without mercy. She laughed. He remained thoughtful.

Well, so many things since then. But the professore has distinguished himself in many countries, certainly in our so-called country where he has held a chair at his alma mater, Cambridge University. Recently he has come home to Italy.

To die, muttered the professore.

Well—the signora laughed—one must do that somewhere, Renzo. Better here in the nicer climate, but certainly not yet. And not when we need your help. We must solve a mystery.

What mystery is that? he asked, eyes still hooded, motionless.

Matteo? she said.

Matteo, taken by surprise, gathered himself. Reluctantly, I thought.

It is a fresco in the upstairs salon, he began, uncovered by damage to the plaster, still mostly buried but emerging. We think it may be early sixteenth century; it has the look of Bellini's school, the younger ones. We can identify nothing yet, but the application of the paint is unusual and the subject, if we can call it that at this point, is provocative. Mythic, poetic, suggestive, but not clear. A woman in classical dress, perhaps, a lion, a landscape possibly.

A woman, a lion? the professore repeated. He looked steadily at Matteo with unexpected bright green eyes.

So it would seem, said Matteo.

Here in this casa, an unheralded masterpiece? Out of the blue?

I don't know.

I don't know either, the professore responded, turning away to the signora. How exciting your life has become, he remarked with some irony.

She smiled and said nothing.

I ventured into the impasse. We wondered if the fresco might have been done by the same person who painted the woman in the upstairs bedroom. Matteo shot me a cold look.

The woman in the upstairs bedroom?

Renzo, the signora said, there is a small painting in an upstairs bedroom, done on plaster long ago, probably when Ca da Isola was a convent. It has a frame around it. I had forgotten it was there, but Nel noticed it and mentioned a similarity when we were looking at the fresco. We marched up to see it, and, I must say, there is something about it.

What is there about it?

It gives off distress, I said. Matteo thinks the figure in the fresco is also a woman. I didn't look at Matteo.

And on the basis of this morning's investigation you imagine it is the same woman?

We don't know, Renzo, the signora replied. We know nothing, and I don't begin to know how to find out something. That is why I hope you will help us. A simple thing for you and difficult for me.

What date did you say you assign to this fresco? the professore asked, turning his head very slightly in Matteo's direction.

Perhaps early sixteenth century. We doubt it's earlier because of the technique, possible overall landscape elements. School of Bellini, as I said.

I see. School of Bellini. Giorgione, Titian, frescoed the wall of an obscure convent when these gentlemen were enjoying noble commissions?

We don't know, Matteo replied, with a tight smile. It seems unusual.

I don't doubt it, the professore answered, pursing his lips and nodding. He turned to the signora and smiled wearily, as if she had lured him into a tiresome game.

Matteo is highly regarded; he has several degrees in art history and is a graduate of the Istituto Centrale in Rome. I'm sure you know what that implies, Renzo, the signora responded, unsmiling. We are not children larking.

In that moment I realized how much I was enjoying this.

Well, I suppose we ought to have a look, the professore murmured. I suppose it's not impossible. The Venetians are terribly fond of new treasures. A bit late in the game, but one never knows. And what was this convent? he asked, gazing at the still-solemn signora.

I don't know, she replied. I am not a historian. It was established, I believe, sometime in the fifteenth century to deal with the plague. The casa was given to nuns to care for the dying. It was a minor asset of the family. They probably made the gift to gain some sort of favor or indulgence for whatever had recently come to light. I know very little about it.

And there are records?

I don't know.

The signora had taken on an almost girlish obduracy, motionless, defensive. She sat very straight and seemed suddenly a haughty beauty, an unmanageable, willful girl. I tried to imagine how beautiful she must have been at sixteen. This was not lost on the professore, who was watching her with so much interest that Matteo and I seemed no longer present in the party.

Where might the records be? I attempted.

The records? she said, turning to me. I have no idea. Where

are such records kept? she inquired of the professore, recovering herself.

In the archives, of course, he answered curtly, also turning to us. The spell was broken; we were back in our conference.

But you would have to know the name of the convent; it would certainly make it easier. There is nothing here to tell you?

You would think there would be something, she said, frowning, restored to her gracious manner.

Annunziata entered with a tray, sandwiches, and a bottle of wine. We were now having whatever comes after *colazione.* They seemed to eat and drink all day long here.

Nunzia, the signora said, *ce per caso qualcosa nella casa che reconta la storia del convento che stava qui. Conoscete qualcosa in qualsiasi camera dove possiamo trovare il nome del convento? O vecchie cose? O qualcosa interessante, speciale?*

Sì, sì, Signora. Nella camera di sopra ci sono vecchissime cose. Sono sporche, molto sporche. Vecchi bauli e scatole. Al inizio, quando siamo arrivati, pensavo di pulire la camera, ma adesso non vado su. Penso che ci sono i ratti, ma soltanto. Non facciamo entare i ratti. Niente ratti, Signora. Annunziata folded her hands and looked concerned.

What did she say? I inquired.

No rats, the signora answered. But a room with old trunks.

What room is this? Matteo looked incredulous.

She says she meant to clean the room fifty-five years ago when we moved in but hasn't gotten around to it. She thinks there are rats there but nowhere else. I am not aware of this room. There are storage rooms on the top floor above this section of the house; I have seen them. Perhaps this room is in another hall above the kitchen or office section. As you know, Renzo, I was mostly in Verona for many years and not here so often. Now, of course, I live here, but mostly in these rooms. I have not explored every nook and cranny. I have been busy with my own work.

Her own work? How mysterious she was. Did I imagine that beautiful, intelligent, healthy women of eighty sat about with hands folded or amused themselves with small dogs? And what was my work? If I wasn't doing it now, what would I be doing at eighty?

Yes, yes said the professore. Well, someone ought to have a look at this filthy ancient vault. It's unlikely that much will be found there, but with no information we can do very little. The location itself is a place to begin an inquiry in the historical records but much more difficult without a name. If the casa was given to the nuns during a fifteenth-century plague, that is a clue; we know when the plagues occurred. Was it always Ca da Isola? Or did it come from the woman's family?

That's many generations ago, Renzo.

Yes, yes, we'll have a look. Now shall we also have a look at this provocative fresco? I must soon be getting back.

Later the signora retired for the evening. She found the afternoon's interview trying, I thought. The professore stood silent in front of the fresco for some time, had a few words with Matteo, and left without further comment. After he had gone, the signora and Leo led me downstairs and through a door in the courtyard into a garden I had not, of course, been aware of.

We did not speak of the encounter with the professore. Enough of that, was all she said. She did mention that we should wear masks when we went to the attic room; mold and rat droppings could be dangerous. Her enthusiasm for our project seemed to have flagged, but she regained energy in the garden. The garden was astonishingly beautiful, a large square enclosure. It didn't seem the work of an amateur; it was other-worldly in its perfection.

The signora pointed out a mulberry tree in one corner, in another a pomegranate, both gnarled, venerable trees; magnolias and lemon trees; espaliered pear and apple trees that lined the walls. In the center was a fountain, pocked granite or lava, ancient; fat putti blew metal horns out of which water splashed into the wide basin. Surrounding the fountain on patterned mossy stones were huge pots, also ancient-looking, primitive and rough, each filled with a profusion of grasses and flowers, some recognizable to me and others quite exotic, most still in bloom. The signora touched the blossoms fondly and told me their names as she expertly deadheaded malingerers. The light was wondrous: cool dark corners, afternoon sun lavishing the fountain and pots; color, fragrance, all dense and lush; stone benches here and there—a miniature paradise. I looked at her in wonder.

Yes, I have always had gardens, she said, smiling. This little cloister is all I can manage now. I have not lived here always, although I came back in the winter. We had a country house outside Verona where I had grand gardens; finally it was too much. Easier to live here. Expensive as Venice is, it is nothing to the cost of two houses and a staff of gardeners.

She looked sad.

It is absurd and embarrassing to know so little about the history of this house. Renzo thinks me a fool. I do sometimes try to imagine the nuns living here and wonder about them, wonder if they kept a garden, if one perhaps may have been a gardener. I would like to know. The fountain has been here for many years, I think. I wonder what it has seen.

My sense of history is the same, I said, I don't have references

I wish I had; it makes me feel lazy and romantic. But information isn't everything.

We were silent, gazing across the green space. I imagined the two of us in white habits or whatever nuns of the fifteenth century wore, wondered what sort of conversation we might have been having then. God, politics, the difficult novice, men? I already felt devotion for this remarkable woman who had admitted me to this house, this garden. My abbess, I thought. I laughed.

Why do you laugh?

Because I'm surprised and happy to be here.

And I am happy to have you. There is very little company I enjoy; it's nice to have a girl here; it makes me remember. Tonight I think I will rest. Matteo will take you to La Barca, very good fish. Leo and I will retire and prepare for tomorrow's investigation.

At the sound of his name, Leo, who had been dismembering a leaf, stood, stretched his front paws, and looked up at us expectantly.

Caro, the signora said, lifting him into her arms. Here is a good little man, clever, tender little man. Leo gave her a single heartfelt kiss on the cheek.

Matteo and I set out through the streets. We had both showered and changed for the occasion. I was not wearing black, not at that moment in disguise or in mourning for my life. I was wearing beige instead, my other option, beige slacks, beige linen shirt, sandals, coral drop earrings. Matteo looked understated and Italian. Black pants, a gray-blue long-sleeved jersey with sleeves pushed up to his elbows. Handsome. His blond hair was darker, still wet. He smelled of some lovely soap. He was preoccupied.

He led me through the usual maze in silence. Finally I made an attempt. So, the professore?

The professore, he replied. Too much time in England.

What do you mean?

He is arrogant. Contemptuous.

Italians are not contemptuous?

It is the particular British style. No one who has not been baptized in those waters knows anything of importance. We are simple Italians, imagining masterpieces everywhere.

What did he say?

That as yet there is nothing to say. I must keep at my work; when we see more, he will pronounce.

He's a strange old man.

He is famous.

We arrived at La Barca, a café on a remote embankment of the Grand Canal emitting divine aromas. The brooding sky was a milky dark blue. I noticed that I had not attempted to cheer Matteo, my usual role; it must be nice for men not to be allowed to be sad in the company of women. My heart wasn't in it. Although he did smell very nice and his skin looked inviting, warm and tawny. It was pleasant to be with a strange man. La Barca, he said, extending his attractive forearm, indicating the café with a wan smile. He was upset. The professore had upset everyone. Everyone but me.

Over a spectacular meal of aglio olio pasta, grilled fish, and salad, we struggled to make conversation. I tried harder, he was withdrawn; the dinner had not been his idea. At last the wine, two bottles of it, began to release us. I asked about the signora's history, did he know it? He knew some things. That she married, very young, a Venetian count, older; the marriage was a bit of a scandal for her British aristo family. He was, in fact, a black sheep, a playboy and race-car driver who died in a car wreck within ten years. She's a well-known gardener, has published on gardening in pots, her specialty; is more famous as a botanical painter, known mostly in Italy. She never remarried. No children. He didn't know about her family, she doesn't mention them, probably all gone. She's private, almost reclusive, rarely entertains, is regarded as a celebrity of another era. The scandal of the marriage, remembered in Venice, lends her mystique. Most of this is known about her; she does not discuss it. She got the palazzo and the house in Verona when the count died. There was no one else to inherit; the da Isola family had annihilated itself. She's been on her own for a long time.

I was fascinated, but that was all Matteo knew except that she had been exceptionally kind to him. The professore was probably a gift that backfired.

We talked about his family and his work. He had been expected to be a doctor or a lawyer and studied medicine briefly at Padua. His family was not particularly artistic, he said, but as the youngest son they finally supported him in his interests. They're wealthy and live in Milan. His father was trained as an architect but is now an industrialist, like his own father, the family business. Matteo disapproves, he loathes the corruption of Italy. He thinks that with its wealth of treasures, every apparent effort to preserve and restore is a cover for making money from gullible foreigners. He has spent years studying and training, has done well in his field, is respected; the conundrum this fresco presents gives him the opportunity to distinguish himself. He is distressed by the professore's arrival and interference. If the fresco is anything, the professore will claim it as his discovery.

You think the fresco is important? I asked.

I know it is, possibly of major importance. I will do the work, and the Honorable Renzo Adolphus will take the credit. That's how things are done. I don't blame the signora, but I wish things had remained as they were.

I'm sure that includes me, I thought. What about the attic? I asked.

Oh, who knows. It was no longer a convent at some point. It could be crinolines from the nineteenth century. It was a da Isola outpost, used for strangers and guests, visiting English.

Matteo did not embrace his English heritage. He told me that he had been there but the hostile influence of his father had prevented him from feeling comfortable. His British mother had become entirely Italian to please her apparently tyrannical husband. He had relatives somewhere in England but didn't know them. He preferred to think of himself as European. He found America distasteful. Then he remembered me.

I don't mean you, of course.

I don't mind.

Why don't you mind?

I don't think of myself as that.

How do you think of yourself?

What a question.

I think of myself as Nel. Even that may be going too far.

We sat in silence. I felt a great deal more sympathy for Matteo in spite of his crankiness. I recognized myself in his unwillingness or inability to overcome his disappointment and fears and put up a charming social front. I saw that he felt his life was somehow at stake and that what mattered to him mattered intensely. I liked how serious he was. I understood why he would hate the pretensions and entitlements that Renzo Adolphus embodied, why he might distrust the Brits. I wondered what he was like when he was happy.

Well, Nel, if that's what you are, thank you for listening. I'm sorry to be despondent. I'm sure the signora wanted you to have a nice time, instead we've discussed . . . whatever.

I don't mind, Matteo. Although I must say that I've found that things are not always so inevitable. Renzo may by now be such a glorious personage he can no longer take in what's in front of him—blinded, you know, by his massive excellence. He may assume that anything on that obscure wall in that obscure house is beneath his notice. He may miss it.

I doubt it. Maybe.

Matteo paid the bill and we set off to find our way back to the house. A few blocks passed in silence. I began quietly to sing. *Rule, Britannia! Britannia rules the waves, Britons never, never, never shall be slaves!* Matteo looked at me with surprise and to my astonishment began to sing. We grew expansive, soon we were shouting; we had, after all, enjoyed two bottles of very good wine. We sang the same two lines over and over again; every time we arrived at *Britons never, never, never shall be slaves!* we laughed out loud, all the way home.

CHAPTER THREE

Coming into the room that night—my room, our room—I felt chagrined to be in so silly a state because there she was, waiting for me. Matteo and I had collected ourselves and said a polite good night, but I was still laughing. I sobered up at the sight of her. She exuded such loneliness. She'd be a sorrowful roommate, but gaiety, after all, hadn't been a conspicuous component of my own experience for a while.

There was also something fervent and courageous about her. How many complicated emotions were communicated by this modest, unembellished little painting. A skilled hand must have made it. And all in her body, not even a face to see. It looked swiftly done, nothing about it was labored; it was a fluent gesture of pain. Who understood grief so well?

Alone in an empty frame. Perhaps that's why she seemed so compelling. People make so many concessions to belong to something, anything. The question "What do you do?" had inspired such alarm in me of late, my reflexive self-protective answer, even to myself, was that I was married to him and he was doing something, so I must be as well. A meager evasion. How distasteful I found it that my life had come to this impasse.

I knew how it had happened. Everything familiar and recognizable had been abandoned on the far side of an abyss I could never recross. It would have been braver to step through the huge tear in my life and find out who and what was on the other side, but I was marooned in a frightening present, brushed by the wings of death. I needed protection, to belong to something, not to be left alone in an empty frame.

If we were going to share the room, I felt she should have a name. I'd call her Angelica. Angelica, I whispered. No doubt we both believed we knew what we were doing, I thought. No doubt we had hopes.

Tomorrow I would find a flower in the garden and put it here for her.

After *colazione* in the salon, Matteo, restored to himself and impatient, opened a plastic bag and produced masks that looked as if we were going into a quarantine zone. I suppose we were, although it had been fifty years, not forty days, since the room had been opened.

No, no, my dears, the signora said, declining a mask with a wave of her hand. This is an enterprise for the young and able. You will come and report. Also Leo must not go up there and eat an ancient, disgusting thing.

Annunziata, however, was prepared. Wearing a huge beige housekeeping smock of some kind that covered her entirely, she had a broom, dustpan, mop, and a bucket that gave off a nasty stink. Also a large ring of keys. She too brushed aside the mask that Matteo offered, but the signora insisted, becoming quite angry until Annunziata accepted it with a stubborn face.

The three of us set out. Matteo carried the broom and dust-pan, I the mop, and Annunziata the bucket. I thought of the Seven Dwarfs, heigh-ho. We followed her to a spotless old stone kitchen, Annunziata's domain, and through a door she opened with a key into an arcaded hallway with large grimy windows facing the larger canal. Another locked door at the far end and we entered a big, empty, windowed but airless room in what Matteo said was the office wing of the house. Annunziata crossed determinedly to one more door at the opposite side of the room, unlocked that, and we proceeded up dusty wooden stairs. On the first landing there were two more doors to either side, closed. The whole wing was deserted. We continued to the next landing and confronted a final door, this one so primitive and foreboding that it suggested something out of a fairy tale.

Annunziata fumbled with the ring of keys, muttering all the while, until she found a massive skeleton key that she plunged into the irregular rough-looking keyhole. Matteo and I put on our masks. Annunziata resisted. With our masks in place our protestations were muffled, so we stamped our feet to remind her of the signora's insistence. She complied finally, looking resentful and ridiculous in her smock and vizard, an unlikely reveler at Carnavale. She turned back to the door, wrestled briefly with the key, and pressed the heavy wooden panel. With a low groan, as if untimely awakened, the door swung open, tearing a huge thick cobweb to dangling shreds.

In spite of the masks, the air that flowed out to meet us was suffocating, tomblike, malodorous with the bitter aroma of an abandoned past. The room was dark, even after the unlit staircase; I felt nearly blind. I could make out vague shapes here and there in the gloom, something immense looming in a corner. Matteo and I stood immobilized. Annunziata, undaunted, crossed the room, unbolted and threw her whole weight against the jamb of a dust-caked arched window, which gasped explosively and fell outward. Light and fresh air streamed in like grace bestowed. I expected everything to disintegrate from sudden exposure to the daylight of another eon. No obvious rats, but they heard us coming.

Annunziata tore off her mask, thinking the window reprieved her. Missing the point, she took the broom from Matteo and began to whisk it furiously in the appalling detritus on the floor—inches of dust, rat droppings, dead insects—sending up clouds of toxic matter into our horrified faces. We fled down the stairs to the landing.

Annunziata! Matteo shouted through his mask. *Non respirare quell'aria!*

Annunziata, no! I cried.

Mouth set, she continued to sweep, pushing piles of filth into the dustpan and tossing them out the window. She was swift, effective, and proprietary. Matteo and I rushed down to the lower room to escape the flying pollution.

She'll live to be a hundred and fifty and we'll die young, I mumbled into my mask.

I hope she opens the other window, he said. We heard a vigorous thud.

If only she were in charge of my life, I remarked. Then we stood quietly like two severely asthmatic children waiting to see the doctor.

Fifteen minutes passed. We heard thumps and bangs; a new wave of poison wafted down on us, the filthy stench of whatever was in the bucket. She must have been whirling around like a possessed exterminator. It occurred to me that she regarded this attic as a dereliction of her duty, one she was forced to admit to under interrogation. Annunziata was not a woman to take responsibilities lightly, and she was proud.

Matteo and I remained in our trance state until she reappeared on the landing clutching her implements and the empty bucket.

Entra! Entra! she ordered, rattling down the steps and brushing past us.

We heard her clumping her way through the rooms; a distant door slammed in what must have been the kitchen. We regarded each other, eyes only, and began a timid ascent to the attic room, Matteo first.

The room smelled terrible but of ammonia not time. A surprising amount of dirt was gone, the floor for the most part looked nearly clean, and she must have taken the broom to the cobwebs. Both windows were open. Outside a clear September morning shone in bright contrast to the contents of the room, which stood exposed like disinterred coffins. Trunks, five of them, with heavy straps, four lined up in a row and one standing alone; in the corner, a massive armoire.

We crossed to the armoire, a black, carved, Gothic-looking thing with a conspicuous keyhole. It was, in fact, locked. We turned back to the trunks.

Which one? Matteo asked.

After years of being what I considered too impetuous, now when I make choices I try to be calm for a minute to let my intuition speak. I did that and pointed to the smaller, reddish trunk sitting a little distance from the others.

Matteo knelt and tried to loosen a leather strap so desiccated and rigid that a piece broke off in his hand. I began to feel like a vandal. What remained of the strap passed through the buckle. He was agile with the other strap, easing it through intact with the deftness of a safecracker. There was a lock on the front of the trunk. Matteo tried pressing the lid upward, and, to our astonishment, it began to give, and then, with a creak like a little cry, it sprang open.

My God! I gasped.

Although it was impossible to tell from the tarnished exterior, the inside of the trunk lid was a rich, red, creamy Moroccan leather, and there, in intense contrast, laid across the top, was a lush violet fabric that must have been a dress or cloak of some kind. The shock of color in the gloom of the attic was breathtaking. I knelt beside Matteo and ran my finger across the sumptuous surface. Not a trace of dust. An excellent trunk, no doubt.

Not Victorian crinolines, I said.

Not nuns, he replied.

What then?

Don't know.

Should we move any of this? Will we damage it? It must be very old.

I don't know. I should ask someone.

So beautiful. Just a little look?

I lifted a corner of the velvet and saw crimson silk and a piece of nearly transparent white fabric. The trunk smelled sweet.

Matteo, do we dare?

Let me ask someone, said the conservator.

I watched him close the trunk, and we moved on to the last in the row of coffins.

His skills honed, Matteo unstrapped this one without incident. It wasn't locked either. No one was being very careful when they left these things here. This trunk was not so finely made, sturdy brown leather. We opened it and saw more gorgeous fabric. Matteo restrained us. Conservators of ancient frescoes do not lack patience.

I'll find out tomorrow what to do. I'll call a friend, he said.

The room was restored to drabness, but morning light filled it as if an aura had been released from the trunks themselves. Matteo closed and bolted the windows. We descended the stairs and walked silently back into the present century.

The signora was delighted with our discovery. Who could imagine such a thing! So old! But very fine things? Not nuns' habits, which I always think of as burlap, although I know they were not poor. Very different, the convents then. Not docile creatures. I know only stories.

We were having aperitifs in the salon. The windows were open; the gossamer curtains lifted in the evening breeze; the light, as always, was soft and pink. Leo was visiting on my lap. Matteo reported that someone would rush up here from Florence tomorrow to view this find. He seemed expansive, smiling and more relaxed than usual.

However, said the signora, I have had a call from Renzo. He put one of his minions to work in the archives, and the minion was unable to identify a convent at this location. He did say there was a record of the house being offered as a gift to another famous convent, Santa Maria delle Vergini, a rich convent. The gift was surely accepted, he thinks; they were enthusiastic about real estate. This would be mid-quattrocento.

Didn't you say it was given during a plague? I asked.

Yes, I think so. That is what Alvise said. He found it amusing that we were offered the plague house, since they regarded him as a plague. There was only his mother left by then, the daughter, and an old uncle or two living in the Canal house. His excellent older brother had been killed in the first war. The countess could never forgive Alvise for being the one to survive; she didn't want to see us.

How did the family get the house back from the convent? I asked.

Probably divested and returned during a papal crackdown, Matteo suggested. There were years of ongoing power plays between the important convents and the authorities. The old struggle between Rome and Venice. The nuns at Le Vergini were noble; I remember someone telling me that that they gave orations in Latin. It's long gone. A piece of it is left out by the Arsenal, if I remember. They're studying these convents now, women's studies. No one cared very much about the nuns before, although they had important collections. They were patrons. Patronesses.

Patrons, I said. We don't say conservatoresses.

Matteo did not smile.

The signora laughed. Poor girls, she said. One lucky sister, and the rest end up being religious. Too many dowries. The married ones did not have such a great freedom either. A little fling and into the fire.

I suppose we're very free today, I remarked. Convents aside.

As they say, the more things change, she replied. It is handled differently, but still the men. Although, as Matteo said, more women scholars. You are an educated girl; I do what I like. The problem always is with the hearts, I imagine. We hand them out a bit generously.

And have them handed back, I replied.

Yes, but sometimes they come back as a gift. I was finally happy to have mine back. Now I am free to give my heart to

Leo. At the sound of his name, Leo exchanged laps, playing the field.

Why do women imagine that only women suffer? Matteo remarked, refilling the signora's glass.

We both looked at him.

Men are not nice to men either, and women are not eternally kind and generous, filling mine.

No, I said, but they're treated differently. Men didn't require dowries. They weren't burned for adultery.

I don't know that women were burned for adultery, do you? There were plenty of prohibitions about sex for everyone in Venice, men and women.

I don't know much about Venice or the Renaissance, I replied, but in spite of all of that generous humanism there weren't a lot of women artists, were there? Not that we've heard of.

There were a few.

An inconspicuous few.

Darlings, said the signora, let us not debate this. We are a lucky few here, and we'll have a nice supper. She crossed to the table and rang a small bell.

Matteo and I, eyes averted, exchanged a little interesting tension. Annunziata, restored to her traditional black ensemble, arrived with the tray.

After the signora and Leo had retired, Matteo and I sat on in the salon over the unfinished second bottle of wine. We had chatted amiably enough through supper; left alone, we were quiet.

I glanced at him; he was looking down at the table, so I too looked down. I glanced up again and found him watching me, unsmiling.

Sorry, I said, patronesses is fine with me; worse things have happened. It's just reflexive.

Probably my mistake, he murmured.

I used to be a warrior. I'm not one anymore. I don't know if people can change the way they think, anyway. Life is short. I didn't mean to lecture you.

What became of the warrior?

She retired.

Once a warrior, he said, what do you do in retirement?

I don't know. Fiercely not be one.

Given up?

Maybe. What about you? You're a safecracker.

What?

The way you did those trunks, I said, emptying my glass. The light touch, Matteo. Safecrackers have it. Clever hands. A little criminal.

He smiled at last, refilled my glass and his own.

And patience, you have patience. Thank you.

I did not always have patience. I learned.

Your work taught you?

My work and other things.

I think you're patient about having me here. I think you wanted things to stay the same. I won't be here long.

Maybe yesterday, but not now. I'm not sure any of what's happened would have happened if you hadn't stayed in that room. You must be a gift. The signora obviously thinks so.

Did you want to be the only gift? I think I like to be the only gift. I like being a gift at all.

Maybe everyone does.

I'm grateful, anyway, that you'll share it for a little while. It's wonderful for me: mysterious frescoes, mysterious trunks, magical clothing, arguing with you about Renaissance convents, and all in this glorious house. It's like an Italian wonderland. Leo led me to wonderland. Or you did.

New York is not a wonderland?

No, I wouldn't say so. What's your life like, Matteo?

My life?

I felt suddenly shy, as if I were inquiring about his availability, the last thing I meant.

I live in Rome. I have an apartment there. Friends. Colleagues. He paused. And a son.

A son?

Yes, he is six years old.

He's with your wife?

No, with my parents at the moment. My wife is gone. When my son was born.

I'm sorry.

Yes.

We were silent.

A complicated situation, he said.

Every situation is complicated, I replied.

Yes.

We could now tell each other everything or stop. I preferred to stop. I could think of no way to talk about my own life that would not leave me feeling as pried open as those chests on which we trespassed this morning. Warrior, indeed. I was suddenly desolate and close to tears.

Well, I'll see you in the morning?

We'll meet, yes, in the morning.

We stood.

It's good that you're here, Matteo said, you mustn't think not. He reached toward me, put his hand on the back of my neck and kissed me fleetingly on the cheek.

Perhaps this was what Italians did to make people feel welcome, but my own body flashed, a sensation I blithely called *meltdown* in the days when this sort of thing happened to me, the unbidden response, more than unexpected at that moment. I felt heat in my face. I felt shocked. I found it hard to look at him. I felt absurd.

I'm glad you're here, he said. Did he know what happened to me? Had I once again missed something?

Thank you, I managed. Then, even more awkwardly, I'm glad you're here too. Was I a child? This was perhaps one surprise too many. I'll see you in the morning then. I turned to the door. The thought of Antony arrived with the impact of a blow to the face. Where was I?

He watched me leave.

I made my way to my room, unnerved, and found my tormented friend. This doesn't end, does it? I said.

I had forgotten to bring her a flower.

Her name was Pia Vanni and she was beautiful. Slim, dark, probably twenty-five. They seemed to know each other well. They leaned over the red trunk together, and she sighed with admiration.

It is so extraordinary, so intact, she said. I think you are right.

She had spread a huge plastic sheet on the floor. They lifted the beautiful violet garment from the trunk and laid it out. It appeared to be a sort of open dress with ties and sleeves, intricately made with edges of gold cloth. How exposed it looked, bodiless and forsaken.

Yes, yes, she said. So extraordinary. So perfect.

What is it? I asked. They looked up, surprised to find me there, I felt.

It is an overdress, a very fine one.

It's the same period—same as the fresco, we think, Matteo added.

And so intact, so perfect, she repeated. I cannot believe it.

How did it stay intact? I asked.

I don't know. A miracle. Fine sturdy trunks, no light, a reasonable temperature somehow, herbs in there that prevented insects for all of these years. Years? Centuries. It is so astonishing.

Like the corpse of a saint? I said.

Really, like that, she said, smiling her lovely smile.

Why do you think they're here?

Who can say? Matteo has seen that none of the trunks were locked. They were left here in a hurry.

Matteo stood and opened each of the trunks. There were the beautiful fabrics. I thought of pirate's treasure. Pia gasped with delight at each exposure, and Matteo smiled at her as if each one were a personal gift arranged for her pleasure.

What will you do? I inquired.

If Signora da Isola approves, I will remove all the fabrics to Florence, to examine and to preserve them, she said, without turning to me.

Can we look in the trunks now?

We can look in the trunks and we can look in the armoire, Matteo said.

Whoever had unlocked it had come and gone; the door of the old cabinet stood ajar.

The three of us began to lift out each lovely article, wrap it in tissue paper, and slide it into an individual plastic bag. Pia gave instructions. We uncovered every sort of exquisite clothing: soft cloaks, linen camisoles, gossamer shifts, all redolent of exotic herbs. I found it disturbing and violating to handle things that were certainly precious to living people once. What sort of a day was it when they put them here? Who were they?

Finally we had packaged everything and carried the bags down into the house. It was not so huge a collection as I had imagined; we made only one trip. We brought them to the salon where Pia opened various bags to show the signora what we had found.

Ma che bello! Sono magnifico! Incredibile! she exclaimed, as each piece was brought to her. Of course you must take them. How lovely they smell! Leo was sniffing with an astonished face. Annunziata dragged in two large cardboard boxes, into which we packed the bags.

The four of us sat down to lunch. Pia talked of her work at a costume museum in Florence, collecting and preserving antique clothing. She regarded this as a neglected aspect of history, but so revealing, so important. What a windfall this was! She cast fond looks at Matteo. How happy she was to see him again, how grateful that he had offered her this extraordinary opportunity, how delighted that he was here in the signora's house engaged in this exciting project, how lucky they both were, the signora and Matteo, how thrilling she found it all. Sweet and enthusiastic as she was, I was picking up the faint aroma of the devotee, a scent I knew well, one that drains my own enthusiasm. Matteo looked pleased.

I was happy when Annunziata arrived to say that a cart was at the door to carry Pia's treasures to a water taxi that would transport her to the parking lot near the train station. Matteo would accompany her to Florence to help with the boxes. A bit more gushing, and they were gone. The signora and I folded our napkins without speaking, exchanged a glance, and smiled small smiles.

The signora retired to her studio, which I had never seen, to spend the afternoon. I was inclined to go back to the attic but felt the need to be away from the house, by myself in the streets.

Once out, I realized I wouldn't mind being lost; I'd find my way back. Another lovely afternoon. I was inhabiting a zone of enchantment.

I loved this part of town. I didn't know what it was called but it was clean, quiet, and private. Birds were singing in enclosed gardens; even the canals seemed to sparkle. I'm always cheered by singing birds. I felt empty and airy, unfocused; none of my usual preoccupations presented themselves. But I would have to call. It would be strange to talk to him, as if I were calling from Venus. Venice. How many days had I been here? It felt impossible to count, not very many.

And what about Matteo? Nothing much to excite me today. He seemed a stranger in a stranger's life, more predictable than before when his reserve was intriguing. Today he had been a professional, the love object of innumerable conservatoresses, no doubt, a man who had a defined existence in a world I knew nothing about. A man with a son. I was curious about that story. But what had happened to me? I had reacted. And not with disappointment. Probably nothing to do with him, hand-

some as he was. Others had tried. Once a glamorous British
rock star found me alone and bored in the green room at a large
New York venue during some charity fiesta in which Antony
was featured, walked up to me boldly, and kissed me on the
mouth—a man women would kill for. I felt nothing, except
how absurdly vain he seemed. And who did he imagine I was?
I had been loyal to Antony. When I was younger I was not so
loyal to Nils, as much as I loved him. I liked to think of myself
as free. After he died, seduction lost its charms.

Still, I felt something last night. Last night? Time was taking on a strange dimension here, so long ago. I felt something
with someone I hadn't thought of in that way at all. It wasn't
that Matteo wasn't attractive; obviously Pia had noticed, but
he seemed conventional to me. Is that what it was? I was used
to recognizable men? Men with apparent power? And power is
what I liked? For how many years did I argue against male
power? Yet I seemed to like it myself. Safe in a sinecure and
free to have opinions? Well, I'd learned my lesson.

And the lesson? That I was no longer among the living? I
was still young, young enough, anyway. She is not yet so old
but she may learn. Burnt child dreadeth fire. And so on. But
why should Antony's disinterest signify some final pronounce-
ment when I knew very well he didn't give anyone or anything
much thought? What would I like to do? I had no idea.

I had arrived at something, huge towers and entrance gates.
What was this? The guidebook was still in my bag. I leafed
through the ample illustrations but there were too many. Wait,
wait, I saw that I was in the Campo Arsenale. This was the
Arsenal, the shipbuilding establishment. Venice, queen of the
sea. The guidebook told me it was an efficient factory; in 1574
they completed a ship for Henry III of France in the time it
took him to "partake in a state banquet." Three wonderful

lions guarded the entrance. Venice, city of lions; there are lions everywhere, not just in San Marco. Didn't Matteo say that a piece of Le Vergini could still be seen at the Arsenal? I'd never find it but felt moved to think it was nearby and had some connection to the events of the past few days. I didn't want to go inside; it looked deserted anyway. I wanted to walk.

I came out on the Grand Canal. It felt wonderful to be moving. Suddenly there was a green oasis, a public garden, shady paths, grass, birds. I was happy to see big trees and turned to enter when I noticed a large bronze figure lying on the steps of the embankment, a curious sight in this city of triumphal statues. It was a woman, collapsed on the shore among the moorings. I turned to the guidebook, tried to locate the gardens, and there it was, tiny on the map. This was La Donna Partigiana, a memorial to the women who died during the Resistance in World War II. A powerful tribute to be sure, but she seemed flung there, helpless, discarded, her body dismayingly prone. The guidebook said she is covered with water and can only be seen at low tide. How odd, no trace of her noble efforts, nothing, she seemed an utter victim, sprawled. And drowned. There must be a concept behind this choice; the book didn't say, but I found it disturbing that this was the monument chosen to commemorate courageous women. It looked so much more like defeat.

I left an unspoken blessing with her and went into the gardens. Peaceful there, no one about, the smell of earth and growing things, red benches, a green thought. I would miss nature if I lived on this island; no wonder the signora preferred Verona. And then, just off the path, there was another great statuary lion; bestride this one was a goddesslike woman with arms raised in what appeared to be a large gesture to crowds no longer there. Who was this? The book had nothing to say. She was, nevertheless, an antidote to the tragic heroine on the shore, the very template of woman or goddess triumphant, albeit anonymous in this case. Anonymous in both cases.

Pleasant as it was in the gardens, I thought I should try to find my way home. Furtively, although there was no one to see me, I picked a few stems with yellow blossoms from a late-flowering shrub. I would bring them to Angelica, another anonymous woman. A tribute from the happy goddess and the green earth.

The signora? I asked Annunziata. Smiling, so kind to me now, she took my hand and we went up the stairs to the second landing. I could hear Fabio and Alberto talking in the fresco room, but we headed down the hall to another door. Annunziata knocked and the signora called. *Entra.*

She was seated at a table in the middle of a room, smaller than the salon next door but with two of the same big windows that lavished the space with golden afternoon light. On the table in front of her were little pots of watercolors, brushes, large sheets of paper, and an exotic flower I recognized from the garden in a glass vase.

Non è sparita! È tornata! Annunziata announced triumphantly.

Oh, good, good, said the signora. We were afraid you had lost yourself in the rat maze.

What a wonderful room! I said. What a wonderful place to work. I reached into my bag and offered her one of the flowering shrub stems, a little the worse for wear. I was in the public gardens.

Buddleia, she replied. Lovely. I never go to the gardens and should. I miss the open spaces. Would you like tea, my dear?

Yes, thank you, I would love that.

Annunziata understood *tea* and hurried away.

I crossed to the table and saw what she was working on. It was the flower in the vase. The painting was exquisitely delicate, a perfect rendering.

How beautiful.

Yes, a tricky one, so many things going on inside that little cone.

Matteo says you are famous.

Well, famous. How many look at botanicals?

I envy your skill. And your knowledge.

It is a lovely avocation for which I am immeasurably grateful. Now come and tell me about your day. We went to the low white sofa by the window.

I told her about the Arsenal, the statues, the peace of the gardens, birds singing. She listened attentively, lovingly. I had no other woman in my life like her. My own mother would have preferred not to be a mother at all, would have preferred to be an empress. But the signora was not like a mother; she was, somehow, at eighty-whatever, glamorous and not matronly, more like a greatly enhanced friend, a sophisticated, obliging, invaluable friend.

Signora, I said, you've given me so much happiness here.

You may stop calling me signora, my dear, I find it aging. Everyone I know has always called me Lucy. I would like you to do so as well.

Matteo doesn't.

He can't get used to it. Proper family, proper boy. Have you spoken with your husband?

Only in my mind. May I call him?

Of course.

He won't be there.

You will have tried. You will not seem petulant.

I don't know how to tell him about all of this. It's so entirely not in his sphere.

Tell him every little detail.

He'll sink into a coma.

That is his problem. He should know that you are interested and cared for here, not a runaway, not a bolter. You are having another little life.

But I *am* a bolter.

I know. That is your business only. That is what you will pay attention to.

Advice! I was having advice!

A great and acclaimed actor, my mentor actually, made a film while he was ill, recovering but bedridden; the scene was, in fact, in a bed. The nervous director approached him between the long takes to offer his thoughts. Are you giving me a line reading? my renowned friend demanded in his gruff voice. Oh, no, sir, replied the director. Damn! No one ever gives me line readings! he roared. He told me this story, shouting with laughter.

No one ever gave me advice.

I should think about myself?

Someone should.

And if not me?

Precisely.

The signora, Lucy, difficult but I did it, and I went on to spend what I will remember as one of the happier evenings of my life. We proceeded from tea to cocktails to supper. Leo was in bliss, going back and forth between us. Annunziata, reappearing with drinks and food, became a sort of household goddess bearing gifts.

Lucy told me about her own marriage. As a girl she had been bored with the courtship of the young men who pursued her; she longed for something, someone, to hold her attention. Such people are usually the wrong people for passionate girls, she remarked, and so was he—Alvise. A count, a playboy, a race-car driver, a charmer, fifteen years older than she. Things came easily to Alvise, but he was rapidly using up his credit and credibility, so to marry the lovely sought-after eighteen-year-old daughter of a family of distinction helped him enormously to regain repute. She adored him. And he loved her devotedly, for a time. They lived a gay bohemian life in the early thirties. The marriage lasted for six years, until he was killed racing with friends on the corniche near Monte Carlo. Another man's wife was found dead in the car.

How awful.

Yes, awful, terribly awful then. I was twenty-four; Alvise was forty when he died. He had slipped back into his old ways and I was devastated to lose him—lose him, I mean, to his other life. And then, of course, to actually lose him. Also, the war was beginning to be upon us. Yes, an awful time.

What did you do?

I suffered. My parents were worried; things were not good here. They had friends among the fascist supporters in Rome but were against the government. My father sent my mother and me to Switzerland, where we spent the remainder of the war, in Zurich. Irresponsible to say so, when many suffered terribly, but it was a wonderful time. I attended an art school. I learned to paint. I had new friends; I began to fall in love with nature in the beautiful mountains. I seemed to be on another, much nicer planet. After the war, the countess gave me the houses, Verona and Venice. Her daughter had died by then, part of the Resistance, I was told; I was moved to hear you speak of that monument today. I didn't know Gianetta well but I admired her courage. The countess was alone; there was no one left to have these places, so she gave them to me and died not long after—in a convent, actually. She had sold the Canal house and most of what was in it. It was the end of the da Isolas, an old and interesting family. Always rather doomed. But the countess, God bless her, was proud. She used the funds from the palazzo sale to establish a da Isola foundation, so the name would not be forgotten in Venice.

Did you think of marrying again?

No, oddly, I never did. The same old problem, no one of any interest, although one would think I had learned my lesson. I'm sure the limitation was within myself. I have loved my gardens and my work, having no one to answer to. I suppose I became spoiled by my solitude. Perhaps marriage was not for me. I seem to prefer seclusion; I like to experience time passing. I might have enjoyed children, I'll never know. I'm sure I've missed a great deal, but I do not believe so much in regrets.

Nils was thirty-three when he died.

Oh dear, so young. These deaths. They are terrible but full of riches, as you must know. They take a great toll on the usual delusions, don't you find? The fictions we live by? We know we are powerless and so are more free. We simply live through it or not. If we live, we see ourselves more clearly, for better or worse; our values change. It's as if the love comes back to us in a new form, larger, wiser, more generous. A kind of blessing. Only if one feels it, of course.

I thought Nils was the only one who could understand how

it felt for me to lose him; he was also the only one I couldn't talk to. I felt such guilt; I was afraid he hadn't known how much I loved him. I was hard to handle then, unruly—maybe just young, I don't know—but what you say is true; something inside cracked, a new self began to emerge, a better one, I think, but so fragile. I married Antony too soon. I was frightened. I was a coward.

No, no, my dear, everything happens in its own time. You had to find out what the new girl liked and what she didn't. She must begin to know; that is why she got off the train. You must be patient and alert. Find out what you enjoy, what interests you. Most important, be alive, always life over death.

She reached toward me to pat my hand, but Leo, on my lap, swiftly inserted his head under her extended palm. Oh, these boys! she exclaimed. The two of us rubbed him all over until he was rolling around like an indulged little princeling.

We talked far into the evening. I asked her if Renzo Adolphus had been among her suitors. Oh, my—she laughed—yes, that's quite another story. Renzo apparently had more information and was coming to lunch tomorrow, when Matteo would also be back. I almost regretted having them here again, this time with Lucy had been so affecting for me. The Sufis say that when you are ready for a teacher, a teacher will appear. But Lucy was not like a teacher; her authority was subtle; she was a generous, graceful soul capable of paying attention to others. Perhaps that's what a real teacher is. I adored her. Except for romance and dogs—I had to smile—few attachments had seemed so immediate and certain. Matteo didn't want to share her either.

I had taken a glass from the bathroom earlier and offered

Angelica the buddleia sprig from the gardens. I moved a small table to just beneath the frame. The room was dim now. She continued motionless; she had no release, not even in the dark. There were photographs of Nils that I scrutinized relentlessly after he died. I became irrationally angry at them because they refused to move, to change; instead, they seemed deliberately to petrify and drain away the life I was searching for. I grew to hate them. And I needed their help. Because of the evening and what it had meant to me, I wanted somehow to reach Angelica, to comfort her. I hope there were better times for you, I said, turning off the light. I hope you had a chance.

It is a circular arcaded temple, the sense of a hill, the sea nearby, night. The temple is dim, smoky; fumes are rising from beneath it; there is no floor, only planklike passages laid across an open, dirt-filled, denlike space in which lions are prowling, making deep sounds in their throats. I feel I should be frightened but am not. Standing in the shadows, I'm wearing a togalike dress. I can smell the salty, damp air. In an arcade opposite I see an old college friend of mine enter, a now-eminent doctor, also wearing a toga or robe and leading a lion on a leash. At first I think he has come to threaten or punish me; he seems calm but I feel anxious. I realize then that I too have a lion on a leash; she is behind me, huge and tawny and alert. I put my hand on her head and feel a shuddering thrill. She's carrying a rag doll in her mouth. We step out onto a plank and begin to cross the abyss of the den. The rag doll is gone; my lion is in front of me, walking with a soft, majestic stride. I feel the pressure her strength exerts against the leash and somehow I'm aware in my body of how her massive paws make contact on the narrow board, their sureness. We're out in the middle of what feels like empty space, above the other lions, which seem more real and menacing, skulking beneath us, batting their paws, but I'm irradiated with clarity and joy. A bird cries and the temple fills with light.

In the morning, after coffee, I persuaded Lucy to come with me to the attic, which I assured her must be spotless by now. She laughed and agreed to come so we started out through the many passages, with Annunziata opening all the doors. Leo frisked about in the empty rooms, sniffing every corner.

My, my, I have not been in these parts for so long, Lucy said, how abandoned they are. The offices were the busiest part of these houses at one time, she went on, when the city was alive. The merchants were the real heroes of Venice. No great art without great riches.

She was remarkably lithe and strong, taking the stairs with no hesitation. What a dashing girl she must have been.

Annunziata opened the attic windows and another brilliant morning shone in. The trunks sat mutely, looking like unanswered questions.

Here they are, I said.

Here they are.

Come and see this one, it's the most mysterious. I opened the lid; the rich leather gleamed out, but it was not, as expected, empty. There was a box inside, a painted wooden box, a pretty scene in a green landscape.

How lovely! Lucy exclaimed.

We lifted the lid and found papers and smaller boxes.

A treasure trove! she said.

Can we look? I asked. Are we qualified?

We own it, my dear.

I lifted out a yellowed page and unfolded it. It opened stiffly; the paper was heavy. It was a letter.

Can you read this? I asked, handing it to her.

Lucy looked over the text with a concentrated frown. Not quite, she said, the handwriting is archaic. I can make out words here and there. It was sent to someone called Clara, something about a *regalo,* a gift, devotion to a gift, perhaps, deepest admiration for—something, my heart has never—something, *una perla,* a pearl, *una benedizione,* a blessing, *una speranza,* a hope, difficult to see, signed with an initial, a *Z.* Matteo will know. What else is there?

I lifted out more papers. What's in the boxes? Lucy asked. Open that one.

I opened a small green leather box and found a pearl, a huge rosy-gold natural pearl. In the other leather box was a simple gold band set with a sapphire. A bigger rectangular paper box contained used, stiff paintbrushes. Enclosed in a small piece of folded patterned paper was a tiny lock of fine, pale hair. The rest were papers—more letters, it seemed.

Someone's life, Lucy said, looking down at the two small boxes in her hand.

And her beautiful clothes. Which were gone now. I found myself resenting Pia and her enthusiasms once again. But why should she not have them? Clara, the golden pearl, would not be back.

In the armoire we found stacks of dry rippled papers and bound books, too many to examine. The other trunks were empty now except for desiccated herbs scattered about at the bottom. The sweet scent was less present, gone with the clothing. One trunk was shallower than the others; a different pattern of paper covered its floor. They all looked like ravaged tombs.

I felt sad. Lucy touched my shoulder and picked up the painted box. We will take care of this for her, she said. It will remain with her friends.

What do lions symbolize, Matteo? We were having lunch.

Lions?

A lion, my dear, is the symbol of Venice, offered Renzo. He was chipper today. The winged lion of the evangelist Mark, whose holy remains were liberated, shall we say, from their resting place in Alexandria by two enterprising Venetians in the ninth century and carried here to Venice to become our sacred relic. *Pax tibi, Marce, evangelista meus:* Peace to you, Mark, my evangelist. Someone must take you to see the Carpaccio, he suggested, forking grilled fish into his mouth.

There's also the lion of Saint Jerome, Matteo added, made gentle by the compassion of the sainted scholar. Many lions in Renaissance paintings. Dosso Dossi's *Circe,* where the lion is like a familiar.

Symbol of the old sun god and Apollo, Renzo went on, still eating, worshipped from Persia to Rome, became then Christ, the Lion of Judah. Strength and courage, the insignia of the Roman legions. Alexander wears a lion's head on one of his coins. The lion of Britain. And, of course, here in Venice, the *bocca di leone,* nothing more powerful than that.

What is the *bocca di leone*? I asked.

The lion's mouth, he replied, repositories placed around the city, lionlike masks with open mouths in which one could deposit a complaint, demand garbage removal, expose a criminal, and denounce an enemy—or just as likely a friend. Very dangerous, very much abused, a charming innovation of the Council of Ten.

I have heard, Lucy remarked, that at one time there was an official state lion, a live one, who lived in a golden cage in the piazza. So cold in winter, poor thing.

But also light? I asked, since the lion is the sun? Illumination, not just power? Do you know who the female figure is that sits on a lion in the public gardens?

The public gardens? Renzo repeated.

It's Minerva, Matteo offered.

You mean Athena?

The Roman Athena, yes.

Who made the statue?

I don't know. A humanist sculptor, no doubt, rejoicing in his classics. Or probably it was looted.

Minerva. I would have thought Venus here.

Well, my friends, Renzo said, wiping his lips with his napkin, perhaps we can abandon these interesting lions for the moment so you may hear my report. I have had my best scholar hard at work in the archives, someone who knows very well how to do this.

Graduate students come here to work with Renzo, Lucy interjected, he is so renowned. She gave him a smile in which perhaps only I could detect humor.

Yes, yes, he said, whatever. At any rate, as you know, from the fourteenth century onward there were recurrent outbreaks of the Black Death. Sometime in the mid-fifteenth century an outbreak occurred. Not a devastating one, as in the fourteenth century or later in the sixteenth, but enough to cause alarm. These outbreaks were continual, every thirteen years or so. At any rate, it was at this point, 1465 apparently, that the da Isola family offered this palazzo to the convent of Santa Maria delle Vergini, also known as Le Vergini, for use as a hospital. The nuns of Le Vergini were, as you may know, noble, extremely well placed, and closely connected with the civic power structure. It's likely that the offer was made to gain favor or to make amends for a disgrace of some sort, appealing to the important relatives, we can assume. These noble nuns were perhaps not so interested in nursing the dying; they were busy holding dinner parties and having lovers and bearing illegitimate children. At any rate, the convent was on a small island not far from here, near the Arsenal, on the Rio Le Vergini. Undoubtedly they would have accepted the offer of the house, very nice real estate, and set up a hospital, run doubtless by the less privileged nuns; also, it kept contagion away from the convent itself. After the outbreak passed, we have discovered, the house was used as a school of sorts, for novitiates perhaps, students, but also for nuns who did weaving and scribing, that sort of thing. A more centrally placed location than out there on the island, but nearby. Why should they give it back? They owned and controlled plenty of property. Apparently it would revert to a hospital during outbreaks of the plague.

Renzo, Lucy exclaimed, how well you've done! How illuminating!

The delight in her praise that I sensed through his smug authority was touching.

Well, of course, he demurred, the life of Venetian convents is hardly my area of expertise; I wouldn't have known these things. Ronald, an excellent young scholar who is working with me here pursuing his own research, has been kind enough to divert himself in our interest. He has offered to write up a brief précis of what he has uncovered, and then he must return to his own fascinating labors. It is Ronald who's to be congratulated.

Ronald must come for a drink, Lucy suggested, so we may all thank him for his time spent on our behalf.

Perhaps, perhaps. The professore turned to Matteo. How are things coming along with the mystery masterpiece?

Matteo barely winced. Fabio and Alberto are excellent restorers; the veil is thinning.

You are able to see more?

Not a great deal more, but it's becoming clear that there's an all-over landscape element. Also—turning to me—we are sure of the lion. The later plaster was unevenly applied and in a haphazard manner; the plaster itself is crude. Nevertheless, progress is being made. We shall see.

Ah, yes, replied Renzo, with a thin smile, we shall see. He offered the smile first to me and then to Lucy.

For some reason no one had mentioned the trunks or the clothing to the professore. Lucy and I returned his thin smile and then laughed. A coven within a coven.

Well, this has been delightful! Lucy exclaimed. So many years in this house and only now do I begin to learn a thing about it. A hospital! A school! Marvelous.

And soon a masterpiece as well. Well, I must be off. He rose and kissed Lucy's hand. Mine too. A delightful diversion all of this. It lets me know I'm home in Italy. You must come to me for supper one night; you may meet the intrepid Ronald. Brilliant young scholar, appalling stutter. Ha-ha! Good afternoon, Matteo.

Good afternoon, sir.

Hello?

Antony, it's me. I'm surprised to find you there.

I think the itinerary says it's a day off.

Oh, so it does. A day off in Bologna.

Yes.

Hi.

Hi.

How is Bologna?

All right, I guess. I've been mostly resting. Worked out a little, trying to get my ankle back.

How is it?

Better. Still sore. Stiff. Where are you?

Where? I'm still in Venice.

Still with the countess?

Yes.

I tried that number, wasn't able to make myself understood. *Pronto? Pronto?*

Oh, that was Annunziata. She doesn't speak English. Thank you for trying.

You're still investigating whatever it was, the plague?

Now for the experiment. Yes, Antony, it's been incredibly interesting. I was taking Lucy's advice. I started with Lucy herself, talked about Leo, my room, Angelica, went on to the fresco, the attic, the clothing, the nuns, the park, the professor. I noticed I didn't mention Matteo. I talked on and on; silence reigned at the other end of the line. I sensed him lying on the bed, eyes closed, drifting off.

Antony?

Yes?

It's interesting, isn't it?

I guess so. It must be. I think my mother's family came from somewhere around Venice.

I didn't know.

I think so. Are you coming to Rome?

I think so. Probably. In what, two weeks?

You have the itinerary.

Silence.

Do you want me to come?

Sure I want you to come. You said you'd come.

Why, I wondered, do you want me to come? Because you love me, you want to make me happy?

Then I'll come, I said.

Good. You'll be a sight for sore eyes.

Good.

Listen, Nel, I'm glad you're having a good time. It sounds interesting and I know the tour is boring for you. I think we've established that, he said, laughing, but let's not make an issue of it, okay? Boris says this is good for you, and I know he's right. Go ahead and enjoy it, and we'll meet up and go home, okay?

We'll meet up in Rome. Okay. Thanks. I look forward to seeing Rome. I'll be glad to see you. What are you doing tonight?

Going out for dinner, Boris and Juan and me with some press people. Supposed to be a five-star restaurant. Nicola somebody, this blond woman who's been around relentlessly, organized it. She's a PR person and a fan, knows everybody. Disregard publicity, there's nothing going on.

I haven't seen publicity.

Well, you know how it is.

Yes. I did know how it was. The inevitable, hostile-eyed, aging ingénue lurking somewhere on the periphery whose ambitions are temporarily thwarted by the presence of the dreaded oppressive wife. The inevitable Nicola. International this time.

Well, have fun. Don't eat clams.

Oh God, no. Remember that? I don't want to go tonight,

you know I hate these things, but I'd better catch a nap, Nel.
I'll try again to call you.

Me too.

Love you.

Love to you.

Okay. Be good.

CHAPTER FOUR

Good morning, my dear! Lucy exclaimed, laying down her newspaper. Such exciting news! Renzo telephoned this morning bright and early, still in remarkably high spirits, I was delighted to find, and we are to attend our first dinner party! Renzo is not only going to entertain us but he is going to produce Ronald! Ronald has a great surprise for us.

A great surprise? What would that be?

Lydia!

Lydia?

Ronald has found this wonderful Lydia in the archives, or Lydia has found Ronald; at any rate they had tea and Ronald, our hero, revealed our research project to Lydia, who is, it seems, an absolute authority on Venetian convents, doing research here herself. She has agreed to speak to us; Le Vergini is very well known to her. Lydia has been sent to us by the gods! And Ronald, of course. I have told Renzo about the trunks to give her more information. She's an American. Imagine. We go this evening. Matteo knows.

Where does Renzo live?

Renzo, in tribute to his academic grandeur, she replied, pouring coffee for me, occupies a flat owned by his university, a lovely large flat in a house on the Grand Canal. I believe the house is a sort of club and for students on important fellowships. Very nice for Renzo. We'll have a pleasant stroll if the weather holds. As an added inducement, Leo is invited. A very grand event.

How exciting. I have such terrible clothes.

Go shopping. No, I will find you something. Are you disturbed?

Just a talk with Antony.

How many weeks?

Two.

Fine. Two weeks is a long time in Venice. Now, what will you do today? Matteo says he must stay with Fabio and Alberto; they are coming close to the true surface; he is excited. A matter of days, he thinks. We must also show him the box. I have been looking at Clara's box. I think it may be something.

Something?

The painting on it is quite beautiful and also familiar. We were too overtaken to notice. I think it may be something special. There is also a little mark on a stone in the foreground. It looks like another Z. It must be from him, the one who wrote the letter, the one who loved her.

The one who loved her?

Well, there is the Z again. Who else would sign it? Artists

of that period decorated such things, I believe. It was made for her, surely. She loved an artist. Don't we all? We must show Matteo the box at luncheon. Now, what will you do?

I don't know. Maybe I'll go to the attic, look at things.

Good. We'll meet again at one. Isn't this exciting! she exclaimed with an impish smile, her eyes wide.

She was so charming in her enthusiasm that I reached across the table and took her hand. I was back in wonderland. Two more weeks.

Is there a word for *wonderland* in Italian? Like Alice? I asked.

Not that I know of, not a single word, *il mondo fantastico*, perhaps, not quite the same. Alice in *il mondo fantastico*. She laughed. Our fairy tales are a bit less fey, not so many rabbits as the British like to imagine, here wonderful transformations, everyone seeking love. I remember from my childhood that the King of Love was a green bird who flew away, and the witch who gave the beautiful Angiola the face of a dog until a real dog, a noble little dog like Leo, released her from the spell. I loved that one, and all the kingdoms that are bewitched and must come back to life.

Oh yes, Happy Valley. I listened to records of some version of that story endlessly as a child, turning the pages of the book. The big black cloud finally went away, the sun came out, and the trees grew leaves again. I was always greatly relieved. That's the point, I suppose, to appreciate the sun, the light.

Appreciate it, yes, and perhaps to learn that the cloud is also there, a useful lesson for children. Also to hear what birds and trees and dogs have to say, but you and I already know that. Now we will go back to work. I will bring the intriguing box to luncheon and we will see what Matteo thinks. Have a lovely morning, Nel, dear. I think my clothes will fit you, don't you?

• • •

I'd opened the windows and a softly clouded, less blazing day cast pale sunshine into the room. Sitting on the floor I felt almost among friends, as if these boxes represented women of my acquaintance, as if we were all at school together and shared this space. Excepting kindergarten, I was always in female institutions until graduate school, when men suddenly appeared on a daily basis. A different sort of youthful madness was finally possible, not just the wildness of girls locked up together from childhood through adolescence. And what could convents be like, where it was like that for life? Politically and sexually complicated was my guess. The unknown Lydia would tell all.

I think I had a better education as a result, in seclusion, as it were. We worshipped Miss Kingly, our melancholy English teacher, who had us writing Chaucerian verse in seventh grade, and tried out our allurements on the rare male teachers we were treated to. What was it like for them, young men subjected to mass seduction by twenty-five kilted and knee-socked girls? Tempting, no doubt. Likewise the confessors in convents? I wondered. These girls, after all, did not choose the religious life; at Le Vergini, apparently, they came from privileged backgrounds, had a taste for pleasure, and what other pleasure is there, really, at seventeen? Confessional boxes are dark.

How old was Clara when she left her beautiful red trunk here?

I wandered over to the armoire and regarded the shelves stacked with books and papers, inaccessible to me, all in Latin or archaic Italian, yet the room had an intimacy and energy that I wanted to be part of, so I opened the brown trunks again to catch the now faint aroma of sixteenth-century herbs.

One trunk was not like the rest. I'd noticed that yesterday, it was shallow and had mismatched paper lining the inside. Leaning into it, I could see that the paper on the bottom was not flush with the corners; it seemed a separate piece of wood laid into the trunk. I'd need a tool to move it. There must be something around. Nothing. Nothing but Pia's barrette over there on the floor, which she had removed at the end of her labors, releasing abundant shining hair in a burst of girlish enthusiasm.

I bent the barrette open rather mercilessly and pressed the metal side between what had to be a shelf and the side of the trunk. I could get a bit of leverage, but it was a weak tool at best and nothing moved.

Frustrated and mad with curiosity, I ran back to Annunziata's kitchen where she stood at the sink and began frantically miming a fork and a knife, which she produced with a look that suggested she might have to have a word with the signora.

Come! Come! I said, *Avanti!* beckoning her to follow, which she did, hurrying along, drying her hands on her apron and shaking her head. Back in the attic I slipped the fork into the space previously occupied by the barrette, Annunziata hanging over me, watching. Ah, ah, she said, and while I applied pressure with the fork at one end, she inserted the knife at the other, and with the two of us pressing, the wooden tray began to move until I was able to drive the fork farther under and give it a vigorous shove. The shelf lifted half an inch. Before it had a chance to fall back, Annunziata applied her knife to jerk it upward and got a grip on the loosened edge, very deftly done.

Bravo, Annunziata! I exclaimed, and we lifted out the false

bottom. Lying on the floor of the trunk was a flat wooden box. Oh, well done!

She smiled with the satisfaction of an expert completing a simple task. Showing no interest whatever in what we had uncovered, she returned to the kitchen.

I lifted the box out and put it on the floor. There was no lock, just a lid with pretty mitered corners, elegantly made. Lifting the lid, I found more inscrutable papers, a small leather-bound book, and, inscribed on the inside of the lid, what seemed to be a name: Taddea Fabriani, if I was reading it correctly. Hidden so carefully, this would have to be interesting. I was desperate with curiosity and helpless. Taddea, a lovely name. Taddea and Clara. I had the uncanny sense of the three of us here in the room with only time, centuries of it, to keep us apart. Perhaps I might have been banished to a convent; perhaps we might have been friends, Taddea, Clara, and furious Sister Cornelia. I was sure I would have responded to the handsome confessor's suggestions, would have been happy to remove with him to a dark corner. I felt inexplicably angry on their behalf, and I knew nothing, nothing, except that Taddea Fabriani had a secret that I had uncovered.

I fell back onto the floor, lay there burning up at the ceiling of the attic as if it were the ceiling of my cell, as if it were eternity itself. Pale ethereal light shimmered in the air. I longed for my impassioned confessor. I longed for freedom and release, the epiphany of a supremely clarifying moment. My body was burning. To Carthage then I came, burning. I could understand how this feeling might be mistaken for religious fervor. Or perhaps it was the other way around. Nel, suggested a small, rational voice, you must get up now and go to lunch.

. . .

But this is extraordinary! Matteo exclaimed. Absolutely extraordinary! He appeared overcome.

You know, I thought so, Lucy replied.

Look! Look! This landscape, these trees, the bridge, the town, the sky, this woman! This might as well be a sketch for *La Tempesta*, or perhaps an homage, but so recognizably that, so clearly a reference, a miniature, a maquette almost, unmistakable. Astonishing! Matteo's hands were trembling.

Clara's box sat on the table between us. Lucy had produced it after our luncheon, as she called it. Matteo had been expressing his enthusiasm about the progress being made on the fresco; he was in high spirits. I would have to say that his excitement about the fresco was lukewarm and passionless compared to this.

This was in the trunk? *This* was in the trunk? he demanded.

I didn't see it either, I ventured, Pia must have unpacked that one, maybe she was focused on the clothing and didn't notice. The lid was shut when Lucy and I went up.

My God, my God, Matteo muttered.

Matteo, Lucy inquired, when you say *La Tempesta*, you mean *La Tempesta* in the Accademia, don't you? Giorgione himself? I don't suppose there's another. That's what I thought.

Himself, or someone who painted as well as he did, which is hard to imagine, unless, of course, we're looking at a Titian here. But there's no attribution issue surrounding *Tempesta*, one of the most extraordinary pictures ever painted. My God! This is astonishing!

We all sat in silence for a moment, riveted by the astonishing box.

If it's Giorgione, why is it signed with a *Z*? I asked. Lucy noticed the little *Z* on the stone there. We looked at a letter in the box, and it was also signed with a *Z*. Lucy assumed that *Z* must have made the box for her as well.

Letters? There are letters? He was becoming wild again.

Yes, letters and a pearl and a ring and a lock of hair. And paintbrushes.

Paintbrushes! He threw up his hands. I had never seen Matteo so Italian.

You will see all, Matteo, Lucy remarked, but what about the *Z*?

Signora, this is the Venetian language; as you know, it is not Italian, everything is *X*s and *Z*s. The single inscription we have of Giorgione's is on the back of the *Laura* portrait, where it is rendered as Zorzi, George in the Venetian style. These letters are signed with a *Z*?

Yes, I replied, at least one of them. Do you find it astonishing?

Nel, Matteo snapped, you have no idea how important this is. He was stern. Giorgione is the most undocumented and elusive of the great Venetian geniuses. We know almost nothing—he revolutionized painting, he was a musician, he died young—little more than that. These days they want to give everything of his to Titian; some want to say he did not exist at all. But if here we have letters, an attributed work, a private life, objects, documents, it is of unimaginable importance; it is beyond belief! We must proceed carefully. We must share this with no one. This is enormous.

He was quiet, motionless, staring at the box.

I glanced at Lucy. And Clara? I asked.

Clara?

He made the box for her. He called her his pearl.

Also his hope and his gift—a gift, at any rate, Lucy added.

He was a man for the ladies, we do know that.

In a convent? I asked.

I don't know. We must look at these things carefully. We must do it ourselves. We will not hand it over. He looked ferocious.

No, Lucy agreed, we will not hand Clara over.

And Taddea Fabriani, I said to myself, she won't be handed over either.

I glanced at Leo on his pillow, head on paws, eyes very big, watching. He had not seen such carrying on in his life, I think.

It was turning dark as we set out, the cloudy pastels of the day given way to a night sky cleared and filled with stars. I had seen little of the night here, just that walk home with Matteo when we weren't paying attention. Venice seemed transformed, suggestive, glamorous in a new way, a little dangerous. We were headed on foot through dim narrow streets toward San Marco, where the bands would be playing, the lights glowing, and the crowds milling about. Lucy had taken Matteo's arm and I was escorted by Leo. I remembered that evening, long ago, when Leo and I, Giacomo then, sat at our remote table at Florian's, both of us so lost and bewildered that we never heard the music. Now here we were, he on his braided leather leash and I with these two friends, three, Leo, my dear, almost a family.

I was wearing something from the thirties—Mainbocher, Lucy said—it amused her to see it on me; she clapped her hands and laughed. Navy blue with white polka dots, silk, a "day" dress although it wouldn't seem so now. Used to less enhancing clothing I felt positively alluring, a white cashmere cardigan with rhinestone buttons, Mainbocher of a different era, draped over my shoulders. I looked like someone who spent her life stalking the resale shops in Paris. I looked charming.

We all looked charming. An interesting group. We had never come out together this way before. We were united in our secrets. I was walking through an extravagantly wish-fulfilling dream; every step, every stone was wondrous, Leo lifting his leg at each corner an enchanting touch.

We crossed the piazza. The lights, the wisps of music floating about in that huge sublime space stirred us; we smiled at each other and at Leo, proud and tiny, leading us forward. We turned right at the Canal and crossed a bridge where a gondola arranged by Renzo awaited us, the full Venice experience. We didn't travel far, just a few blocks, if that's what they're called here. This was my first gondola ride. I was exhilarated to be on the water, the brackish smell of the sea close and arousing. The gondola pulled into the landing stage of a narrow, handsome Gothic building wedged between two larger, grander palazzi from a later period. This was the University Club, a shining brass plaque informed us, as we went up the steps to the glowing entrance.

We were met by a young Englishman, suited, deferential. *Buona sera,* he offered, with a barely perceptible bow to Lucy. Come this way, please. He showed us up a staircase and then down a hall to a polished wooden door. He knocked smartly and opened the door. Professore, your guests, he announced. We entered the chambers of the great Renzo Adolphus, most eminent Renaissance scholar.

The room was breathtaking. Huge windows overlooking the Grand Canal—one could see the water glistening and lights opposite—a faded but lovely frescoed ceiling, angels with trailing wings ascending into extravagant pink clouds, elaborate plastered surfaces everywhere, a frenzied mantelpiece, ancient paintings stacked up every wall. Near the windows a large table was spread with a gleaming white cloth, set with crystal and silver, candles already burning. By the fireplace a circle of venerable leather chairs were pulled up to a low carved table where three people were seated.

The professor rose from one of the chairs and came forward with a wide vulpine smile. Welcome, welcome, he exclaimed, taking Lucy's hand and lifting it to his lips with exaggerated devotion. My kiss was briefer and Matteo was slapped on the shoulder. His spirits had prevailed.

Marco was there at the landing? he inquired.

Yes, he was, Renzo, so considerate you are. We had a lovely walk to the embankment and a charming ride. Leo was very brave in the piazza and is grateful to join us. May I put him down? Lucy inquired.

Of course, of course, one happy family, Renzo replied, casting a doubtful look at Leo, unleashed and sniffing the enormous Persian carpet. But you must come and meet our other guests of honor.

He led us toward the fireplace where a low fire burned and two tall thin creatures stood smiling shyly, nodding their heads almost in unison.

Ronald MacAlister and the blessed Lydia Fairbanks, he declared, extending his arm in their direction. The introductions went round, we shook hands, all of us nodding now; then we were given wine and settled at last into the remaining chairs.

Polite inquiries were made and responded to for some time. Renzo found it jolly to have two beautiful "Yankee girls" in the company. Lydia and I exchanged glances. I liked her at once. She was tall with limp but wonderfully shiny blond hair to her shoulders, a plain, open, pleasing face, and a huge transforming smile that appeared often. She was from Wisconsin, attended Bryn Mawr, and went on to become a groundbreaking scholar in her field, which was essentially the examination from a feminist perspective of marginalized women's institutions of the medieval and early-modern eras, among them Italian convents. She was already much published. All this according to Ronald, the telling of which required an effort; he did, in fact, stutter, not appallingly as Renzo had suggested, but enough to challenge him fairly frequently. He appeared courageous in carrying the burden, however, determined not to be marginalized by it. I liked him as well. He was pale and freckled, with wispy, sandy hair but a handsome, intelligent face and a charming, gangling body that seemed, in every position, to sprawl.

Ronald's area of expertise, I learned from Lydia—these two were already a team—was Renaissance painting with a specialty in the Venetian masters; Titian was his passion. He also had published, also groundbreaking, in his case a radical rereading of thematic reference. Renzo believes he will make waves, Lydia remarked admiringly, offering Ronald one of her dazzling smiles. He bowed his head, muttering something. They were very sweet. Thank God, no one inquired about my own area of expertise; we were called to dinner.

The meal was divine, many courses, many wines, all served by a silent, rather dour gentleman in black sweater and slacks. We spoke of England, Cambridge, Rome in the twenties, the quality of vegetables in the markets, Renzo's forthcoming book, and Ronald's heritage, which linked him to Sir Walter Scott. Matteo took Leo outside briefly; then we sat over glasses of brandy by the renewed fire. The moment had come.

Now, my dear Lydia, said Renzo, tell us what you make of

the information Ronald has given you on which you were kind enough to reflect. We all turn to you. We all did, in fact, turn to her.

Lydia composed herself as the guest speaker, uncrossed her legs, leaned forward with a thoughtful expression, regarded our attentive faces, and smiled.

Yes, yes, she began. First I will tell you a little about Le Vergini, your convent, the most interesting of places, an extraordinary establishment.

She told us more of what we had already learned, that Le Vergini was small and elite, never more than fifty-five residents, exclusively patrician and patrician at the highest level. They claimed as their founder Guilia, daughter of the emperor Frederick Barbarossa. At the inauguration of the convent, she was symbolically married to the doge; the pope also was in attendance; this was in the twelfth century. These three great powers had laid the first stone of their institution, or so the nuns said. They had a proud and noble tradition that they believed guaranteed them independence and special prerogatives, protected as they were by both the papacy and the Venetian authority.

They gave orations in Latin? inquired Matteo.

Yes, they did deliver orations in Latin, and before the doge, at the installation of each new abbess. Very unusual for women to compose in Latin at that time—to read it, perhaps—but to write Latin as well was extraordinary. They knew their classics. Also, for a nun to address a chamber of men was highly unusual. These nuns were not "observant," in the sense of being invisible and deeply cloistered; they were what's called "conventual," a much more liberal contract. They didn't take vows of poverty and obedience but agreed to go into the convent because that's what their families required of them; usually they had relatives there. They stayed in close touch with the goings-on in the outside world, wielded considerable civic power, and kept their own names. Being, in a sense, independent women, one might say they occupied an exceptional position.

And men? I asked.

Oh yes, men. Among the advantages of being conventual and not observant was to have the freedom to leave the convent and even to remain sexually active. No vows of chastity. There are amusing stories of men climbing ladders and vines to get over the convent walls, nuns cross-dressing to make assignations, all quite lively and jolly, although there were certainly abuses perpetrated on these women as well: drunken young nobles breaking in at night, finding the idea of a houseful of unprotected women irresistible. Naturally there were illegitimate children as a result. The author of the wonderful Le Vergini chronicle was the mother of several herself.

What is the chronicle? Lucy inquired.

Ah, now we come to it, what I think may have bearing on your discoveries. The year 1519 was a very bad one for Le Vergini and for all the convents of Venice. There had always been male critics crying for reform, calling the nuns whores and so on, but in 1509 the battle of Agnadello was lost to Pope Julius and the League of Cambrai, a vendetta against the power and, one might say, arrogance of Venice. It was an enormous wound to Venetian pride; cries went up that Venice had lost the battle due to its own decadence, some, of course, pointing to the convents as the root of all evil. Immoral independent women offended God, hence the defeat. Civic and ecclesiastic authorities determined to reform the convents—easier, of course, than reforming themselves.

As I said, the worst came in 1519 when the vicar of the

patriarch of Venice imposed *clausura,* enclosure, on the convents, including Le Vergini. Observant nuns from less prestigious convents were brought in to live among them and conventual life ended; the doors were slammed, literally, and rigorous prohibitions imposed. All of this is recorded in the chronicle. The outraged abbess rails against this usurpation of authority and rains down insults and even curses on the head of the vicar, the villain, who seemed to her to be a nobody, an upstart. How it all unfolded is a long story, a brutal struggle, but the nuns were, of course, eventually defeated. The conventual nuns were walled up in half of their convent, observant nuns were allowed to run the place, and the authorities waited for the old nobility to die out, as eventually they did. There is that sad inscription left at the Arsenal.

What is that? I asked.

Oh, a fragment of the convent, an arch, and under it a plaque with the inscription *Hope and Love keep us in this pleasant prison.* How pleasant, one can imagine.

How very, very sad, Lucy remarked. The same old story.

I'm afraid so, Lydia replied, but finally we're learning their stories, hearing their voices.

What has this to do with Ca da Isola? Renzo interrupted.

Well, Lydia replied, turning to him, Le Vergini was divested of its properties, including the palazzo, and the nuns were sentenced to enclosure, forbidden personal possessions. In their hasty removal, I believe, they left behind their beautiful clothes and most precious things in the hope of reclaiming them in better days. The convent lost its considerable art collection, books, everything; no impious art allowed. Utter lockdown.

Impious art? Matteo inquired. Such as frescoes with classical imagery? They would have been plastered over?

It's unlikely there would be such a thing in a convent, Lydia replied, but if there had been it would have been removed by whatever means.

So they fled, or were taken away, and left their lives behind, I said, how completely frightened and heartbroken they must have been. I'm always trying to imagine those last moments in the attic; this makes it awful. Did their families help them?

Yes, certainly, there were appeals to the authorities and many from the nuns themselves—they put up a vigorous fight—but it was too late; they had to lose their freedom to salve the indignation of the Republic. The observant nuns who were installed came from another class; they submitted to poverty, chastity, obedience, utter seclusion; this then became the only permissible model. An era was over. They were literally starved; our nuns tore a wall down at one point to supply themselves with food. Awful.

Awful, echoed Lucy.

Women like ourselves, I said.

Yes. Imagine.

There was a moment of silence until Renzo exclaimed, How very interesting! It's quite true that we know very little of all of this! Fascinating! The mystery of Ca da Isola is solved! So, he remarked, turning with a wicked smile to Matteo, it was a nun who painted the mysterious fresco! After all, if they wrote Latin, why not do everything else? Ha-ha!

Indeed, Lucy replied. Well, my dears, what an extraordinary evening. Such wonderful hospitality, such disturbing information. Lydia, thank you so much. How happy it makes me to know that you are doing this work. Now we must take a sleepy boy home. She lifted Leo from her lap and stood. Renzo, so kind, how can we thank you? You must all come to us one evening.

We made our farewells and gathered our things. I found a moment to speak to Lydia and asked her to call me, scribbling the number on a telephone pad. We looked at each other and exchanged weary smiles.

Back on the landing, Marco was waiting. Our ride home was otherworldly, the only sound the water and the oar, everywhere around us the sky and the sea. At one point, Matteo spoke. We're passing the Arsenal, he observed quietly.

Lydia had agreed to come to us in the morning to look at Taddea's papers. Matteo thought that would be all right, although he wanted no one to know about Z's letters. He would spend the morning reading those himself. At luncheon, as we all now called it, he would take me to the Accademia to see *La Tempesta;* we would find something to eat on the way home. In the afternoon we would discuss Z's letters with Lucy. Lucy was reading up on Giorgione, consulting Vasari's *Lives* and whatever else she could find in her library. We were regimented now, committed to our tasks. Matteo was our general. We deployed at *colazione.*

Lydia responded to the attic in the same way I had; she stood silent, and after a moment I could see tears in her eyes. It did feel tragic now, the rush to conceal these things, the fear, the despair, leaving one's precious possessions behind. They must have dragged it all up here themselves. Women, young and old, struggling on the stairs with trunks and armfuls of papers and books. The miracle was that nothing was discovered before the da Isolas reclaimed the house.

We opened Taddea's box. Lydia traced the inscription of the name, as if to conjure her, then picked up the pages and with a furrowed brow read steadily through them. I sat watching her.

At one point she turned to the leather book and glanced through it. We sat like that for an hour or more.

At last she laid down the last page and looked up at me. She was smiling but her face was full of emotion. Nel, this is unbelievable. Intimate papers from this period are unusual; a woman's diary is unimaginable.

There's a diary?

Yes, Taddea preserved it.

What about Taddea?

What about her? Well, quite a girl, our Taddea. No more than fifteen, probably younger, very bright, full of life, devoted to her family, especially her brother, and to a friend, someone indeed called Clara. These are not so much letters as a record of her correspondence, a kind of loose-leaf journal. Clara had a difficult time. This other book, the diary, is hers. Taddea must have concealed it with her papers after Clara died.

Clara died?

Yes, in childbirth, or shortly after.

Does she say what happened? I asked.

Not really; she's writing to herself and doesn't need to explain, but you can sense her transforming from youthful enthusiasm to real sorrow.

Can you piece anything together?

She's known Clara most of her life. Unlike Taddea, Clara hasn't been placed in the convent but still has ties. Taddea's brother is a friend of Clara's brother; they are trying, as Taddea says rather enigmatically, to make her dream come true. Later, Clara seems to be in love and Taddea is concerned for her. Look at this.

She held out a page; I could see strange little symbols reappearing in the text.

What's this?

A code, I think, a code to conceal a name.

The name is shocking?

Perhaps. I don't know.

How do you know that Clara died?

Taddea says so; she's heartbroken. It appears that the symbol, whoever he is, is also dead. And Nel, they both died here, in what she calls the "house."

Is there any indication what year this is?

She mentions in these later pages that the city is in despair, with both the defeat and plague coming at once. My best guess would be 1509 or 1510, just after the defeat at the hands of the League of Combrai that we spoke of last evening. There may have been a plague outbreak at that time as well.

Ten years before—what was it—enclosure?

Yes. Just as things in Venice began to change.

But Taddea was, no doubt, enclosed?

The writing breaks off. I think she was saving these things in memory of Clara. She loved Clara. Nel, I'll translate these for you; it's not so much, you can see for yourself.

And Clara's diary?

I think you should keep that and give it to Matteo. It may have something to do with the fresco.

The fresco? Why?

Because Clara's name seems to be Catena. Taddea speaks of this family, a stepmother and so on. There was a fairly well-known artist named Catena, Vincenzo Catena; he may have been Clara's brother. The family was well-to-do, and he was known in humanist and artistic circles. They could certainly have had a daughter educated at Le Vergini. It may be a clue. How extraordinary to find such things!

Oh, Lydia, these lives!

Yes, I know. It makes one wonder if this wonderful, heartfelt Taddea was among the ones tearing down the partition at Le Vergini in the attempt to find some food. She would have been little more than twenty-five by then.

Her friend dead at eighteen, maybe twenty.

Yes. And what became of the child?

The day was clear and breezy, bright blue, but we did not meander. Matteo marched me purposefully through the streets until we crossed the Accademia Bridge. I had a swift, glorious view of the Grand Canal. Matteo took a brief pause to point out the Palazzo Barbaro where Henry James wrote the *Aspern Papers,* a name I supplied to his description of the book about letters. Then straight on and into the imposing Accademia itself.

I was rushed past glorious altarpieces, up a short flight of stairs and into a low room, then into a another little room, and there it was, *La Tempesta,* much smaller than I would have imagined.

Well? Matteo asked.

The likeness to the painting on the box was astounding, but so was the painting itself. To my eye nothing quite went together; the voluptuous nude woman seated on a little hill-side nursing her child on the right of the picture seemed to me to be in a different proportion to everything else; the brooding landscape behind her, the entranced young man at the left who gazed not so much at her as into space, while she regarded us directly with a gentle, knowing look. The disproportion some-how wrenched the eye back into the landscape and the explo-sive sky, lightning, the town, the river; everything came suddenly to life, as if one could feel the wind and smell the bitter stormy air. I found it physically shocking to be almost violently swept into what seemed a pastoral scene.

How extraordinary.

Yes, one of the greatest pictures, I think, Matteo quietly remarked. You can understand my emotion at this discovery, if it is what we imagine it might be.

We stood gazing for some time.

This is not the real world, I finally remarked.

No, he replied, this is the realer world.

We lingered a bit longer without speaking and then turned to leave. I noticed a shocking portrait of a wizened old woman. This is also Giorgione?

La Vecchia. The old woman. Some attribution issues, but almost certainly.

This looks more like the real world, I must say. What is this inscription on the paper she's holding? COL TEMPO?

With Time. Gather ye rosebuds. As I am, so shall you be. That sort of thing. Gather ye rosebuds, Nel. Don't forget.

Matteo said he would like to go to the Zattere, the quayside around the corner from the Accademia that looks across at the island of Giudecca, but we were late so we found the nearest café and ordered coffee and sandwiches.

It's magical, isn't it, that picture? I said.

Oh, yes, Giorgione created miracles. He revolutionized technique, of course, but no one has ever been able to lay a finger on the mystery. It's the mystery that matters.

What is it about, *La Tempesta*?

Centuries of speculation, he replied, eating his sandwich, everything from a gypsy and a soldier to a portrait of his wife, although he had none; Troy; Mother Nature herself. Interpretative fashions change; the art world on the march. That's what Ronald is doing with such apparent success.

What do you think?

I think it's allegorical, about nature, Arcadia, a vision of perfect unattainable harmony, a state of mind that reaches for that essential something, the essence of life. The Renaissance was very interested in the nature of love—divine love, platonic love, physical love, the futility of desire, the ideal of beauty. There were iconographic traditions for expressing these things, but Giorgione is rarely conventional or literal. I think that what you feel when you look at the picture, the effect it has on you, is what it's about.

It made me feel off-balance and—what would the word be—aroused. A little ecstatic. It came as a shock.

Imagine being able to paint that.

Imagine being able to feel that and also to paint it.

Very rich lives those people had, so many beginnings.

So much danger.

That too. But so much passion. That's what we need more of. He finished his coffee, not looking at me. We must go. The signora will be waiting.

What little I can find suggests that he was a nice man, a talented man, a marvelous musician as well as a great painter, certainly handsome from what seems to be his self-portrait as David. Humbly born in Castelfranco, Giorgio Barbarelli—most doubt the Barbarelli surname—came to Venice, moved in refined circles, entertained with his lute, and became friends with a sparkling crowd. Vasari says, "From the nature of his person and the greatness of his mind, Giorgio came to be

known as Giorgione"—Great George, that is, "he was not otherwise than gentle and of good breeding throughout his whole
life." He was physically large and of an amorous nature. Lucy
was reviewing her notes. Revolutionized Venetian art, admired
and emulated da Vinci, died young, at thirty-three, from the
plague, apparently contracted from his mistress. She looked up
at us.

There are scholarly issues and questions of attribution, she
went on; someone who knows these things would be useful. *La
Tempesta* is certainly his. Vasari is interesting about the frescoes
at the Fondaco dei Tedeschi, the German factory that burned
down; Giorgione frescoed the outer walls upon its restoration.
Entirely lost except for a preserved scrap of a nude woman.
Vasari couldn't understand them; there were no scenes or stories, just large figures of men and women in various attitudes,
one with a lion near him, one with a Cupid. A lion, Matteo,
and you, Nel! Isn't that interesting since we think we have a
lion? Vasari adores him. I think I do too.

Do you have a picture of the self-portrait? I asked.

Yes, here in this book. Also, in Vasari, this etching. A handsome and compelling face, no?

Passion? Here was a face full of passion, an aquiline nose,
sensual lips, chin thrust forward, eyes guarded, probing, self-
aware, looming out of the darkness, a challenging face, reticent
yet intensely present, the face of a hero, hair to his shoulders.
The red fur on his collar seemed to ring him in a circle of fire.
If a lover, what a lover he must have been. To see that mouth
smile. Goodness, I remarked.

Yes, said Matteo, a powerful man at the height of his powers
in every way.

And the letters, Matteo, what do the letters say? Lucy
inquired.

If Z is Giorgione, he was everything to her. At first her friend, finally a lover and soon to be her husband, he seems to suggest. A great friend of her brother. Praises her excessively. She is not the gift in that first letter, the gift is hers. It's hard to decipher what things mean when people are so intimate, but there's no doubt they were in love and that it was a revelation to both of them. It doesn't sound conventional, not simple flirtation, certainly.

And the diary? I asked.

I haven't done the diary; these letters were hard enough. The diary is dense, at least at the beginning.

I suppose we'll never know if the box was made before or after the painting of *La Tempesta,* if she was some kind of inspiration, Lucy said.

No, but there is something else. He often calls her his Laura; that, of course, is a trope referring to Petrarch's Laura, the paragon of beauty and virtue in the Renaissance, the equivalent of Dante's Beatrice. But most amazing, one of Giorgione's greatest masterpieces is his portrait *Laura,* which I mentioned to you, signed by Zorzi himself. No one knows which Laura, if it was any Laura at all or simply the metaphor, but one can't help making the connection to Clara if she was his inspiration. But the portrait is daring. It's hard to believe it could be a wealthy, respectable Venetian girl from a good family, let alone his fiancée. Everyone has assumed it must be a courtesan. On the other hand, the face is extremely tender and Laura, or whoever, is not a staggering ideal beauty but recognizable as a real person, intelligent, intense, sensual in a soft way, baring her breast. Or covering it, no one knows. She's crowned with laurels and, oddly, wearing what seems to be a man's fur-lined coat. She also wears a thin white veil, the symbol of marriage. Awfully suggestive, I think.

Fascinating, said Lucy, perhaps a liberated woman, if there was such a thing; there were certainly women intellectuals. She might have been a poet. Or possibly just a girl madly in love and willing to do anything for him.

Lucy, I said, *Laura* must be in that book.

Of course, of course. She found the picture. We gazed at her face.

Not a witless child stunned by love, Lucy remarked.

No, I said, not a great beauty either, but a clear, strong face, someone who could hold her own. And brave, something brave about her. My God, do you think this may be Clara? Matteo, you must read the diary!

It's hard going. Unfortunately, or fortunately, the fresco is just now coming into the light as well. The thought that it might be Giorgione is more than I can bear to contemplate. But why would he paint this thing in an obscure convent? What are we to make of all this?

We need help, I said.

Not Renzo. Please, not Renzo.

No, no, not Renzo, Lucy agreed.

Wait, I know! I exclaimed. Ronald! Why not Ronald? He knows as much as anyone. Ronald again! Bring in the Scotsman!

Can we trust him? Lucy asked.

I'll speak to Lydia. We know, don't we?—I do—that we can trust Lydia?

Yes, Matteo agreed, that might be all right. Speak to Lydia. In confidence.

The atmosphere around us was charged; we sat staring into space, possessed. Leo had lost interest and was asleep on his pillow.

Clara, are you Clara? I asked. You died here? Died having a child? His child? Who else's child could it have been for a girl like you. You're eighteen? Twenty? Who painted this? Him? We know about Taddea, we know about him. We're looking; we won't give up. This is news from Nel, Clara. This is from Nel. I wonder if I saw you today.

Lydia, may I take you into my confidence?

We'd spent the morning together, walking and walking through Cannaregio, which I now understood to be my district, my *sestiere*. We walked to the Ghetto, where Venetian Jews were required to live beginning in 1516, Lydia told me, *ghetto* deriving from *gettare,* to cast in metal; there had been foundries here, hence that unpleasant word. It happened more or less at the same time that the convents were ghettoized, a civic purge. Confine the nasty elements and feel cleansed, Lydia remarked dryly.

We crossed a beautiful wrought-iron bridge, walked on for another great stretch—Lydia was energetic—crossed a few more *rios,* and arrived at our destination, Sant'Alvise, a convent contemporary with our long-gone Le Vergini.

This will give you some idea, Lydia remarked. These nuns also came from the nobility, not quite as old as Le Vergini but distinguished. The buildings were Gothic and imposing.

We entered the church and immediately encountered an incongruous brick structure looming overhead supported by columns. The nun's choir, Lydia explained. It connects to the living quarters, and as you can see, the nuns would have been completely invisible behind that wall. That's where they heard mass. Their singing must have seemed faintly celestial. This, of course, would have been after enclosure. They were disappeared.

The brick wall was so crude and impregnable in the otherwise lovely church that I began to feel physically uncomfortable. Ghastly, I whispered.

Le Vergini was a distinct target, she said, abhorred for their conspicuous freedoms. Also La Celestia and San Zaccaria. It's amusing, she remarked, laughing; San Zaccaria is now home to the carabinieri, the police of the Italian army. Little ironies.

With an expansive sense of liberation, we left the church in search of a place to have lunch. Lydia took me to a trattoria in a quiet, unpretentious part of town that seemed another world from San Marco. She knew Venice well. We took a small table and ordered pasta and wine. I asked my question.

And may I tell you things that remain between us?

But, Nel, of course.

Lydia, it's extraordinary. We've made what we think is an astonishing discovery. Truly astonishing, if it's what it seems to be. Matteo knows a great deal, but he's a conservator, a good scholar but not a historian in the sense that Renzo is, or Ronald. We need someone with that expertise. We don't feel ready to share this with Renzo quite yet and wondered if Ronald might speak to us, answer our questions, without feeling that he's betrayed Renzo?

Lydia laughed. Ronald is grateful to Renzo, she replied, but Renzo is not his only mentor. Ronald is superbly clever. I have no doubt that he would be interested and informative about whatever it is you're speaking of. Do you know the art world, Nel?

You know I don't.

Well, let me just say that whatever world you do know, it's like that.

But Ronald wouldn't make this his own, take it for himself?

Ronald is an exceptionally decent man; I'm very fond of him. More than that, if you want to know. Do I sense here that you're protecting Matteo?

I realized I hadn't thought of it in that way. I imagined I was protecting our secret. But for whom? It means a lot to him, I said. He thinks of this as his chance, with the fresco, with everything. This has all happened so fast. It ought to belong to him. Yes, I think I am protecting him. I think he's a good man. And not bad-looking, no?

She laughed. No, indeed.

But Lydia, do you know that I'm married?

Nel, I know almost nothing about you but what I know.

I am. Not a particularly happy situation.

Not unusual, sadly. How long?

The marriage or the unhappiness? Eight for the first, about five for the second. My husband feels like a black hole into which I've disappeared. It's more complicated than that, of course, but I'm certainly not thriving, and I don't think it matters to him. It doesn't feel like my life. It doesn't feel like life. It's probably not his fault, but being here has been a revelation for me. I don't want to go back to the state I was in when I got here, a thousand years ago or whenever it was. I can't just vanish. He doesn't seem particularly fulfilled either but carries on happily with his own things regardless. I don't mean to be pouring this out. Forgive me.

Don't be silly. I'm not without experience of these relationships, for want of a better word.

I don't know what to do. I'm supposed to meet him in Rome in less than two weeks and go home.

Can't postpone?

I don't see how; I've already postponed. It would be a sort of showdown and I dread that. The idea of discussing anything with him makes me afraid I'll be lost again. He has a way of doing that.

I see. Well, my advice to you, if you want my advice—she refilled our glasses—is to remember that stories have chapters. I've had a few myself. Some are more drawn out than others, but the story continues unless the story is stopped. I would hate to think of you clawing down walls to find some nutrition like our friends at Le Vergini. I say if your heart is ready to take a leap, take a leap. The moment comes to be brave and then it goes by. One life. You have friends, you'll survive. I have no doubt he will. You might actually be happy. Imagine that. The smile.

Lydia, I said, what a fine old American you are.

You too, kid, she replied, laughing, lifting her glass.

I was walking again. Lydia would speak to Ronald and be in touch later. She must certainly be part of this adventure herself, I thought. How could we do without her? Her strength and optimism were inspiring, I felt confident with her. Alone again, I began to fill up with dread and an unexpected tenderness for Antony. It was strange to talk about him in this clinical way. There was a time when he seemed not only my salvation but my best friend. The thought of going over it all again in my mind was nevertheless deadening. When he went away on tours in recent years, I'd regain my energy and believe that I could make it work again, just by staying strong and alert. It never happened.

I remembered sitting in painful isolation while he whistled around the house, returning phone calls, going to the gym, taking his daughter out, meeting with collaborators and secretaries and agents. I don't believe he ever once asked me, "How are you, Nel?" No. No. I would not go back. I would not be sentimental. This wasn't enough to survive on. But what would I do? Divorce? I couldn't even imagine what that must be. Perhaps he wouldn't care; why would he? How would we begin this? What would I say?

Lost in thought? said a voice behind me.

Matteo! I cried, turning around to him. You startled me. What are you doing here?

What am I doing here? We live here. I saw that I was, in fact, in front of the house.

You were out?

Books, he replied holding up a paper bag. Lucy's are a bit outdated. Also dog food. Annunziata forgot and Leo was distraught. We can't have that. What's the matter?

Nothing.

Really? You look a little bleak.

I couldn't speak.

Come on, he said, come in here. He opened the door to the courtyard, put down the bags, and opened the door to the garden, making a gesture to enter, which I did. He closed the door and we sat down on a stone bench.

Something happened? he asked.

No, not really, I said. Just thinking. Thinking about my life and becoming confused. Do you become confused?

That's why I prefer work, he replied.

You don't like thinking about your life?

I don't know how to. Plaster is easier.

I used to know how to think about my life, I said. I seem to have lost the thread. This is a nice life. Maybe we should ask Lucy to adopt us, attempting a joke.

What is your life?

My life? What is my life? Well, I guess my life is in the throes of collapse. My life seems at the moment to be eight years of a marriage I don't understand. An abandoned career, no foreseeable future, lost identity, paralysis. Nothing much really, nothing to worry about. I was looking at the mulberry tree to avoid crying. I turned to him.

Matteo smiled for the first time in a way that allowed me to see him, not the handsome person, not the cavalier of conservation, a real smile, a sad one. How hidden we all are.

That's what you were thinking about?

That and feeling entirely displaced, jealous of Lydia, wanting more, afraid of wanting more, wishing I were a nun. I don't know. Again I couldn't speak.

Wishing you were a nun. Why a nun?

Not a nun, maybe an artist, to live in the sixteenth century, I guess.

To be more alive?

I suppose. Would you wish that?

To be more alive? To live in the sixteenth century? I would like to have known what it was like to live in so exciting a time. Every time is in some way the same, I think, but I would like to have been inspired, to have felt that newness, be passionately involved, part of something changing. We spend our time searching out what was everywhere then. We all feel it, even Lucy.

Some people do all right with things as they are, I said. Or seem to. Seem to flourish. I wonder if some of us miss things from previous lives. If there *are* previous lives. Things I've never seen before often seem familiar to me. I read a poem in *The New Yorker* once about the sorrow string on the violin, the one that speaks to things we can't remember and grieve for, a longing that has a life of its own. Maybe life is a longing that has a life of its own. It's hard not to be trapped. Hard to stay free and hopeful. I don't feel very free or hopeful right now. Being here is like a dream, very much like a dream, entirely unexpected and a message I can't decipher. I expect to wake up. Probably soon. Do you know what *The New Yorker* is?

Yes, Nel, we have heard of New York.

We were quiet.

What about your life, Matteo?

My life. Also a difficult marriage. My wife left when our child was born. She actually went to India to follow a guru. Things come late to Italy, I suppose. He laughed. Better late than never. She couldn't manage much of this; we were children together and then everything changed. I don't mind. I wish her well. I love my son. I cope and work. Nothing much, as you said.

But you're very admired.

Very admired?

Pia.

Oh yes, well.

Well?

Well, what? Have you never been admired?

What was wrong with me?

We finally looked at each other. I saw an older face; I don't know what mine must have been. Nel, he said, taking my hand, listen, whatever this adventure we're having may be, be glad and grateful that we're here to be part of it. Look at the three of us—we're touching something extraordinary. Doesn't it feel fine to you to be given this? It's the finest thing I've had a chance at, I know that. Perhaps it's true for you too. Don't be sad and distracted; do that later. We may never have such a good occasion again.

I knew that he meant the work, the project, but something in his smile and his changed face moved me. I was so awkward at intimacy now. I touched his cheek. Thank you, Matteo, I said. Thank you for this. You've been kind. I'm sorry to be dreary. I'm sorry.

Dreary? he said. Kind? Nel! He gave me a perplexed look, leaned toward me, took my face in his hands, and kissed me. It was a kiss without inquiry or doubt, an unexpected kiss, a kiss that to my surprise flooded me with comfort and heat. Then, looking away, without speaking, he put his arm around my shoulder. We stood and turned back to the house.

CHAPTER FIVE

Lydia was coming in the afternoon. She had called first thing in the morning to tell us that Ronald had gone to Rome but would be back tomorrow and would happily speak to us. She also asked if we would permit her to look through the papers in the armoire to see what might be relevant to the history of Le Vergini. Lucy said we would welcome her to look through all our drawers if she pleased. We'd have a small dinner here.

I was feeling odd and disoriented. I had nothing to do until Lydia arrived. Matteo had not appeared; Lucy was painting or reading, so I took Leo for a walk and, like Matteo, we also found a bookstore, a serious-looking, ancient-seeming one. I made inquiries and then bought what the bookseller assured me was an important monograph on Giorgione, rare and expensive, three copies left in French and one in English. I paid a startling amount. With my credit card. Spending Antony's money on Giorgione. A strange limbo. I called him last night, hoping he wouldn't be there and he wasn't. Nel called. No word from him.

I had had another lion dream. I was walking with Leo through dark streets. Not on his leash, which caused me anxiety, he would run down alleys, reappear, and disappear again. I looked for him but had the sensation of something following me, something large and sinister. Leo, Leo! I called, moving faster and faster, looking back. I felt water rising; whatever was behind me was moving faster too. I ran, frantic for Leo, terrified, and emerged into the Piazza San Marco, brightly lit, where couples in fabulous costumes were dancing, everyone was laughing, some were taking off their clothes and dancing naked, wearing only masks, water everywhere. I fled and was suddenly in the countryside; the sun was shining, surreal light. I met a lion in a meadow, sleeping; he rolled over and showed me his beautiful furred tawny stomach. I touched it; it was warm. The lion reached up and took my face in his claws and showed his teeth in a sort of Cheshire cat smile, a mocking smile, a smile like Renzo's. I lay down beside him and turned into a nun; he became a passionate dark-haired man tearing at my clothes, a man I adored. I didn't want it to end, but the sun was in my eyes, Leo was licking my face, and then I was awake, alone in my room in Lucy's house, shaken and confused, no Leo, no light, not even dawn. The aura was still around me. I wondered if Giorgione had entered my dreams. Was I dreaming for Clara? Or Taddea.

On our way home, Leo and I passed the Asian art shop and encountered Enrico the bulldog once again, back in his studs. He plodded and drooled in greeting. Having nothing better to do, we entered the shop and found the same attractive blond woman and the same wonderful bronzes of Siva dancing. She was thrilled to see Leo and friendly to both of us this time.

Years ago Nils gave me for my birthday a beautiful bronze of Siva and his consort Parvati pressed together, both beautiful and voluptuous, surrounded by a halo of symbolic arms, each carrying an emblem of their attributes. One could see Siva's handsome face because half of Parvati, the upper half, was missing. In spite of this, the statue gave off an intense delicate passion, a sacred passion, oneness, expressed through their embrace. Parvati is the soul seeking union with the divine. Sometimes they dance. Siva dancing is Nataraga, Lord of the Cosmic Dance; he dances in a circle of flame, the energy that creates and destroys the universe, his dancing feet trampling the demon of ignorance and forgetfulness. Nils was fascinated by Eastern thought; he had a spiritual fineness as well as a dangerous wit. He was also raised a Catholic and was in phobic flight from it. And he loved to dance. After he died, the things that I had learned about Buddhism and Hinduism from him were all that really helped me. As if he knew. That and drugs. Not even drugs.

Strangely, the statues made me think of *La Tempesta*. Transcendence, if that's the word, conveyed through voluptuous physicality, plentifulness. That beautiful naked woman, her abundant flesh, yet nothing remotely salacious about her. Laura too, exposing her breast but with a look of such clarity and tenderness it could never be mistaken for enticement. Something metaphysical about the way both were imagined, what Matteo called the realer world. Somehow Giorgione managed to convey the spirit, the divine, whatever the word may be, illuminating the mortal creature. Even *La Vecchia*, with her less than happy news, was beautiful. Clearly he understood something and found it everywhere in the physical world. Perhaps my outrageously expensive monograph might help me to understand this.

These are exquisite, I said to my new friend. I wish I could afford to have one.

Oh, I have smaller things, she replied, much less valuable but not less delightful. She brought out a drawer of small bronzes, some worn so smooth they seemed like gleaming stones. With Leo on my lap, we sorted through them. Two spoke to me, one a dancing Ganesh, Siva's candy-giving elephant-headed son, the other a small worn female figure carrying a spear of sorts. Who is this? I asked.

That's Durga, a goddess, very powerful, destroyer of demons. This one is quite old.

Can I afford these?

Oh yes, I think so. They are not yet rare in India. I think you must have both. Ganesh will bring luck and happiness and Durga will keep you safe. Durga will keep you safe too, she added to Leo, making a face at him across the desk.

We bought both. On the way home, we also bought a black cashmere sweater and a pair of black flats—the nights were getting chilly for sandals—lilies for Lucy, dog biscuits, and a pretty red leather notebook for my thoughts. By then I was feeling better. I allowed myself to remember the kiss but part of me refused to dwell on it. I walked home talking to Leo.

Once again we were having cocktails in the salon. Lydia had been in the attic all afternoon and Matteo in the fresco room. I had been in my room with Clara reading the monograph, recording my dreams and offering myself suggestions regarding the future in my new notebook. The monograph had little more biographical information than what we already knew; speculation as to his intentions, however, was abundant. I had barely cracked that heavy tome.

Lydia was eager to see the fresco but Matteo wanted to wait. I thought he might let Ronald have a look if the energy seemed right, although he hadn't said so. I knew he was torn between wanting knowledgeable input and the fear of having his discovery swept away. I could see the dilemma in his face. Who would be allowed to behold the box, which was currently secreted in Lucy's studio?

I shared his feelings. I felt protective not only of him but of all events that had taken place over the centuries in this house. I included our own interactions. Lucy seemed the appropriate heiress; strangers would be unnerving, at least for now. I wondered how we could understand anything with so little information and all of it circumstantial. All we really knew was that Taddea lived here, knew someone named Clara, who died in this house, as did her lover *Z;* their child was removed, and *Z* can suggest Giorgio in the Venetian dialect. And the box. It was all slim, as they say, without the box. On the other hand, if even some of this was true and verifiable, it would be, as Matteo said, beyond belief.

Well, there's quite a lot of material there, Lydia replied to Lucy's question about the armoire. Another treasure trove. There seem to be records and journals of the workings of both a hospital and a school, business accounts, and lists of what, I suppose, were patients or students or both. There are piles of beautifully copied Latin texts from a scriptorium, mostly classical; I think I saw a bit of the *Aeneid.* Those would have been left behind as forbidden. There are packets of personal letters as well as scraps of historical information about the convent written by the nuns. Nuns were often wonderful writers, although we're not supposed to think so since women were considered too weak and untrustworthy to be historians. This in spite of the fact that they were much better educated than many men, had time on their hands, and knew everything going on in the world through their important families. At any rate, there are masses of fascinating material, and I hope you'll let me go through it. It would be a great gift to our field.

But of course, Lucy replied. Think of those voices waiting there. How interesting it will be to discover what they have to say. Women of all ages?

Yes, one would think so, if this was both a school and a hospital. There may well be interesting theories on the treatment of the plague somewhere in those documents. It was primitive, of course, mostly herbs and prayers, but their idea of the plague was revealing of the period.

Why was that? I inquired.

They thought the abscesses were caused by poisonous vapors in the air, vapors caused in turn by movements of the stars. A lot of medicine was based on astrology and astronomy, so they read portents in addition to bleeding and other ineffective techniques. When the plague struck, most people just ran away or went on pilgrimages. As someone said, that was no less effective than the treatment.

The outbreaks continued for centuries, she went on, which would explain why this establishment went back and forth between being a hospital and a school. By the time of the really devastating plague in the seventeenth century, it would have been gone. That time, victims were simply sealed up in their houses or removed to islands or ships in the harbor. It must

have been horrifying. The Salute church was built to commemorate the deliverance of the population from that particular nightmare.

How little I'd seen of Venice, I thought. I didn't mind. I
seemed to be learning about it from the inside out. We had
moved on to the table; Matteo poured the wine. Lydia, he
inquired, if someone were to come down with the plague,
would he go to a hospital rather than stay in his home?

I don't really know, Lydia replied. It seems likely, to avoid
spreading contagion.

Oh dear, Lucy interjected, I think I would rather not discuss
the plague during supper. Tell us about Wisconsin, Lydia,
where I think you grew up.

Where will I start? she said, smiling. The glories of Wisconsin. Nel, wouldn't you rather speak about the splendors of
Maryland? The pleasure domes of Baltimore?

Now don't laugh at me, Lucy objected. I have been not only
to New York but also to San Francisco and Boston and Texas,
and there was much to admire, except perhaps in Texas, which
I felt I didn't understand.

You wouldn't be the first, I said. What were you doing in
Texas?

It was a meeting of a botanical society that gave me a little
prize, quite a while ago, in a big hot city. I don't believe I saw
a single flower except in the center of the table. I liked New
York very much, so sophisticated and busy. Boston was charming and San Francisco delightful. I don't suppose I'll ever go
back. I prefer backwaters such as Venice.

The quiet life we're leading in this dull place? I inquired.

Yes—she laughed—I can't take too much excitement. She
smiled at Matteo; blue eyes shining, she looked twenty years

old. I'm much too ancient for intrigue, she remarked, reaching for his hand. Matteo took her hand and lifted it to his lips. We'll try to remember, he replied.

And yet I was an American and so was Lydia; how different did that make us? I think we were still astonished to find ourselves on this side of the ocean, as Matteo said. I wondered if one ever got over that. I was sure Lydia knew a great deal more about Venice and Florence and Rome than she did about Wisconsin, yet Wisconsin would figure in everything for her forever. Expatriates like Lucy's parents, did they ever feel truly Italian? Maybe not, but that was a time when such people could feel at home anywhere in the world.

How much feeling at home anywhere at all was possible these days? No place felt entirely real, as Mr. Eliot had observed early in the century. Everyone knew it now. Unlike most places, Venice still looked the same, but even here the past hadn't reached into the present; the past was entombed, and with it an authentic reality. What was left seemed to be speculation about that reality. The present was managed, displayed, devoid of much intention beyond gestures at preservation and the endless rounds of tourists. There was a Disneyesque quality to ancient places now; they'd become entertainment; they no longer entertained. Not that I imagined myself as anything more than a tourist. But difficult as life may have been in those old days, Matteo was right; he longed, and so did I, to live a life where the past and future seemed connected to the present, vital, sustaining, an inspiration. How many wonderful cities had I seen, however briefly, and soon after how many airports, neutral nowheres that gave the lie, as Shakespeare would say, to the imaginary experience of having been somewhere. For us an airless waiting room and uninterrupted television, the century we live in.

Matteo was Italian. He had ancient history, at least, he grew up with it. This other thing is American, our gift to the world. No wonder I fell into ecstasies over the scent of sixteenth-century herbs; no wonder I was moved by this fervent man. Like everyone, I'd been starved by the evaporation of authenticity. What seemed authentic now was more like mind control or the effect of a mood-altering drug, an antidepressant. A lonely time to be alive. Especially without love. Lydia knew this. She grew up in Wisconsin.

The night was cobalt blue and a little cold; I was sitting in the garden wearing my new sweater. I went out there to smoke a cigarette when everyone had gone, my first in years, an illicit purchase made that morning. The cigarette gave me the pleasant sensation of enjoying my own company; they do that. Somehow, passing through this not particularly eventful day, I felt I'd arrived somewhere. Where, I couldn't say. I was happy to be alone. Alone and knowing who else was in that house, that my own room was waiting for me.

There was a knock at the door. I was deep in my monograph, rapidly losing ground in a rising tide of provenances, attributions, and dueling theories.

Yes?

Nel, called Matteo, come with me!

I opened the door and there he stood, looking triumphant. We can see it! It's faint but it's there, he declared.

The fresco?

Of course the fresco, it's glorious! He threw his arms around me and suddenly we were kissing again, this kiss rather more arousing than comforting. No, no, come, we must go!

In the fresco room, Fabio and Alberto were working close to the wall with small brushes. They stood aside as we rushed in, smiling enormous smiles.

I hadn't been in there for days, not since the first time I saw the fresco when so little had been uncovered. The change was miraculous.

Six months! Matteo exclaimed, six months of plaster and now look at this!

The figure that had been so partial was revealed, still through a veil, since the last thin layers clung to the surface in a powdery veneer. It was indeed a woman, a woman in pale-green nearly transparent classical dress, a white scarf flowing across her body as if she were walking into the wind although she appeared to be standing still. Her head was noble and serene; her eyes gazed out to some point in the distance. She was young, a wreath in her dark hair; her right hand rested on the head of a seated lion who looked up at her, and in her left hand was a scroll unfurling. She stood on a hilltop, a column or stele near her, small flowers and grasses at her feet, a few delicate trees. Behind her the landscape opened into a valley, mountains in the distance, a small town, a bridge, fields. Most extraordinary was the sky, a vast sky filled with churning clouds, the sun bursting through, backlighting her with a golden aura, almost a halo. The color was soft but intense, dimmed as it still was by the last of the dust.

Oh, Matteo, my goodness!

Yes, she's something, isn't she?

Do you think?

I don't know. There are certainly suggestions, not to mention the sheer gorgeousness of it.

Can you make out the writing on the scroll?

Not yet, but soon. It's Latin.

Has Lucy seen it?

No. I'm going to find her now.

Left alone, Fabio, Alberto, and I smiled at each other, having no other way to communicate. We smiled and made gestures toward the wall. They were clearly proud of the meticulous job they had done uncovering this remarkable painting. Did we call a fresco a painting?

Matteo returned, leading Lucy. She lifted her hands to her face. Oh, my dears, who could have imagined? How ravishing she is, a goddess! Look at that sky! Transcendent! How lovely! And the sweet devoted lion! So intense, lovely, lovely beyond words! My, my!

She's arrived, I said.

Yes, Matteo agreed, his face full of delight, she's here.

Ronald had come. There was tension in the air. Lydia was with him. It was late afternoon. I didn't believe that we had sufficiently prepared for this; we hadn't compiled questions. We sat around the low table in the salon with tea before us. No one knew how to begin. Leo was sitting on Lucy's lap with ears erect. He was not used to so much company and could tell that something was going on. Pleasantries were exchanged.

How was Rome? I inquired.

Always a delight, he replied. And always useful.

You went in pursuit of your Titian studies? Lucy suggested.

Yes, just that. To speak to some authorities. He had trouble with the word.

Who would begin? Matteo took the lead.

We have questions, he said, that we hope we may ask you without implying more than that. Will that be all right?

Of course, Ronald answered, looking down at his lap. Lydia smiled at me.

Our questions regard Giorgione. I understand there is little to know but I'm sure, given your field, that you must have more information than we have: dates, details, new theories, if there are any.

Giorgione is a mystery, he replied. A phenomenon but a mystery. I imagine you're acquainted with the debates?

Yes, Matteo said. However, I do believe that there was such a person and that the work that is attributed to him is the work of an actual person and not a stylistic innovation.

I agree.

How to go on from here without mentioning something? Matteo was bold.

We have uncovered a fresco and found a painted object, a box—both are suggestive—and other things as well: letters, references. We understand that the idea of finding such things at this point is unlikely, incredible, and yet they are, as I said, suggestive.

I see, Ronald replied. What a dance this was.

He died in 1510, I believe, of the plague?

Yes. Gossip suggests it was contracted from his mistress. He was thirty-two or thirty-three. We know little more, virtually nothing, just where he was born, a few associations and patrons, that he was a musician, an attractive, powerful personality. He transformed Venetian painting, apprenticed with Bellini, but there's no indication of any real discipleship; he never ran a workshop of his own until quite late. Some think he was a sort of autonomous genius, not painting much but painting it with transformative insight. Humbly born but moved in patrician circles, very famous in his time. Vasari makes him out to be as important as da Vinci. An early connection to Titian, who may have been his pupil or apprentice but who certainly carried on and perfected, in a sense, his remarkable innovations. Some suggest they shared a studio at one time, but that first decade of the century is obscure, even regarding Titian, about whom we know so much more. I'm sure you know all this. Ronald barely stuttered.

Yes, Matteo replied. You would put *La Tempesta* around 1504 and the *Laura* portrait around 1506?

Yes. We think so.

Naturally, because of the things we've discovered here, we're trying to make a connection to this house, which seems to have been an adjunct to the Le Vergini convent. Lydia has given us a quite feasible explanation for some of what we've found, that these were personal effects left behind when enclosure was enforced in 1519. Of course, 1519 is too late for Giorgione, but there was another trunk, different from the others, which could have been left at an earlier date and which contained the relevant objects. Some of the letters we've found in it are signed with the initial Z. All very tantalizing, as you can imagine.

And Matteo, if I may, Lydia interjected, in the pages that Nel and I looked at, the notes of Taddea Fabriani regarding her friend Clara, there was a reference to the Catena family; she calls Clara's brother Vincenzo. Wasn't Vincenzo Catena a contemporary of Giorgione's, Ronald? Of course, that could be an entirely different person, a different family.

Vincenzo Catena? Well, that would be interesting. Catena was a wealthy citizen, not noble but prosperous; the family traded spices or something like that. He was a painter of some real merit. His connection to Giorgione is documented. It's the *Laura* portrait; on the back there's an inscription identifying the painting as being done by Giorgio of Castelfranco, colleague of Vincenzo Catena, spelled Zorzi, of course, in the Venetian style, one of his few documented pictures.

We know they knew each other? I asked.

Yes, that's established. Giorgione painted on some canvases that had already been sketched on the reverse by Catena. Their connection is one of the few things we do know.

Really, Lucy remarked. And that was Clara's name? Catena?

Apparently, Lydia replied.

The assumption has been that Catena and Giorgione had some sort of partnership, Ronald went on; at least for a while, Giorgione worked out of Catena's studio. This was before the major commissions. Catena was influenced by Giorgione but not until later in his career. Giorgione's self-portrait, the Braunschweig self-portrait as David, was one of those painted on reused canvas from Catena's workshop. It was around the time of this portrait, some say, that he changed his name from Zorzi to Zorzon, Giorgione, the great George; others think it was a posthumous honorific. I rather imagine that he felt he had slain the giants with his enormous gifts. I suppose he had. The Venetian giants, anyway.

How was that? I asked.

Well, as I said, Vasari equates him with da Vinci. He was certainly influenced by him, *La Maniera Moderna,* but Giorgione was innovative in every area: technique, subject matter, color, vision, everything, especially the light. Venetian painting was changed for good. He was interested in the pastoral, which takes the extremely complex and places it in the apparently simple, as Empson succinctly put it regarding literature. He was a genius and a real poet, a painter of poetry, a poet of light.

How lovely, Lucy said, a poet of light.

He was, as you know, greatly attracted to allegorical depiction; his foremost interest was the mind and spirit behind the image. That's da Vinci as well. His own allegorical self-portrait was the first of its kind in Venice. At any rate, if it is the same Vincenzo Catena, and if this Clara that Lydia mentions was his relation, there would be every reason to imagine that she could have known Giorgione. Was she a nun?

No, Lydia replied, but she had a connection to the convent. Taddea was certainly her good friend and also knew Vincenzo; they all seem to come from the same circle. Clara had a child and died in this house; so did Z, whoever he may be. Oh, forgive me, am I saying too much?

No, not at all, Matteo answered. You can see, Ronald, we have these circumstantial fragments that cry out to be connected. Due to the dearth of historical information, all that we have appears to be what's in this house. But what's in this house is compelling.

There was a pause. Would Matteo show him something?

Too bad we have no handwriting samples to compare, Lucy observed.

We have something better, Matteo said.

Another pause. The box or the fresco? Both?

Ronald, Matteo said quietly, may we take you into our confidence? This means a great deal to us.

I assure you, Ronald replied, without a trace of the stutter.

Lucy, Matteo continued, may I bring in the box?

Let me, Lucy replied. I'll just be a moment. Leo followed her out.

The four of us sat silently until Lydia said, Could they have been married? Would there be documentation of that?

I suspect someone would have found it by now, Ronald replied.

Are there legal documents pertaining to the Catena family that we could look at?

As you must know, Lydia, the daughters are not always recorded. I did read a monograph on Catena once. I vaguely remember something about a will; he kept changing his will, as I recall. I could have a look at that. He lived into the 1530s so the wills would have been later.

We still haven't really seen the diary, I remarked, Clara's diary, and, Lydia, there are those records of what went on in this house. Maybe some of it was left here with the intention of suppressing it. You can imagine that the women living here were a close community, attached to each other and protective. I wonder how many there were?

We can find out, Lydia said, but given how few were at Le Virgini, there would have been even fewer here. A small community, you're quite right. There were, after all, only four similar trunks. I suspect those belonged to the younger women, of whom Taddea was one, but who knows? Maybe the others got caught.

Clara's trunk would have been left in 1510, the year she died, I said. Perhaps Taddea put it up there. Odd that no one claimed it. Maybe she was in disgrace.

There had been plague, Lydia replied. Perhaps it was left for reasons of contagion and then forgotten about.

We heard Lucy coming down the hall, and everyone turned in her direction. She came into the room with the box in her hands, looking like a priestess bearing a sacred relic. She placed it in the center of the table, creating an effect that could only be described as stunning.

The box seemed to glow. It was a perfect miniature of the

painting, the same proportions, smaller, of course, no more than ten inches on its longer side, less worked over and finished, more like a sketch, a likeness, but unmistakable all the same. And there was the little *Z* on a small stone in the foreground, certainly not found in the picture at the Accademia. Matteo was watching Ronald's face.

Oh my, Lydia murmured.

Ronald examined the surface of the box with intense focus for some time; he narrowed his eyes, frowned, grimaced, sat back, looked away, and covered his mouth with his hand. I don't know what to say, he finally remarked. It's certainly commanding. This is the box that contained the letters?

Yes, Lucy replied, the letters and other things, including paintbrushes.

He did decorate furniture early in his career; his wonderful *Judith* was a cupboard door of some kind, so a piece like this wouldn't be a complete anomaly. This would have been later, but made as a gift? A token of regard? It's not impossible. It certainly suggests his hand, no doubt about it. It's hard to think who else could have done it. It carries a beautiful message to one's beloved, indeed it does. Well, Matteo, I see your dilemma. Something like this turning up, with letters inside and paintbrushes! He laughed. It's unheard of. It has all the earmarks of a hoax, but the hoax seems to be four centuries old. No one has been in that room, we know that?

As Matteo has suggested, Ronald, Lucy answered, we believe that this house was returned to the da Isola family at the time of the enclosure. Perhaps they demanded its return, I don't know; for them it was a minor property, used only for guests, storage, nothing much, until it was given to my husband and me over fifty years ago. My housekeeper knew of the existence of this attic room, but she is not the type for sophisticated forgeries, and truly, everything else up there was untouched. Why would anyone leave behind such beautiful things if they had been discovered? Quite a lot of money to be made if nothing else.

Also the letters and the diary and Taddea's things, a fair bit of work for the hoaxer with little hope of enjoying the outcome, Lydia said. He'd have to be a terribly talented painter as well and could probably have done better elsewhere. I agree that it defies credibility in some ways, but stranger things have happened.

And do you believe he may also have made the fresco? Ronald asked.

Right to the point, I thought. I could see that Matteo was stymied. Were we going all the way?

Of course I can't say, he replied. There are stylistic congruencies. If you don't mind waiting a few more days until we have completely cleared the surface, I'll let you see it and you can judge for yourself.

Matteo, Ronald said, I will give you every assistance in this matter. I do grasp the stakes and understand your concern. Let me assure you that I am not a pirate. I think, probably, everyone here shares a distrust of the ways of the world as we have come to know it; it strikes me as that sort of group. A glance to Lydia. These discoveries, whatever they may be, are yours. I'll be happy to sign an affidavit, he said, and then smiled, having had a great deal of trouble with the word.

He means it, Lydia added. That's why we're engaged.

Engaged! Lucy exclaimed. How wonderful!

Sudden, yes, Lydia said, but these things happen. We must never quail before miracles. Ronald was looking down at his lap, blushing and still smiling. She was blushing too; these two towering, brilliant, attractive people were reduced to embarrassed children.

With my terrible imagination I tried to picture them in an ecstatic embrace but forbid myself to go on with it.

Well done, old man, Matteo said, the first Briticism I had heard from his mouth.

We must celebrate! Lucy said. We'll have champagne! She crossed to the little bell on the table and rang it above her head as if it were a tiny church bell.

In a matter of moments, Annunziata reappeared, with not only champagne but also a dish of caviar in a bowl of ice, toast points, lemon, chopped eggs, everything. We laughed and toasted each other, devouring in no time the most sublime of luxuries.

Here's to Ronald and Zorzon, the enviable lovers! Lucy exclaimed, lifting her glass.

Great George and Great Ronald! Matteo seconded.

And to the women who love them! I said.

Yes, declared Lydia, to Clara, and to Taddea, all the brilliant souls who never had our chances! God bless them. There were tears rolling down her face, but by now we were all a bit looped and emotional after the day.

We talked and drank; the second bottle was nearly empty. I glanced at Matteo, caught him looking at me. We smiled and made a discreet toast that I thought no one noticed. I felt a flush pass through me. Was I falling in love with Matteo? Was I drunk? Or was I just in love with this excitement and joy? Early in my acting career I fell in love, as everyone does, with every costar I had. Some of these attachments were more real than others, but none lasted. Once out of the magic circle of work it was hard to remember what one had felt and why. The encounters became tedious; I gave them up. And this? We were not actors, but we were, after all, in wonderland, I was at least; how could I believe in this? There was nothing but confusion ahead for me, no glorious smooth-sailing revelations like the one Lydia and Ronald seemed to have enjoyed. I noticed that Matteo watched me withdraw. His face was serious. But not resentful. I probably was a bit drunk. I wouldn't be alone in this company.

Well, Lucy said, we should go out and dance, but I will have a tray in my room; this has been such a day! How happy we are for you two and how pleased to have you with us on this adventure. Aren't we all terribly lucky? Especially me, to have such exceptional young people around me. We must have many more celebrations, and we must find Clara. To think that we are privileged, perhaps, to know the great Giorgione! I am overcome. You too, Leo, you are overcome although you don't say so. Good night then, she said, rising. Good night, sweet friends, good luck to us!

Matteo rose and smiled and so did we all.

The four of us sat on talking for a few hours. Annunziata brought sandwiches and more wine. I couldn't remember having such a sweet, friendly time in many years. Antony didn't really have friends, and mine weren't part of our life. We—I—had lived in isolation, nothing but fans, hangers-on, staff and business people. No constant friends as interesting as we imagined we were, no independent people. Other celebrities sometimes, most as dull as anything could be. Nothing as genuinely celebratory as this felt. Nothing celebratory at all. Was I being unfair?

We talked about our childhoods—Scotland, America,

Milan—and other times in our lives, the madness of youth. They had all been married before, although I did not speak of that. We talked about the world as it is now, wanting to live some other way, how difficult that was. We talked about not being truly young anymore; we could not be considered old, I thought, not nearly forty, but that might be denial. Inevitably, because of the engagement, we talked about love and unexpected happiness. We heard the entire story of their courtship, beginning with glances exchanged in the reading room of the archives, blossoming over shared sandwiches, startlingly similar insights, day trips, midnight walks. People in love love to tell the story. They were both apparently from wealthy families and would not be sharing a cold-water flat. I seemed to be the only one not of independent means, also the only one still in round one. But it was kind and comforting and reassuring, and by the end we were kissing each other and declaring allegiance.

After they left, Matteo locked the door. We stood in the courtyard. The night was cold and I was shivering, so he put his arms around me and we remained standing that way in silence for what seemed a long time.

Nel.

Yes.

Are you surprised?

By you, Matteo?

By this. I am, I must say.

This is wonderland, Matteo. I thought we weren't asking questions.

Wonderland, he said.

No, not wonderland. I've always actually hated Wonderland and Alice. I found it creepy and perverse. This is better than that. Although I do believe I'm getting bigger and smaller. More or less at the same time. He had taken off his jacket and put it around me. I've always liked that men seem impervious to cold. My shivering at that moment might not have been entirely due to the night air.

I had forgotten what happy people looked like, he said.

They're very happy. Do you think it's contagious?

No, but it's inspiring. Interesting, isn't it, how you can forget so much. Start thinking of it as other people's behavior, nothing to do with you.

I took my illicit cigarettes out of my pocket and offered them. To my surprise he accepted, took the matches, lit two, and gave one to me. Smoking, he looked like a forties movie star.

Were you ever bad, Matteo? Lucy says your family is terribly proper.

What is bad? What my family might have thought was bad seemed to me the only possible way to live. Yes, I suppose I was bad in the way you mean. Mostly in Rome.

You were bad in Rome?

I spent two of those years having an affair with my professor's wife. She was older than I, a wonderful woman, a sort of Lucy; she probably gave myself to me. If it was bad I don't regret it. Then I came back and married the wrong person. I still don't know why. Bigger and smaller, as you say. Maybe that's how things are done. It probably takes a genius to know what he's doing.

And then?

What? Work. And then this. This place, Lucy, the fresco, the box, everything, you.

When you say *you,* you mean me?

I mean this, whatever it is. For me, the first thing since. Something, anyway, isn't it? Not nothing. Familiar, as you said.

I understand the first thing since. I understand familiar. But, Matteo, we're under a spell, aren't we? I think I am. I don't know what's real.

We were quiet.

All right, let's do that, then. Let's be under a spell. He smiled, dropped the cigarette, put it out, picked it up, and put it in his pocket.

I wish I had known you in Rome. When was that, ten years ago? It seems like another century. I feel like a shadow now. A shadow in front of a mountain. I was never afraid once. By now I was shivering uncontrollably.

You're cold, he said. We'll go in.

We walked back into the house, kissed briefly on the landing, and went to our rooms. I was exhausted.

My God, he's right, Lydia said. It's like hieroglyphics, beautiful to look at and impossible to decipher. The writing is so small at the beginning. It loosens up bit later, but I don't think she was interested in anyone else reading this.

We were in the salon; I had a yellow pad and was prepared to take dictation, but we weren't getting far. We were seated at the large table. Outside, a luminous day was shining. The light was changing, so was the season. How many days since the incident of the train? And how many left? Seven? Eight at the most? Antony was strangely quiet.

Let me see, let me see, Lydia said, adjusting her glasses and squinting again at the first page of the small red book. You know, I think if I go faster it works better, skim across the text and try to pick up some sense rather than focusing on each word. Yes, let's see, the date is fairly clear 1505, June 10. Something about rest, a dream? Vincenzo's name, I think, fruit? A green dress, a storm? Then June 11, she is fifteen, not be what? Destroyed? Gifts? Vincenzo again. This is very difficult. Then June 12, much longer, something about her birthday, a monster, a book! From Zuane. A silk purse, from Lorenzo, someone named Nucca gives her what? A sewing box, I think? A demon, oh, Nucca is the demon? Not clear. Someone named Tonso, Messer Lucca, gratitude to Vincenzo, good news. Oh dear, it's so tiny, obviously he's given her whatever she wanted. Wait, wait, here's something, I shall become, something, something, your amazing, I think, Clara, a joyful heart. I don't think I can do this.

Amazing Clara? I said.

Yes. She must have been thrilled to have this book and wanted it to last so she made the writing small. A diary like this is unusual anyway, as I told you. These must be her brothers, Zuane, Lorenzo, and Vincenzo; Vincenzo seems to be in charge. Who is Nucca? Doesn't sound like a sister. Taddea mentions a stepmother, perhaps that's Nucca? No apparent father at the party. The stepmother doesn't seem well-liked if she's the demon. Good thing she had Vincenzo.

But what is she doing?

Who knows? Getting educated against the conventional wishes of the stepmother? A sewing box? Not the most inspiring commemoration. Lorenzo gives her a purse, a predictable gift, although clearly expensive; money in the family. Zuane maybe knows something more about her and gives her the book, this book, I would guess, and Vincenzo gives her the great thing, whatever it is. Nucca — it means nape of the neck without the extra *c* — has her by the throat, perhaps?

How many pages are there?

Let's see, I would say about eighty; that will take forever. Do you think Matteo would let me give this to someone who can do it better than I can? I can find someone trustworthy; that way we can read it sooner without stumbling along like this. My translation skills are okay, but this is daunting.

I don't think he'd mind as long as it was secure. And confidential.

These people translate hundreds of things. I know someone dependable. I might Xerox it first so the book itself never goes out of our hands. That's a good idea. Aren't you longing to read it?

I am. This is the first moment of hearing Clara's voice. Does she sound like Taddea?

A bit, two bright young women, full of beans. Amazing Clara is touching.

Both hurtling toward ghastly fates.

Yes, I suppose so. But living nevertheless. Are you depressed?

Just realizing I won't be staying much longer. Wondering what I'll do. I wish I had a PhD in Renaissance art history.

There's still time.

Don't be silly. I don't think I'll be a ballerina at this point, and I'd be a hundred before I knew half of what you know, or Ronald, or Matteo.

There are, of course, other things to do. Truly, Nel, I believe you could do whatever you like. You're a smart girl.

Yes, a smart girl with a gigantic boulder in her path. I don't mean Antony; I mean what's coming up. Some people seem to be able to just go on to the next, as they say; I've never known how to do that. It takes me so long to get over things. Do you find that?

Of course. Although it does get easier. Cut your losses. That's my motto. One life, Nel, not to be tedious.

Who could be more tedious than I am?

Will he mind? I mean really, truly mind?

I doubt it.

Well then?

Many acts of courage, Lydia, and in another world.

Take this world with you, then. Take me. I'll remind you.

Where does this happen? On the telephone? In Rome? In New York?

If you're sure, sooner rather than later.

I haven't seen him for weeks. I owe it to him to go there, to Rome.

So? You'll go. You'll come back.

And do what? Live with Lucy forever? Follow you around?

I don't know. You have to have some faith. That annoying thing about closing doors before the next ones open. Unless you just go back, something has to happen; it may not be easy but it won't be forever. When you were fifteen, you probably thought you could do anything, just like our amazing Clara. How much have you really changed?

What happened to your first husband?

He got involved with a tiresome, ambitious girl in his department. He couldn't tell the difference. Poor man, they have four children now. I don't like to think about what his life must be. Maybe he's gloriously happy. I wish him well, but frankly I don't care. I do care that I'm gloriously happy.

Was it hard?

Yes, of course, it was hard, but so long ago now, like something that happened in a school playground.

Oh, Lydia, you do inspire me.

Good. I'm happy my own mess proves instructive. But look at me, Nel, there is hope! A huge smile.

If hope were that easy.

. . .

Lydia and I set out to find a shop with a Xerox machine; then she went off to deliver the pages to the translator. Securing Clara's diary in my bag, I diverted through San Marco on the way home to enjoy the day. The air was crisp, glinting with sunshine, the throngs and pigeons reveling together.

I wondered what San Marco was like when Clara was here. Were there pigeons? I wondered where the Catena household was located or if there was a way to find out. Fifteen years old, five years left to live, and yet she was soon to be the object of a great passion and had ambitious plans for herself, an exceptional girl for her time. Here was I at thirty-five, floundering in confusion. Mozart was dead at my age. So was Giorgione. *Col tempo,* wasn't that it, the message of *La Vecchia?*

I would go to Rome. And what would I say? Antony, let's be honest? A trial separation? I can no more? Could I do this? Did I want to?

Suddenly a thousand pigeons exploded into the air with a great *whoosh;* something had alarmed them. The sky was filled in an instant with fluttering wings; some dropped back down at once; others wheeled away, out over the lagoon and back, gleaming in the sun, glittering as they circled to land. Shocked, looking up, I was blinded by the blaze in the sky. *Old chaos of the sun,* Stevens said; we live in an old chaos of the sun. Dazzling brilliance seared off every thought in my head. I was abruptly and entirely released into the spectacular present beauty of the afternoon, the world, being alive. Lightning in the head, nothing but poetry was left, poetry and light. Everything inside and out of me seemed to shudder and shift. One life, Lydia had said, and here it was, delivered like a command

from the universe—Wake up! Look up! Out of the shadows
and into the brightness—it doesn't last long. The pall lifts,
the spell is broken, broken now by a crowd of startled pigeons
and words, as Beckett said, *not many.* I stood in the middle of
San Marco transfixed and transformed, staring up at the heavens. I didn't care who saw me or if I looked mad. Life! Take it
or leave it, and I would have it. I would. Amazing Cornelia!
What a gift! And you, Zorzon, poet of light, you painted this!

CHAPTER SIX

The writing was cramped and archaic. Xerox reproduction didn't help; the machine must have been low on ink. Giuliana Datini pulled the lighted magnifying lens she used for these sorts of texts into place between her gaze and the papers. Giuliana was among the elite sought-after translators who could be depended upon for discretion and accuracy; her tiny dark office drew distinguished historians and scholars. Lydia had discovered her early in her stay and the two had become friends, so Lydia was granted access in Giuliana's pressing schedule, the schedule Guiliana found oppressive. She missed daylight. She missed having a life. One had to make a living.

Nevertheless, handwriting from centuries ago still affected her, even the tedious legal documents and official records that made up her usual tasks. She had come to recognize scriveners of various eras in the employ of the Republic and felt admiration for the artistry of some. This writing, however, had none of the flourishes of civic penmanship; it was tiny, neat, fluent, and pretty. She knew without knowing the content that it was a woman's writing, a thing she rarely saw. She assumed it would be the work of a nun. They were doing nuns now, Lydia was; this would be a convent record or history. Her back was tired. She was fitting this in after a long day as a favor; Lydia was a new and amusing friend, one of few.

She opened her computer and set to work, hoping to get a few pages finished before she was too tired to see straight. *June 10, 1505. Last night I dreamt once more of Riposa.* Odd, Giuliana thought, more like a poem than a chronicle. Dreams of a happier life? Well, why not, poor things. She adjusted her glasses and went to work.

JUNE 10, 1505

Last night I dreamt once more of Riposa. Papa was there, Vincenzo also, so young. We were in the apricot orchard; a fierce sun blazed. In the dream Papa lifted me from the ground and swung me into the air; I raised my hands to the golden fruits. I was small and barefoot and wore a green gathered smock I can nearly remember. Great Nico pranced at Papa's heels. Reach, *cara*! Papa commanded. I felt his strong hands, but even as I stretched out my arms at once a howling wind whirled up, an angry black sky swept suddenly down, all the fruits and leaves were swirled away in the precipitate tempest. I cannot reach! I cried in terror, Papa, I cannot reach! But Papa, I knew, was gone. I awoke in wretchedness.

JUNE 11

I am fifteen years and shall not be vanquished. On the graves of my dear parents, this portrait of her I never truly knew, I vow that they shall not have borne me in vain. They have bestowed upon me gifts. Vincenzo says so. Also upon this day I abjure forever meager souls. Neither shall I be false to myself. Never.

It is three days since my birthday, a cold and gray day for so lovely a month. A dreary celebration it was. Today it is bright and warm. Tonso whistles at the window; a part of me is singing too. I record here in sweet Zuane's gift, a handsome leather book chosen, he earnestly spoke, to collect herein my intimate imaginings. A most uncustomary and inspired suggestion. Zuane is a dedicated reader. He hopes I shall emerge a poet. Lorenzo gave me a patterned silk purse on a golden chain, a luxurious gift from my dear brother. To what festivity am I to carry it, I wonder? The little girls painted flowers on a folded paper; I opened it to find their names in a confusion of inkblots. Angela's eyes were wide and mischievous, Gemma with her plump hand upon her mouth to cover her delight. How Papa would have loved them. Nucca's gift was the largest, wrapped in patterned paper. A sewing box. She watched my face. How I should like to fall upon her with all my strength and strangle the demon within her. I shall certainly look for time to sew, I meekly said. That would be a welcome improvement, she returned, a tone pleasant enough and eyes like frozen lakes. Vincenzo gazed down, a miserable smile on his kind face. He cannot bear it but does not speak. But later, as I sat speaking to Tonso, he came to my room, my only haven in this changed house, to give the best news of my life. He has arranged, now I am fifteen, that I may study with Messer Luca, here at home. If I do well and am skillful, I may be invited to visit the studio. Visit the studio! I threw my arms about him. Thank God for you, my good Vincenzo! I cried. I shall become, I promise you, as you have always called me, your amazing Clara. He laughed and kissed me. I will sew slippers for him to keep the jackal at bay. Tonso is covered and quiet; the moon is waxing above the lagoon; for the first time in as many years since, my heart is joyful.

JUNE 13

Nucca has told Vincenzo that she will not open the house to Messer Luca; she does not care to have unclean artisans tramping about spreading contagion. Furthermore, if I wish to defy the proper bounds of a gentlewoman's education in addition to my disobedience and ill-tempered mien, she will be happy to gather the five hundred ducats and pack my *cassa* so I may return to Le Vergini and paint there, not in her house.

All of this I heard; I was reading in Papa's study, where I go to feel what lingers of his kindness. They were in the hall, her voice shrill, as is usual when she speaks of me. Why does she hate me so? She was never kind, but when Papa died she seemed to turn upon me afresh. How have I provoked her? Perhaps it angers her that my grief was more terrible than her own. Almost at once upon his loss, beloved Nico, Papa's dear companion and my great comfort, was exiled to Riposa, where I pray Viola cares for him, and Bini, my kind orange cat who did harm to none, was banished as well; his fur made her unwell. I wept in triple agony. Only Tonso is left to me. Him I will protect with my life.

Nucca has told me that my sewing skills are so lamentably poor that until I have demonstrated improvement, I may devise my own clothing. She can in her despair for me contrive no less strict a method. My time is habitually wasted, she says, pursing the tiny lips in her porcine face; for my own welfare, I must be led. She cannot think through what indulgence I have declined to this lamentable state. My father would be shocked. I am obstinate now but will someday be grateful that she has dedicated these efforts toward my improvement. I stare as if to murder her with my eyes; I do not speak.

She longs to slap and beat me as she does the young serving women but dares not, as Vincenzo stands between us.

This morning as she raged I crept behind the drapery in the study so she could not come and accuse me of listening. My body trembled. I pressed my hand against my mouth to stifle my sobs and heard a great ringing in my ears. I huddled there for I do not know how long. Oh, Papa, I would give all my life to be for a single moment wrapped in your benevolent arms. Our happy life has perished. Like Tonso, I am trapped in a cage. How, Papa, am I to live without kindness, facing always this granite obstruction, this devil? She throws up the welfare of "the sisters" to Vincenzo and will not allow for the other sister, the one who knew you best and is here bereft since you have entered the glories of heaven. I feel in my sorrow that it would be well for me to go and seek you there, forsake this bleak existence where I must serve the will of an ogress until one of us is dead.

I do not know how the conversation with Vincenzo ended. When I regained this room, I threw and kicked her hated sewing box about until Tonso became frightened and began to scream. I retrieved my senses and took him from his cage to hearten him. Dear Tonso. He pecked and kissed my mouth, then gave a hard bite to repay me, a bite I am sure I deserve because I am a willful, intractable girl. Yet I am certain my heart is honest, my aspiration not simple vanity. I am not like good and pliant girls who yearn only to marry. It hardly matters that Nucca keeps me from gatherings; though I am lonely, I can bear that. I shall not be content without some consummation of my dream. I feel the need to grow capable. God has made me so and must wish it as well.

The wind has come up. It lashes rain; all is mist and fog. The scent of the sea is strong. I pray Vincenzo prevails. Look down, Papa. Sustain your sad daughter.

Giuliana Datini decided to have a little supper at a café in the campo and come back for an hour or two before going home. She was curious. Who was this sorrowful child?

I spoke to your husband, Lucy said. He called while you were out and has apparently grasped enough Italian to convince Annunziata to allow him to talk to someone.

Antony? Really? What did he say?

That he knew how much you were enjoying yourself, that he hoped to meet me sometime, that he was grateful for my hospitality to you, that his mother's family came from somewhere near Venice, he thought, that Italy is delightful, and would I ask you to call him. Very charming. He is a charmer, no?

He is a charmer.

His tour has been extended; he is going to Paris. You are offered a reprieve. He will be in France for at least ten days and you may meet him there. I sensed popular demand, muted, of course.

No doubt.

So, Nel, a few more weeks? I'm very pleased.

Pleased is hardly the word for me.

Isn't it odd? These irresistible men, they look so much more delicious than they taste. I do know. I'm sure he's perfectly fine, but he is an event unto himself and cannot resist whatever will proclaim that. I was able to recognize the sorcery. Alvise was adorable; so many found him so. You cannot expect a peacock to walk on a leash.

Oh, Lucy—I was laughing—is that an ancient Italian adage?

It may be. I can never remember anymore from where I've accumulated all that I know. I am too old and wise. I am a sibyl.

I'll call him. I'm very grateful for this. Maybe he understands that I want to stay here.

Perhaps. Perhaps he has other things to interest him. I wouldn't be too generous. Not without more information.

I had an indescribable day, I told her. I was—I don't know—struck down by the sun in the piazza—no, not down, up, dazzled—it was like an epiphany. I must be under the influence of Giorgione, don't you think?

An epiphany in the piazza? How nice. I myself often disappear into flowers; if you look into one long enough, it too becomes another world. One feels a little shocked coming back to this one. I agree about *Tempesta*. I myself always thought that picture was a vision, but for him a vision that lovely woman represents.

Do you find her bigger? I asked, I mean, proportionally grander?

Her presence is certainly stronger. It's really her and the landscape, isn't it? Perhaps she's the landscape personified. There's a sophisticated theory for you. I'll be in competition with Ronald soon—she laughed—the young man does seem entranced.

That's what it is, *Tempesta,* isn't it, a kind of ecstasy?

Ecstasy that required a great deal of skill to communicate.

He was young when he painted it.

Lively times, my dear. Lots of inspiration about. Now, Nel, I must consult you. I feel a bit guilty about Renzo. We've abandoned him, and abandonment is what he's always blamed me for. What can we do?

Matteo is afraid of him. With reason, I think?

Probably. But nevertheless we must offer him something.

Let's offer him lunch and a lot of unknowns. He'll want to see the fresco but Matteo doesn't want that. First things first, don't you agree?

Of course, she said, smiling. Always first things first.

Taddea is surprisingly unresentful at this stage of her confinement, as Lydia said, chipper and full of interest in the news she's getting from the world. She refers to an aunt who seems to be there and a cousin as well; she's more involved with Clara. There are gatherings with her family in the public room, always attended by her brother Giacomo, how funny; he's the apple of her eye, brings her gifts—a beautiful cloak, paintings of his own devising. She paints as well. They have competitions, also singing competitions, which she believes she wins. He brought a puppet show to the convent. She plays tricks on him, bakes a cake with pebbles inside; he told her he would report her to the abbess for attempted murder. She seems to be no more than fourteen, if that. This is at the beginning.

A few more pages with references to her father and mother, a house she loves, dogs, her married sister's child; then suddenly it breaks off and the rest appears to be from a later time. Perhaps she didn't have room in the box for all of this lively commentary and chose to include only the pages about Clara.

Her tone here is different, more serious and reflective. Her handwriting has matured as well, according to Lydia. I wonder how many years later? She speaks of Clara first meeting the symbol, an event Giacomo also attended. This was sometime earlier; she blames Clara for being secretive. Clara has now revealed more, that there was wonderful music and Giacomo sang; Clara wishes that Taddea had been there to sing as well. Clara says she was taken with the symbol, everyone was; he sang like an angel himself. He's Vincenzo's great friend, exceptionally handsome and amusing. Also very grown up; Clara doubts he will have noticed her. She speaks of Clara's work, which has surprised everyone, although Donna Tomassa always said there was no one to match her. Messer Luca told Vincenzo he was amazed to find such a jewel. What is she talking about? Anyway, to go on, that woman won't leave Clara alone, Taddea says, insults her and keeps the little sisters away from her. How sorry her papa would be if he knew what he brought into that house.

Another page. Clara has asked me to use this symbol for the symbol so I have made corrections, Taddea says. Clara is terrified of *N,* says her eyes are everywhere. Clara has met the symbol many times; she mentions mutual friends—Taddea's longing is palpable here, poor girl. The symbol has indeed noticed her—who would not notice Clara? she remarks—has expressed admiration, sees her often. Clara believes herself to be in love and is what Taddea regards as overexcited. Vincenzo suspects but has not expressed disapproval. He is devoted to the symbol. If *N* were to know there would be trouble. *N* imagines herself very grand, Taddea says.

There are more pages suggesting an intensifying relationship. Taddea worried about secrecy, fears for Clara, afraid she's taking dangerous risks.

No doubt she was taking dangerous risks, Matteo observed.

I wish this were a bit more explicit, I said.

Perhaps Clara will tell more, unless she's writing in code too. With the gruesome *N* around it would seem sensible.

There's more, Matteo, but it's brief and compressed. How many years do you think this is? There are no dates, but time seems to be passing.

La Tempesta was—what—1504 or thereabouts, they think? Clara's diary begins in 1505; she doesn't know him then. They both die in 1510? So, five years, but which years are these?

Taddea's much less expansive in these later pages. She seems under pressure and is even more inscrutable. Brief notes, really, impossible to tell how much time lapses between them. I doubt she was keeping her own diary going; less fun seems to be had by all.

We were on the couch in the salon. I had Lydia's translation of Taddea's notes and was reading to Matteo, who was lounging with his head against the armrest, eyes closed. Briefly, what happens? he asked.

Briefly, very briefly, I said, turning through the remaining few pages, Clara's been back to the house, ongoing problems with *N*, Clara appears to be engaged. Taddea arranges a gift, more problems at home, Taddea frightened for Clara, Clara ill, Clara back at the house, Clara in exile, Clara returns, Taddea joyful, the symbol is ill, appears to come to the house, which is now called a hospital, dies. Donna Tomassa is helping Clara. And that's it. Hardly the story. Terse.

By 1510 the convent would have been under pressure, the League of Combrai thing Lydia mentioned, Matteo remarked, although apparently dozing. Venice was changing, a new mood, tougher, looking to blame. It was the end of something, although things carried on fairly normally until the Counter-Reformation. Interesting, isn't it, how shifts come early in centuries and take a hundred years to play out? Change is slow; no one knows what to make of anything new.

True of life, Matteo, I thought, is that what you mean?

Clara and Z were right on the cusp and they vanished. I suspect they were illuminati of sorts, prescient; they shot through. The rest struggled on. Catena barely registers the influence of Giorgione until much later. Something catches up with him. We should go and see some Catenas.

Do you know, I said, that Lucy's worried about Renzo?

Worried about what?

That he's left out. She thinks he'll take it personally.

So take him to the Accademia to offer opinions on Giorgione, say we're curious about Neoplatonic thought. Suggest we're idiots. It won't be hard to convince him. Say the fresco is daunting, so frightfully difficult.

Neoplatonic thought?

Renaissance theories regarding harmony, the nature of love, the divine.

Love? He will be theoretical, no doubt?

He'd welcome the chance to expound on the nature of love in Lucy's presence. And he is, after all, the sublime authority on the Renaissance. Or one of them. You'll learn something. We'll all learn something if you can remember what he says.

Matteo!

I don't mean you won't remember. I mean you'll be tempted to nod off. Also he'll be loud, and that will embarrass you. Lucy will tell him he's marvelous, and you'll start thinking about getting out of there. Forgive me, I'm being unkind. He makes me nervous.

I'll be attentive. Lucy can manage him.

I don't want him to see the fresco. It's too wonderful.

It is. She's a goddess, as Lucy says.

But we'll show it to Ronald?

Yes. Beyond thrilling.

What?

All of it.

He opened his eyes at last and looked at me. Thrilling, yes, but is it real?

What?

All of it.

Leo skittered into the room, followed by Lucy, who was carrying a book. He rushed up to us, jumped on the sofa, and covered my face with kisses.

Oh, Leo, Lucy cried, not in front of me! Come, you two, I want you to see something. Something struck me; it's not exact but not far off. Come, come. She left the room and headed upstairs to the fresco room. We followed obediently.

Fabio and Alberto had gone for the day, but light was still glowing in the huge uncurtained windows. The powdery surface of the fresco was a layer thinner, the colors even more pronounced. Being buried had not dimmed this work. Lucy stood between us and opened the book. It was the *Laura* portrait. Do you see what I mean? she said. We all looked back and forth from the book to the wall.

Yes, Matteo finally said. I think I can see it.

But she's changed, I said. She's thinner, not so dewy. The bones in her face are more pronounced. She looks wiser and fiercer. The hair is the same, and the eyes.

Yes, and although she is serene-looking, Lucy remarked, there is something in her face that seems—I don't know—transported; she sees something we can't see, something that compels her. She's looking past us.

Something the light behind her is illuminating, Matteo said. The light seems to contain her, almost direct her. We're meant to look there, at what she's seeing, but it's literally beyond us.

The lion is looking at her, I mentioned.

Yes, the lion is watching her watch, Lucy said. Very powerful. Is this Clara, our little girl?

We stood for a few moments considering her entranced face.

If only we could see the face upstairs, I remarked.

That's not the face she wanted us to see, Lucy replied.

If this is Laura, Matteo mused, if we could have a few significant people agree to make that speculation, the tie would be established. There's also that wreath; it looks like laurel, an iconographic consistency, a deliberate reference, possibly. There's something here, given what we know. What we know, of course, is nothing, except for the box, which confounded even Ronald, who is hardly an enthusiastic amateur. We must find out about the *Laura*. There's more to that inscription. It mentions a patron. Who would the patron be if it was a portrait of his beloved? Would he give it away? Sell it?

Also, it's so daring, I said.

Yes, very deliberately daring. He went on to paint the first great reclining nude, not in any way prurient but lost in a dream, spellbound, like this one. And look at this girl, he said, indicating the *Laura* portrait—so sensuous but somehow chaste. She offers herself but in the most aesthetic way. Erotic and virtuous at once. The two Venuses.

Will we ever understand this? Lucy said.

My God, I hope so, Matteo replied.

We have yet to hear from Clara, I said.

And Clara, Lucy observed, is the key. We must show this to

Ronald. We must have his thoughts. Renzo's as well, but we will divert first. She actually winked at Matteo, then wrapped her arms around our waists, hugging us.

You will see, she said, in the annals of art history—laughing—we shall not be forgotten.

JUNE 16

A letter today from Taddea. She urges me to visit. Donna Tomassa wonders how I am faring at home. I have not seen either for months. How ashamed I feel, miserably stitching at this misshapen garment, when at the house they are painting and singing. A nun's life seems jolly. Even dearest Donna Tomassa laughed at my ineptness with this ungovernable needle. Taddea wonders if I have seen Giacomo and if I went to the Bonvincinis' ball. I have seen no one. She invites me to her family's gathering in the public room in two weeks' time. There will be a festive meal; Giacomo has arranged a puppet show. I will ask Vincenzo to accompany me. Nucca will not object; anything that draws me near the confines of a convent delights her. She may allow me a new dress for the occasion, hoping, I am sure, it will be the last I shall require. I pray I do not break down amongst my friends.

JUNE 20

Vincenzo and Nucca were closed all the afternoon in Papa's study. How it reminded me of Papa's conferences with that woman, when she would weep and complain in a loud voice. I was a child and hurried away by Bice, my nurse, but wept wildly myself and cried out to go to him. Today I stood at the end of the hall, hoping to hear something but unable. When the door opened, I fled to my room. Vincenzo left the house. In my flight I heard Nucca shriek at poor Piera.

Vincenzo did not return for supper. The little girls chattered at the table while their wretched brothers pushed and chided each other. Zuane and Lorenzo spoke among themselves. Nucca and I sat in silence. I am utterly defeated by the tyrant.

In the late evening, from my window, I saw a singular white dove fly out on currents of plum-colored air above the canal without a friend or flock. How lone and lovely she appeared. They have excluded her because she is not feathered as they are. I wondered if she knows that she is more beautiful or only that she is alone? I watched her soar and drop until night fell and she returned, I suppose, to her solitary roost. Such are my poor hopes.

JUNE 24

Today is Papa's birthday. As we have done each of these sad years, Vincenzo, Zuane, Lorenzo, and I brought flowers and walked to the church of San Zanipolo. We sat for some time in our chapel. Foolish to say so, but how contenting it felt to be a family together again. The angel above my mother's tomb has seemed always a kind messenger, carrying her lost love to a daughter so soon bereft. Papa told me about the angel when I was small and said my mother was a soul as gentle and beautiful as any the world has cherished. He has found her again; how joyful he must be.

We sat in silence; then Zuane and Lorenzo went off to race on the lagoon. Thinking of Papa, I began softly to weep. Vincenzo laid his arm around me and held my head to his shoulder. Courage, Clara, he said, all will be well. His kindness released me and I sobbed in his arms, crying out my despair.

Vincenzo is kind and dignified, not gay and openhearted as Papa was but just as good. He told me then of the talk with Nucca. Vincenzo will not blame and says his responsibility extends to Nucca as well, but she must not keep me from fulfilling the gift which he is convinced God has granted me and which he means to nurture. Vincenzo is a fine artist and scholar; he reveres the nobility of the human spirit and believes that it reflects the glory of God Himself. He had to insist with Nucca that I be taught, that it was not improper but a blessing, and in his authority as head of the family he required it. She did not simply acquiesce, I cried, she must plan something! Ponies for the boys at Riposa, he declared, and a dancing master for the girls. For fat little Gemma? I laughed, astonished, and sober-minded Vincenzo laughed as well. God bless you, my good brother; you are your father's son.

JULY 10

Messer Luca has come ten times now. Upon his first visit Nucca refused to acknowledge his greeting as I led him to the study. When he leaves, she has Piera open all the windows. He is a small nervous man with thin hair, untidy clothing, and, in truth, a near-fatal aroma. Nevertheless he is kind and skilled. Perspective is difficult, but I begin to master its perplexities.

The vanishing point (or points) must be rigorously adhered to. It is a poetic idea as well, I think, that all things tend at last to the unseen. I long for a true landscape but make small paintings of gardens. I am allowed to visit gardens.

Signora Vidali—she has a tall palm tree—so admired my picture of her garden that she asked to keep it and gave me a pretty bracelet. You are my first patron! I told her. She knew my mother. Messer Luca also is pleased and said so to Vincenzo.

I feel quite crammed with praise. Messer Luca thinks my gift for creating likenesses "remarkably uncommon." I have always been able to do that. Papa had frames made for the pictures of Zuane and Lorenzo I made when I was eleven. Why did I not make a portrait of Papa?

I have no time now to brood upon anything but my own improvement. I have begun to sew slippers for Vincenzo, conspicuously, in the evenings. I would sew him a crown for the happiness he has provided me.

AUGUST 23

I shock even myself! I must conceal this book or face hanging. I told Messer Luca that I wished to study the form of human beings. I do not understand anatomy, but my landscapes are much better. I wish to become poetic, as Vincenzo says Messer Bellini is.

Messer Luca has brought me a wooden doll with moving parts. Such an oddity I had to laugh and he, dear man, laughed as well. I do not aspire to paint puppets! Late last night, as it was too hot to sleep and with the moon shining through my casement making silvery light, I had an inspiration. Taking chalk and paper, I pulled off my shift, looked into my large mirror, and sketched myself in every position I could manage. With the strangeness of the hour and the light, I felt I had entered a forbidden world. I did a handful of sketches and found them illuminating.

I stood then in the moonlight by the window, still naked. All was quiet; the water plashed softly; the sea scent was keen and stirring. My spirit too began to stir. I yearned to sail out into the darkness where I might encounter some magnificent creature of the air who would carry me to celestial regions on great soft wings. I seemed then to feel that warmth and strength beneath me and became dizzied by a sensation of swift plunging in my stomach and legs until I trembled all over even in the heat. Spellbound by such an experience and by the radiance of the purple sky, shaking and watching, I stood until night paled and early barges came by upon the water. I lured Tonso to kiss and calm me, drew on my shift, and lay awake. I must hide these drawings most carefully; she comes searching my possessions. What would ensue if these were found! But how elated I feel, as if I were made of air!

OCTOBER 3

A remarkable week it has been, nearly miraculous. A good angel smiles upon Clara. Nucca and the children have gone to Padua to visit her family and will not return for ten days more. The windows of the house have flown open! Two great events have occurred. The first: Messer Luca told Vincenzo that I am a jewel. Vincenzo laughed and said that we are all jewels here. Messer Luca showed him my landscapes with figures and my much-improved portraits, some three-quarters, one of Messer Luca himself as Petrarch which I made for Vincenzo, knowing he would laugh, and he did so, robustly. Vincenzo venerates Petrarch and has read to me his beautiful poems. He is pleased with me and said that I may come to the studio, since there is no other way forward. I shall be allowed to be a true painter! When Messer Luca said that I was "exceptional," there were tears in Vincenzo's eyes. Surely there were in my own, risen for love of my generous brother and the glorious expectation of what lies before me.

If any event could rival the joy of that afternoon, a most remarkable occurrence befell just two days later. Vincenzo gave an evening's entertainment and allowed—no, requested—that I attend, not merely appear and curtsy as if I were seven years old, which Nucca would have insisted upon, so intent is she upon my isolation.

Vincenzo brought in Ginevra, who made me several dresses, the loveliest a violet velvet gown with gold ribbon. Extraordinary as such a gift seems to me, the evening itself was a visit to paradise. Friends of Papa's came, all dear to us, and Vincenzo's friends, including Giacomo, who has grown quite handsome.

I was painfully sad that Taddea could not be there. I will tell her everything, but we both understand that it is not the same. Wonderful dishes, wine and laughter. Lucia and Augustin, who have served us for many years, were merry to have a celebration in the house once more. At one moment, I seemed to hear Papa laughing. I started and looked about and thought, yes, such was the home he loved; he sends a blessing.

Vincenzo has a friend whom I have never seen before, a big and handsome man, who when he played on his lute and sang, all became quiet and looked in wonder, as if an angel had come down or Orpheus himself. I do not know his name but I dreamt of him. I dreamt that we were on a boat in a dark night. How do you like the sea? he asked me. Is that not strange?

NOVEMBER 7

I feel so glad that I might grow wings. I have been to the studio many times now. Vincenzo has given me a corner in which to work. Huge windows fill the salon with light; it is the piano nobile of a near-derelict palazzo. My space, although not near the windows, is a heaven to me. The others, assistants who prepare canvas and mix colors, and Vincenzo's friends who work there, have been kind and helpful, although they were at first astonished, as if a rabbit or a mermaid had appeared and sat down to paint. When the models came, living people who pose for us, often quite undressed, there was a general embarrassment regarding myself, but soon we were at work again. Now I am taken for granted because I am as serious as they and my work is good. How beautiful these bodies are, the work of God's hand; nothing of them is shameful or corrupting. I laugh to think of Nucca here, what penance she would have to undertake to redeem herself. Donna Tomassa would, I am sure, heartily approve my studies.

It was late. The fluorescent light of the magnifier was making Giuliana's eyes ache. She switched it off and sat in the dimness, thinking of the things she had hoped for at fifteen; being a translator had not been among them. She remembered her own father's death, summer nights in the small town near Padua, soft sweet-scented nights, her solitary young body poised like an arrow. No one had come. She had studied, moved to Venice, opened this little office. Giuliana sighed. She rubbed her eyes, switched off the computer, gathered her things, went into the hall, and locked the door. As she made her way down the dark stairway, she wondered if she would ever be happy.

Lucy and I took Renzo to the Accademia, as planned, to talk to us about early-sixteenth-century painting; we would then take him for luncheon. Looking huge and distinguished in the usual tweed ensemble, he shepherded us about, making declarations in front of various masterpieces, gesturing with his walking stick in a way that made the guards watchful. He guided Lucy with careful attentiveness. We dwelt on the work of Giovanni Bellini and Carpaccio. Soon we would go up the stairs and encounter *La Tempesta*.

Renzo, I inquired, what is Neoplatonism?

Neoplatonism, my child? I don't believe I can tell you in ten words or less.

Briefly? If you don't mind?

Well, well. He sighed. Originally a school of thought derived from the works of Plotinus in the third century, he began wearily, as we made our way through the gallery, essentially a metaphysical hierarchy of the One, the Intelligible, and the World Soul, corresponding more or less to the divine, the perception of the divine, and materiality, which, they posited, emanates from the soul, placing the human mind, you see, in unique relation to divinity as well as to empirical reality and announcing thereby man's singular capacity to connect God's presence to the world of matter. Very important to the Renaissance it was, offering as it did notions of harmony and proportion, beauty as a reflection of the ultimate, implications in mathematics, music, astronomy, mysticism, so on, even alchemy, all systems for approaching the ineffable realm of perfection. How's that?

What did it have to do with art?

Another weary sigh. Ah, yes, well, in a nutshell, beauty in the world "awakens in the soul an inner image," as Michelangelo proclaimed; this image would be the soul reaching back to the divine source. Physical beauty in art will now reflect the beauty of the soul. Love, of course, is the basis of Neoplatonism, divine and profane love, the two Venuses, two paths. Plato argues that love is the force that binds all. The divine manifests as beauty, you see; love seeks beauty and therefore the divine; thus we have many lovely nudes in this period, the body as the inner self. Nature reveals the divine paradigm as well; it offers another path to the seeking spirit; in apparently random motion, we will inevitably discern concealed order, harmony, perfection. Quite refined and sophisticated, I'm sure you agree.

So Renaissance art was more spiritual? Not only religious?

I would say that it became more spiritual, if that's the word you like. Neoplatonism offered a more active participation, beyond the ritual worship of the Middle Ages. The Neoplatonist soul struggled to rise from baseness into clarity, transcendent union, and so forth, ideas taken from the pagans, Christianized to some extent, but placing man at the absolute center. The divine was now immanent in the world, no longer confined to heaven. Artists engaged the struggle to penetrate the sacred paradigm and portray what they had glimpsed. And there, I think, we have the girl's guide to Neoplatonism. Ha ha. I don't suppose you'd like a book list? I'm afraid you'd find it rough going.

Beauty is truth, truth beauty? That is all ye need to know?

More or less. Whatever Shelley said.

Shelley?

We had arrived at *La Tempesta.* I noticed Lucy cast a horrified glance toward *La Vecchia.* How funny, I thought, La Vecchia herself may have been younger than Lucy was now—life was harder then—but Lucy was radiant, still beautiful, her eyes bright and alert, girlish sometimes, capable still, one might say, of turning heads. *Col tempo.* Perhaps that inscription was more ambiguous than it appeared, or perhaps Lucy was a particularly successful manifestation of the divine.

Giorgione's mother, supposedly, Renzo commented.

And what would you say this picture is about, Renzo? she inquired, turning to our subject. I find it so captivating and elusive.

Oh my dear, he replied, who knows? The arguments are divergent to the point of tedium; Giorgione himself was essentially a phantom. A particularly baffling allegory, I would think.

Renzo laid out for us a roster of theories: mythology, philosophy, pastoral-poetic connotations, hermeneutic symbolism.

Bucolic, obviously, he went on, classical certainly, layers of implication, the mind of the artist, and who may penetrate that? What for me is wonderful is the strangeness, so unworldly an atmosphere, such radical structural innovation. There were probably a series of these, figures in landscapes, lost now. Reference is made to them in Michiel, but we've never seen them. Vendramin, Giorgione's intelligent patron, may have exercised some influence, may have wanted something in particular. There are mysteries we'll never solve, and this picture is one of the great ones.

I find it so moving, Lucy remarked, I haven't seen it for years. These figures in the foreground are really in another world, aren't they, barely aware of the wild storm going on behind them. Many worlds here, I think. Even the trees seem to have an interior life, everything responsive, so alive. And the water! More active than a dream, a vision, I've always thought. Magical light. The wonderful half-hidden moon—is that the moon? I had forgotten how lovely. This beautiful woman in her little shawl.

Yes, indeed, Renzo said. Lord Byron admired her too, wrote to a friend about her; we can see why. Ha-ha! Not much more time now, ladies; we must visit the great Veronese and something of Titian and Tintoretto, if only to see what became of your Giorgione's innovations. He was, you know, Giorgione, a great one for the ladies. His mistress gave him the plague. Some say this is her—Cecilia—but never mind, on we go.

Lucy and I looked at each other and moved along as directed.

Over a memorably delicious luncheon that Lucy had arranged at Harry's Bar, Renzo's favorite—where I found it gratifying to see what deference was paid to her by the usually cynical staff, Antony and I had been ignored—the three of us spoke of trivial things until Renzo inquired about the fresco, which he again referred to as the masterpiece. Lucy replied that it was coming along, and soon we would require his expertise. He seemed satisfied and asked no more questions.

The two of them spoke once more of their childhood, all they really had in common, I thought. It became clear by innu-endo that Renzo had always been in love with Lucy and had assumed that one day they would be married. I couldn't gather how much of a romance it had actually been; Lucy was not expansive. It seemed more an understanding on his part, unjustified probably, that because of their childhood connec-tion, they were destined for each other. It was the shocking jolt of Alvise's appearance and subsequent success that drove Renzo to England, still young, heartbroken, angry, into what he called his "long exile." He never married but achieved a weighty reputation and various eminent positions, culminat-ing in a chair at the great university. He clearly enjoyed tortur-ing Lucy with her imaginary treason. Rather girlish. I didn't think she could have considered this man for a moment at any point in her life, although he was no doubt handsome and probably sensitive before all the weight and grandeur had piled on. I couldn't think he expected anything of her now but high regard and some gratifying acknowledgment of her guilt. It seemed to me he had a tidy private life over there at the club that he would not willingly surrender. She offered him tastes of both, regard and guilt, delivered with amusement and utter detachment over a spectacular meal. He seemed pleased; we had a nice time. Renzo had been dealt with. Women's work, I thought, until, in a last remark as we rose from the table, he said he was thinking of giving a talk at the club. He was going to call it "What Remains? Are Surprises Forever in Store?" Ha-ha! He hoped we would attend. Bring Matteo, he said, he'll enjoy it.

As soon as we were alone, walking briskly, I said to Lucy, What does he know?

I don't know.

Not Ronald?

No, I'm sure not. Of course not.

Something he saw the first time?

I don't know. He senses that something is up. He suspects us. He is clever and cold. And has an eye. We did go on about Giorgione.

Maybe he's trying to lay a claim, just in case?

That's possible. Awful man. He saw Matteo's wariness. He knows other experts were there and interested. He knows a great deal. I'm afraid I've made a terrible mistake.

No, without him there would be no Lydia, no Ronald. He doesn't know about the letters, the diary. He doesn't know about the box! He can only be speculating. Trying to scare us, pretending to get there first. We have everything important. He thought a nun painted it.

I suppose.

Do we tell Matteo?

Of course. As you say, the talk can be nothing but self-serving innuendo; otherwise it wouldn't be at the club. Oh, I hope we can accomplish this for ourselves. Awful man, trying to spoil things.

The pressure is on, Lucy.

My dear, it's a time bomb. She took my hand and we marched firmly homeward.

In the morning, Giuliana sat down reluctantly at her computer. This text unsettled her; her night had been filled with disturbing, evocative dreams. She felt restless but had to get this translation out of the way, and there were pages to go. How strange to think that this child's Venice was the same Venice she inhabited, the beauty lost on her by now, her life a drab routine. She wasn't yet thirty. What was it she had wanted to do? So many things. Let something happen, she murmured, anything. Damn Lydia. She switched on the fluorescent light.

NOVEMBER 10

He has come here. He is a painter as well as so fine a singer. His name is Zorzi and he will work in the studio. Vincenzo is proud to have him with us; he is becoming famous, he says. They met years ago in Messer Bellini's studio. Vincenzo tells me he has painted a great altarpiece, religious works, portraits of noble gentlemen, and, most interesting, small paintings on canvas and board, landscapes, usually with figures, which are commissioned from him by noble gentlemen for their collections. These are not religious pictures but speak to ancient subjects and texts that contain, Vincenzo tells me, systems which give access to the perfection of the universe.

I cannot truly understand what he describes, but I have seen a few of Zorzi's landscapes here and they are mysterious and enchanting. What is it that he does to make them look as they do? I asked Vincenzo. He laughed and said that he can see through things; he is a wizard. I would like to understand. I aspire to see through things as he does, and so I watch him at work in as concealed and unobtrusive a way as I am able. He works quickly and deftly and alters the canvas constantly with a swift brush; it is difficult to grasp his method. He has been kind to me, praises my own work, offers guidance, and tells me I am a precocious and nimble child. He jokes with Vincenzo and calls me Clarissima the Unexpected. At first I was exceedingly shy in his presence. Everyone admires and defers to him, and I remember my dream, which makes me blush, but now I have grown accustomed to his being here and am able to speak with him as a normal person would, even to make a joke. Yet when he stands near me, I must clasp my hands hard against each other or I begin to tremble. I have looked up from my work and found him watching me. He smiles and waves his brush in a silly way or simply smiles. It is difficult to regain my concentration. It takes all of my courage to address him as Zorzi. How absurd I must seem. There is gossip and laughter in the studio, suggesting he is sought after by famous women of great sophistication and beauty. He has a wide reputation. I do not wish to appear a plain and foolish girl.

Giacomo also has been here and paints with us sometimes. He has done me an extraordinary kindness. He has given me a commission. He has engaged me to paint Taddea's portrait. What a joy that will be! I will work once more at the house. I shall attempt in my efforts to see through Taddea. That will certainly make her laugh. I am only sorry to be away from this place for even a moment.

NOVEMBER 21

Life here is much the same. Donna Tomassa seems to me always a brilliant, beautiful, kindhearted, and witty saint, if there may be such a thing. Like Saint Cecilia, she will enter heaven in a burst of music and glory. It cannot be easy for these girls, some my good friends, to accept so constrained an existence—not so constrained, I am told, at the convent itself—but these are Donna Tomassa's chosen and live the life of aspirants to virtue and knowledge. I know because I have lived amongst them and am the better for it. I owe myself and my life to her, and yet I cannot make that my destiny. She loves me not the less. Taddea comes to me each morning and we set to work. It is difficult for Taddea to resist the impulse to talk incessantly, but I demand that she concentrate on her innermost thoughts. She tries hard as she is able and is good for some time, until I see what is like a bubble rise in her and know that soon it will explode in a great laugh at our circumstances. I am not disappointed with the work so far. Donna Tomassa joins us occasionally, sits quietly, and makes no remark. Her smile tells me that she is pleased.

DECEMBER 16

I shall see Zorzi tonight. Two weeks ago at the Basegios' celebration of Mea's engagement, I met him for the first time outside the studio. Vincenzo escorts me to these occasions. Nucca scowls but makes no objection; she remembers the ponies. Zorzi and I encountered each other in the crowd and strolled about talking until we found ourselves in a separate chamber. I have grown comfortable speaking with him; he engages me in discussions regarding the nature of painting and poetry. His thoughts are deep and difficult. Nothing is still, he has said; clarity is the child not of reason but of intuition. Light is all. He is often somber when he works but was that evening in a genial humor and told me droll stories to make me laugh. We entered at last a small library where a fire glowed before a long bench and there alone sat ourselves down. I could breathe the scent of his body. Clara, he said, gazing into the fire, you are an amazement to me. I could not at first reply but finally said, You have taught me so much, Zorzi, I am happy to please you. Yes, he replied, my inspired apprentice. But then, as he turned to me and our eyes met, the room seemed to whirl away from me. He saw my discomposure and took my hand. There was a sound of voices in the hall; we rose suddenly and stood apart. When the voices faded he laughed and said, What a gay courtier! I did not understand and turned to look at him, unnerved and barely able to stand. He came to me. Clarissima, he said, bright angel, kissed my forehead and led me back into the hall. Surely I am a fool. He is a hero and I a mere creature, a pupil.

DECEMBER 20

Today a most handsome and noble young man came to the studio. Vincenzo and Zorzi greeted him with humor and affection. He noticed my presence and his eyes widened, all three laughed, and I was thereupon introduced, blushing, as the curiosity that I am. I deduced that he must be a member of one of the societies of young men to which both my brother and my master belong. I have little knowledge of these societies, since they exist for the edification and pleasure of unmarried men. Vincenzo is deeply dedicated to his devout brotherhood but also attends fellowships convened in noble houses devoted to the reading and discussion of texts and poems come down to us from the ancients. Zorzi does as well; they speak together of these things. Zorzi has told me of a confraternity of young nobles who put up entertainments and masques devised upon pastoral themes which give him great pleasure. How dull is the life of girls. This young man sat for a few hours during which my master sketched his noble head; his hair was to his shoulders as is Zorzi's, it is a gallant style, which Vincenzo does not affect. When he had gone, Zorzi laid in a bright pinkish ground for his costume. The application of such a color is unknown and daring. What enviable freedom! But for my few outings, I return each evening to a prison. It is unimaginable to think that a man such as Zorzi is could feel anything but affectionate indulgence for so drab an innocent as myself. Yet he is fond of me, I think.

DECEMBER 31

So much has come to pass in these happy months that I feel I must reflect on so transforming a time, which like all earthly circumstance will further transform and pass away. These days I wish always to remember. I began the year as an unhappy child and am now, by God's grace, no longer unhappy nor, I think, a child. My work has developed largely and productively; I am continually in a state of urgent inspiration and grateful diligence. Taddea's portrait is my finest effort, I believe. Giacomo presented it to her at a Christmas gathering in the public room. Taddea's family, Donna Tomassa, and Vincenzo were all in attendance. Taddea had baked superb little cakes. It is nearly painful to see my friend so glad. When Giacomo offered her my picture, she laughed and gave it back, saying that she knew very well what she looked like. All expressed delight with the likeness and rendering. There is in it, I think, something of the spirit my master has taught me to seek: freshness and tangibility. At the studio Vincenzo and others praised my work. Zorzi shook his finger and said, "You see! You see!" "You see" is the phrase he murmurs continually when instructing me. It has come to have a resonant meaning for us, that I must look closely, see how shape is modeled by light within as well as light without, awaken the inner eye. I hope I have made him proud. My efforts are for him. No one can approach his genius or his kindness. He is a miracle.

Now I must speak of my own miracle. He loves me. He has told me. I cannot comprehend how it can be. It was on Christmas night, a night most sacred of all the year. Vincenzo had a gathering; he seems now to be truly the master of our home. Nucca's acquiescence makes me uneasy but, Praise God, I no longer sit through long days with her. Fifty at least attended, we feasted and sang; Zorzi accompanied on his lute. A merry time it was, and near midnight we prepared to go out to the celebrations in the piazza, which would be ice cold, full of music, and blazing with torches as in all the years that Papa took us. I rushed to my room to gather my warmest cloak and bid Tonso good night. When I returned to the hall, only Zorzi remained to escort me. A happy Christmas, Clara, he softly said as he laid my cloak round me. The warm wave that I feel in his presence surged over me and before I could comprehend I was in his arms, his mouth upon mine, so near to him I seemed to die and be reborn through what grace I could not have dreamed. How can I speak of this? We breathed some other medium, stronger and sweeter than air, one such as I have never known. So we remained for some minutes, then went and walked amidst the revelry of the crowds. I felt myself nearly levitated. We encountered Vincenzo and the boys and strolled far along the embankment, flushed with laughter and high spirits. Has there been such a night? I am fearful all the while that I will awaken from so extravagant a dream. I have not seen him since; it is the holiday; we do not attend the studio. Happiness in such a degree as this confers is near terrifying. God protect me and make this true.

FEBRUARY 10, 1506

What happiness! We do not reveal ourselves to any, not even Vincenzo, yet my brother knows me too long and well not to have an awareness that I am more joyful and enlivened than at any time in memory.

MARCH 15

I find so little time to record here. I wish to recount every instance of my felicity, yet life carries me swiftly along. I think of tomorrow and become agitated to arrive there. I throw myself upon the bed and confide to Tonso until my exhausted heart gives way and I sleep.

Still, I must record that *Z* is working on a most ambitious and wonderful picture of three sages who stand and sit under trees before a great dark cave. Messer Contarini has commissioned this painting for his collection; he is a rich and learned patron. *Z* says that Messer Contarini is knowledgeable in the philosophies of the ancients and wishes to contemplate a depiction of these exemplaries before the famous cave of Plato, each betokening an aspect of arcane wisdom. *Z* brushed in his design but has since made amendments; it changes each day. One sage had a crown like the sun, which I admired; that now is gone. The picture is most powerful for the contrast of the darkness of the cave with the radiance of the sun rising behind a distant hill, emerging, *Z* says, as the supreme good, the giver of life. His structure is complex and fraught with symbol. Everyone in the studio is excited by this picture; there are discussions and debates, each one showing off, I think. All wish to copy him but none is able. I timidly assert here to myself that I am closer at least in technique to my master than any present in our circle and endeavor most earnestly to perceive the world as he does.

I have imagined a portrait of Z as Orpheus but dare not attempt it. I have had two commissions from the house: Mella and Nencia were to be painted. Although I feel changed it was cheerful to be amongst my friends.

I have portrayed Mella in her habit and headdress; she is serious and intellectual and all believe she will be abbess one day. Donna Tomassa reveres her; they have private lessons. Nencia I depicted as Primavera. I hope I have not been too bold, but I am under the influence of a bold master. She is young and pretty as a nymph. I placed spring flowers in her hair and behind her the pink morning sky. She is but twelve years, yet what young man would not adore her? She has sisters, I think, all as lovely as she, poor child. Donna Tomassa is especially kind to her and gives her candy. Taddea tells me that she weeps at night.

And Z? What can I say of him? He is tender and fond. I watch for disappointment and distraction but it does not occur. Our burden is that we are kept apart by everything and have never the privacy I long for. I wonder where he may be when we are apart. I believe that he would indeed be with me were we able, but I live incarcerated. Not even Vincenzo can prevent this. Nucca would never allow Z here except in a crowd; she loathes artists as inferior and will not pollute her home. Vincenzo is spared because he is a gentleman. She regards his work as a mere pastime, and she must respect him as the heir. I shall never forgive her persecution of my father. He was too good-hearted to see more than a pretty widow, as then she was. She is fat now and loathsome, bad-tempered and deceitful, one who senses every opportunity for mischief. Her

great hope is to place me in the convent to free my father's fortunes for her daughters. She aspires to join the nobility but
why would they have her? I am not so benevolent as Vincenzo.
I fear her.

Tonso has gone to sleep; good night, my good green bird.

We were gathered in the fresco room. Lydia gasped when we
came in but no one spoke. Annunziata had placed chairs facing
the wall and there we sat as if wondering why we had been
called together. Her entranced face looked beyond us.

Hmm, Ronald remarked, after long silence. A conundrum.
Very, very beautiful indeed. I don't think it's him, not at first
guess, in spite of having many characteristic elements: the
charged atmosphere, gorgeous light, Arcadian vista, and this
lovely enigmatic figure launched out at us. Something is different, hard to say. I suspect if you had ten experts here, five
would say no, two would say yes, and the rest would make it
early Titian.

What's different? Lydia asked.

An authority issue? The structural conception is strong, I
would say, not bold. The palette is less intense; it doesn't glow
in quite the same way, but it's a fresco. It could be something
early, although it could also be the work of an observant and
gifted apprentice. To my mind it's more a psychological issue.
The woman in *Tempesta* looks out at us from deep within
the aura of the picture; by the time we get to the Venus, she
doesn't look at us at all, she is lost in her own dream. Those
figures are expressions, if you will, of an interior vision. Here, I
don't know; she seems to be directing us out of the world that
exists behind her with her gaze. It doesn't strike me as having
the same interiority that he intended. She doesn't so much sig-

nify a subjective state of being, rather she appears an independent entity, moving beyond her context. Still, I find it extraordinary, as if she's been summoned from Arcadia by some compelling *nextness,* for want of a better word. That in itself is quite innovating in the decorum of these pastoral dreamscapes. This is all intuition, of course. I believe there are many, as I said, who would disagree.

Leaving the frame, I said, I see what you mean. One foot is forward, isn't it?

What about the lion? Lucy remarked. He doesn't seem interested in what she sees, he seems interested in her. Perhaps he can't see it, only she can. I wonder if she'll leave him behind?

Matteo, Ronald said, do you know the *Tarocchi* of Mantegna?

Of course, Matteo replied, those wonderful prints that are not, in fact, Mantegna's. Matteo, I could see, was disappointed but rallying. Ronald had said, after all, that not everyone would agree, and who knew where we were headed?

They're a series of emblematic figures, Ronald went on to Lucy. Neoplatonic esotericism, muses, heavenly spheres, cardinal virtues, and so on. They became a prototype for the tarot deck, which was devised later in the century, but many of the images remained the same, remain the same to this day, I believe, not knowing much about tarot, although I do know the Mantegnas.

Tarot deck? Lucy exclaimed. I've seen those wonderful painted sets of cards, some of them quite elaborate and beautiful. There was a marvelous show here years ago.

Well, Ronald went on, the Cardinal Virtues are all female figures pictured with symbolic emblems and an animal companion. The Strength card, or Fortezza, shows a draped woman near a broken pillar, and next to her is a lion. Lydia, you know more about this than I do. I'm not sure of the interpretation in the tarot deck.

I'm hardly an expert, Lydia replied. I do know that the card represents wisdom or strength conquering the instincts. Not unlike Saint Jerome taming the beast. It would seem to be a reference, it's so explicit.

In the *Concert Champêtre,* once attributed to Giorgione, then to Titian, and now making its way back to Giorgione, Ronald continued, the consensus of critical opinion suggests that the two nude women enjoying a hilltop outing with two clothed musicians, are, in fact, a collective reference to the muse of poetry; they carry the emblems of a flute and vase, just as in the *Tarocchi,* so I suspect the prints were in currency at the time. Educated people would have known about them. *Concert* is undoubtedly Giorgione's picture, I believe; he was a musician, after all. Music and poetry were deeply entwined and in a sort of aesthetic competition. These competitions among the arts were popular and interested Giorgione very much—painting versus sculpture, poetry versus painting, and so on. He enjoyed a challenge.

Wouldn't the writing on the scroll help to explain something, Matteo? I asked.

The scroll is obscured, Matteo replied, some of the writing is concealed inside the rolled paper and what we see is hard to make out, but the inscription on the stele or tomb or whatever says, *Harmonia est discordia concors;* we do recognize that.

Yes, we do, Ronald replied, how interesting. Francino Gafurio. Another Neoplatonist link, music again, deeply rooted in these arcane systems, deriving from Pythagorean mystical numbers, the heavens as a musical scale. Gafurio wrote his treatise at the end of the fifteenth century. It would certainly have been current in Venice long before 1510, if that's the year we're talking about.

What does it mean? Lucy asked.

Gafurio makes this announcement in a woodcut where he's shown lecturing his music students, Matteo said; it comes out of his mouth like a little flag: *Harmonia est discordia concors*—Harmony is discordant concord. Something about intervals.

And musicians would know this book? Lucy inquired.

It was a popular book, yes. Giorgione knew a lot about geometry, we see that in his pictures, his structural innovations, Ronald continued. Geometry too was linked to music in Neoplatonism, perfect numbers, systems of proportion. They were enthralled with the idea of a unified cosmos, flawless and knowable, up to a point.

Why would this be on the tomb? *Is* it a tomb? Lydia asked. Are we to assume that it's the grave of a musician? Or just a motto?

It has implications beyond music, I said. It could be read psychologically, that wisdom is living with contradictions; two things can be true at the same time, or when people get involved, the perfect order of the universe tends to break down.

How true, Lydia said. Nel is right that the scroll is important; it might shed some light.

We'll focus on cleaning it up, Matteo replied. We've neglected it for the rest.

Now, I know I'm dwelling on this, and it may just be my own fancy, but Matteo and Nel did not laugh at me. Once again, Lucy produced her book of reproductions and opened to the *Laura* portrait. Ronald, Lydia, do you see a connection? I feel so sure that I do.

The two of them pondered the image, looking back and

forth as we did earlier; they looked at each other and seemed to reach a consensus.

Yes, Lydia replied, the similarity is there. The face has changed but is recognizable—or could be.

I thought so! Lucy exclaimed.

This is Laura? Ronald inquired of Matteo.

It's maddening, Matteo replied. We have so many loose ends, all leading to a connection we can't quite make. If Clara is Laura, if Giorgione died in this house, if the box and letters are his, if they were in love, if she is indeed Vincenzo Catena's sister—which she seems to be—how do all these clues play out? And what do they have to do with a fresco in an obscure auxiliary of a noble convent? We do think the box is his?

I'd put some money on that, Ronald said.

Have we looked again at his letters, knowing what we know now? Lydia asked. We'll have the diary tomorrow, I hope.

Taddea tells us, I said, that Clara was in love with the symbol—handsome, charming, and brilliant, Clara calls him—and a musician as well. She's overexcited, Taddea feels, at some point taking risks that get her into trouble. She also talks of an engagement, although never a marriage. Maybe Clara expected more than she got, or something went wrong. Clearly they both died here, and there was a child.

It's like an old ballad, Lydia remarked. Something Irish— love, tragedy, and you never quite know what's going on.

Pater said Giogione had a unique gift for poetry "which tells itself without an articulated story." Ronald stumbled on *articulated.* We may be facing a version of that here; he eludes us once again. I so liked that Ronald never acknowledged the occasional crisis of consonants.

I don't think so, Lucy said. We'll get to the bottom of this.

Clara has no wish to elude us; she will reveal all, Taddea too, perhaps the nuns in their papers. The women want this story told. They are, as Lydia said, quite capable of writing their own history and not lost in divine abstractions. The child was no abstraction; what became of him? Or her? Giorgione was real, real enough to die here.

She rose, clutching her book, and led us off to dinner, Leo at her heels.

Discordant concord. Agreeing to disagree? Birds not of a feather? I was trying to think who else had said this and how. It was easier to get to harmony; I had played Portia and knew *The Merchant of Venice:*

> *How sweet the moonlight sleeps upon this bank!*
> *Here will we sit, and let the sounds of music*
> *Creep in our ears: soft stillness and the night*
> *Become the touches of sweet harmony.*
> *Sit, Jessica: look how the floor of heaven*
> *Is thick inlaid with patines of bright gold.*

Lovely. Neoplatonism again, I supposed. The early ecstatic moments of being in love. "Parallel fantasies," Antony called it, as if it meant nothing. Of course he was right, but it was also, ironically, the thing that interested him most— seduction, surrender, the first delicious kiss. Discordant concord was another thing, the second act, trying to make harmony out of mundane disappointments that collapse the fantasy; things that didn't fit together, the aftermath. Perhaps clear-eyed encounters had charms of their own. I didn't actually know. The next place. Is that where Clara was going? Going on her own? Was he buried on the hilltop? But her face had that light in it. This couldn't have been an entirely disappointing man, perhaps a terrible, disappointing fate. She chose the Strength card, after all, not the Hanged Man, the tarot card I did remember, if, in fact, the Hanged Man was a bad thing. It sounded bad.

I was lying on my bed, the window was open, the night air a little cold. We'd had a sweet supper; we'd become a devoted circle of friends. I felt happier than I had felt in as long as I could remember, short of being in love. Unless I was in love.

I sat up. *Chose? Chose* the Strength card? What did that mean? Had I been thinking all along that Clara herself painted this thing? I seemed to regard it as a response; who else would respond? An observant, gifted apprentice did Ronald say? My God, all those elliptical references to her "work." What was her work? The symbol admired her "gift." What was her gift? Messer whoever said she was a jewel, and Vincenzo said, *We are all jewels here.* He was a painter. She was a painter! Of course she was a painter! Clara! You! My God, someone—Taddea—saved your paintbrushes, your paintbrushes and a lock of your child's hair. Or did you live to do that? Live to see your child taken away? No, I didn't think so. This must have been before that, when you had hope that you could go on and take some part of him with you, the child you made together. Is that what you're seeing, the other side of Arcadia?

I got out of bed and began pacing the room, turned on the light and looked at her. Was this Clara, pregnant and turned away, while he died in this room? *Pray for us?* Or did he paint it? Could he have, sick as he was? His last act of devotion? How awful for him. How awful for her.

I wanted to wake Matteo and tell him. Lucy too. It was late. I went instead to the window and breathed the cold air. No, Clara, I may be overwrought, but this is real. You. No wonder he loved you.

Lydia and Lucy were having coffee in the salon before Lydia went upstairs to the attic. I dragged Matteo from the fresco room. They looked at me in bewilderment. It was eight-thirty in the morning. I stood in front of them.

It's her.

What is her? Matteo inquired.

The painter. Clara is the painter.

The painter of the fresco? Lydia asked.

Yes, I'm sure of it. I went on to enumerate my revelations, the references to her "dream," her "work," her "gift," the "jewel," her time in Vincenzo's studio that Taddea mentioned, the paintbrushes, the observant apprentice that Ronald suggested, the musician's grave—if it is a grave—the figure stepping away to someplace outside the frame. *Laura.* Who else could it be? I'd been thinking of all the elements in the fresco as coming from her perspective, not his, and never realized it. What do you think? The fresco was a tribute, a farewell, an homage, the culmination of her skill. And then she died.

No one said anything. They looked at me with expressionless faces. Leo, since I was the only one standing, danced around my feet, thinking we might be going for a walk. I picked him up.

Is it an absurd idea?

No, Lucy replied. A little shift and it does begin to make sense. Not him, her.

Yes. Clara.

Why would Taddea not have been more explicit? Matteo said.

She does say that Sister someone said Clara was the best, or something like that, Lydia responded, and Taddea talks about her own painting, so they must have painted. Taddea's not enormously explicit about anything.

Clara, Matteo said. Clara? Well, if you think so, let's go get the diary and hope to God she makes herself known. If it was Clara.

But Matteo, what do you think? A brilliant undiscovered artist? A great painter of the early sixteenth century? Giorgione or early Titian, Ronald said? A gifted apprentice?

What a story that would be, Lucy murmured.

Something about it feels right, doesn't it? Lydia said. How incredible it would be to make a such a discovery. What do we need to substantiate it? What else besides the diary do we have? The nuns.

But to make anything of this, the *Laura* connection, all of it, we need solid information, Matteo declared. We have to have a legitimate, defensible case or it's just more speculation. Clara. Well, I suppose it might as well be a woman. This is the house of women.

Giorgione got in, Lucy observed. And also you.

Right you are. Anything goes. Not Giorgione, Clara. Good God.

We were quiet for a moment and then rose as a body and went back to the fresco room, where Fabio and Alberto were hovering over the scroll. They stood aside and the four of us contemplated the wall in a new light. I knew without looking that Lucy would have tears in her eyes.

Could it be true? Was this the masterpiece, buried for cen-

turies, of a superbly gifted twenty-year-old girl who would not
live out the year? I tried to imagine her with her ladders and
brushes and paints, there, in that room, so young, with who
could imagine what going on in her heart. Clara.

I was dispatched to collect the translation. The office of the
translator was near the Archives of State where Ronald and
Lydia met. I was following a hand-drawn map that Lydia made
for me, but this was an especially confusing part of town. I
knew I was looking for the Campo dei Frari and the huge
church as the significant landmark. The former monastery
attached to the Frari church housed the archives; the translator
would be in a side street nearby.

I turned down a nameless street feeling desperate, but upon
reaching the end, space opened out and there it was, the Frari
campo and the church. One never arrives anywhere in Venice;
one is delivered with wonder and gratitude.

Using Lydia's map I fairly quickly located the translator's
office, a tiny room in a grim building. She turned out to be a
young woman of scholarly appearance who handed me the
pages in a manila envelope, accepted my payment, offered a
receipt, and then, taking off her glasses and looking at me with
lovely, expressive dark eyes, said, I am sorry, I am only meant
to translate, but I cried. The Xeroxed pages are enclosed here,
she said, patting the envelope. A sad story. My regards to
Lydia. She seemed forlorn.

Thank you, I replied. *Grazie*. This woman knew Clara's
story. She was moved. What would happen to the rest of us?

I wandered back into the *campo* and decided to have a brief
look into the massively impressive church; a few minutes, then
I'd go back. It felt liberating to be released from our obsession.

The day was pleasant and cool, abundant sunshine, people all around living lives with no idea of what an art-historical cataclysm we were attempting to unleash. I was a truant, a feeling I've always enjoyed.

The church was enormous, cavernous, stuffed with elaborate monuments. I located a brief guide and set out. Here on the left was Canova's tomb. I didn't recall who Canova was but admired his pyramidal tomb, which struck me as elegant and modernist amid the frenetic carving and sculpture surrounding it. Up the aisle to the monk's choir, above the altar was an enormous Titian, the *Assumption of the Virgin,* a hugely populated extravaganza. I didn't know enough about painting to say why this was magnificent, this sort of imagery didn't move me, although surely it must be magnificent. With no time to linger I passed back down the other aisle, and there, opposite Canova, was a massive tribute to Titian, a great sculpted, façadelike thing, cold and passionless. I wondered if Ronald would find it affecting. I felt nothing and was happy to be out under a bright sky.

Having missed breakfast, I wanted to be home in time for luncheon, but the light, the air, incited me to wander. I knew I mustn't. I retraced the map and was heading north through the labyrinth when out of the corner of my eye I noticed a sign in the window of a dilapidated house. CHIROMANTE it said and, underneath, for the tourists, PSYCHIC READINGS. TAROT. PALM. Tarot. Lydia and I would have to come here and find out what Clara's card meant, have our own unconsummated fates revealed. How absurd you are, Nel, you won't believe in churches, but you'll be back to see some old imposter to whom you will give utter credence. We haven't seen her yet, I objected, she may be wonderfully prescient. I certainly prefer intuition to doctrine. Who knows, she may be a Neoplatonist. I wrote down the address as well as I was able.

Streets were becoming vaguely recognizable. Titian was a protégé of Giorgione's, was he not? Ronald said so. Here was this exalted shrine to Titian who made Giorgione his own, a genius himself, no doubt, triumphed anyway, lived, got everything attributed to him, and became a towering preeminence. Where was Giorgione buried? Where was *his* monument? He was the original, the innovator, the first genius. No tribute at all? Probably he made no money for anyone; if he were British he would never have been Sir Giorgione. He vanished into his famous dream. What became of his body? Did they burn plague victims?

And Clara. If he was lost, she was annihilated. Buried under layers of plaster, secreted in trunks, gone. These outcomes were puzzling. Not so much hers, that was more predictable. But he was, in his time, as famous as da Vinci and equally admired. It was as if some people belong to another category of history, a concealed category, a category not validated because not—what? Useful?

Having lived with celebrity although never actually being part of it—not that I hadn't had attention or praise in my life but never the glorified, gainful version—had provoked a lot of thought. I'd had time to think. These people were not as interesting as they were made to seem, you'd expect that, but what seemed odd to me was that they defined what was interesting because they'd been successful, which was to say, they'd made money and gained reputation. They'd won.

I remembered that one day—I had no idea what provoked it—I had the image of a black river running alongside history, a wide dark column running parallel to what I visualized as an illustrated time line, one of those tidy, authoritative historical summaries that tells with faces and pictures what happened when, and there you are: that's all, that's what happened. Who decides? History is written by the victors, and all of that, but this river! It was a revelation. The river was not so much black as deep and invisible; it was made up of all the watchers and standers-by, the doubters, the cynics, the wives, the ones who lost the prize, the unwilling, the reticent, the disdainful, the disillusioned, the genuinely serious, the marginal insiders, the disgusted, and the ones who were driven mad. The others. The unheard-from and forgotten. The ones who saw but were not seen. The river was wider by far than the line.

It sounds depressing but was not. I felt comforted by this huge assembly of heartfelt, perhaps witty, disbelievers—many of them women, naturally—centuries of them, who looked on and, needing no authority, understood. I could imagine the expression on their faces. Witnesses. Anonymous witnesses who smiled or raised their eyebrows and that was all they bothered to express. Unless they went mad. Otherwise they probably went on leading the lives they were required to live with whatever satisfaction they were able to manage—children, plants, animals, music, their own minds. Also the unpredictability. A clever friend once said to me that you don't understand the world until someone of your generation wins a major prize and you think: *him?*

What had summoned this memory? I thought Titian was not as great as Giorgione? Ronald would dispute that, and how would I know? I was only thinking about the disappeared, the ones who didn't have monuments to celebrate them. Among them, no doubt, many like Giorgione and Clara, whom Matteo called *illuminati,* with a small *i.* History didn't go their way— or, even if it did, someone else won, or lived—so they vanished, something happened, and with them went the story of another way of being in the world. Ronald said they tried to deny Giorgione's existence. How many others there must have been! The phantoms, as Renzo said. The river was the other life, buried, flowing, full of awareness and vision, never-quite-gone, never-quite-remembered, timeless in its own way. Comforting.

It made the translator cry, I said to Lucy.

And we have news for you, she replied. Lydia had papers and books piled before her.

What is it? I asked.

Well, Lydia said, you were right. It was a small community, twelve or fifteen at most. Almost an art colony, led by Donna Tomassa; remember her from Taddea's journal? The one who said there was no one to match Clara? She ran the scriptorium and painted herself, miniatures recording significant moments in the history of the convent; they appear to be sketches for the chronicle itself, which must have been in the works before that scathing document of 1519. Not bad, the few we found here.

Donna Tomassa was a Grimani, a noble intellectual human-ist family, and what she ran here was an academy for her favorites, Taddea among them, under the guise of producing manuscripts for Le Vergini, which they also did. A pleasant life. Accounts indicate they dined well, ordered plenty of wine, purchased books and supplies, even commissioned paintings. Interesting names come up. They were looking and learning. Serious. Le Vergini's honor students, something like that. Clara remained part of it, although she never took vows. Her name is in the lists of residents but with a little mark beside it. Hon-orary member, I suppose.

And?

Well, Clara actually lived here in 1507—she's mentioned—no mention by 1508, and then she's back in 1510. This is a sort of log, not a diary. There may be more—this is all I've found so far—but it would seem Clara Catena was part of this establishment.

She would have had her own room? I asked.

This is a big house. There were only twelve of them.

It would seem this was her safe haven, Lucy said.

Yes, Lydia agreed, a dependable refuge filled with friends, lively, educated noblewomen. Who heard their confession? Perhaps they made the journey out to the island for that. Made a day of it. She laughed.

What about the hospital? I asked.

There it is in the records, admissions, patient lists. Donna Tomassa seems well informed in that capacity as well. She has a compilation of remedies. Good women, I think we'd have to say. They risked their lives, after all. One or two died, she notes with sorrow.

And Giorgione, is he listed among the patients? I asked.

I'm not sure. There's a record of an outbreak in September of 1510, not devastating but some admissions, five or six. They might have used another name for him. Ronald says Giorgione died in October, so that would have been late in the scourge. Bad luck for him, but he could have been the only one here by the time he became ill. They may have chosen not to record it if it was an issue for Clara. A safety issue.

How long does it take to die of the plague? Lucy inquired.

Not long, Lydia replied, a week perhaps from the onset. Flu-like symptoms at first, then it becomes horrifying. Abscesses appear everywhere and burst and stink, terrible pain, awful, ghastly. Appalling to watch, no doubt.

A twenty-year-old girl watched the man she loved die like that? Lucy was shaken.

And these women saw it happen over and over again? I said.

Some recovered, Lydia replied.

Clara couldn't possibly have painted the fresco after he died; she was hugely pregnant. It's not physically possible, let alone whatever her emotional state must have been. She must have been shattered.

I don't know, Lydia answered. Only Clara knows.

Twenty years old, Lucy said again.

I was certainly a child at twenty, Lydia replied, but if Clara was this greatly gifted person and the lover of Giorgione, a most desirable man, she was exceptional in every way. Girls married early then.

Married, yes, I said, but she didn't simply leave the safety of her own delightful home to join another family in their delightful home. She seems to have been a sort of outlaw. Taddea thought so.

Well, Lydia replied, amazing Clara.

I don't know how I can go on living in this house, Lucy exclaimed suddenly, so soaked in tragedy. It's unbearable. Her face was desolate.

But Lucy, I said, you're her savior. Without you we'd know nothing about her; she'd be lost. You're her last great friend, like Donna Tomassa; she saved her once and you've saved her now. How could her spirit not love and protect you in this house that was her refuge? It's still a refuge! Think of me! You carry on the tradition of a noble enterprise! We're all here together!

I rushed to her chair, knelt down, and put my arms around her. She began to weep. Lydia and I, embracing her, started to cry as well. My God, I said, thank God for Ca da Isola! Thank God for you, dearest Lucy! You're like an angel!

Leo was alarmed, he pressed in among us, kissing everyone he could reach, until our attention turned to him and with tearful faces we offered reassurances.

Oh, well, Lucy finally said, laughing, wiping her eyes, *Ad ogni uccello il suo nido e bello.*

What is that? I asked.

Lydia was laughing too. There's no place like home, she said, more or less.

CHAPTER SEVEN

*L*ast night I dreamt once more of Riposa. Only Lucy had seen it; she kept it through the night. In the morning she handed me the pages without speaking. I carried them to my room, closed the door, sat on the bed, and began to read. Clara's words. *Last night I dreamt once more of Riposa.* I read on.

APRIL 1

I am grown weary of this imposed partition that keeps me from my desires. My work changes as my life does not. All at the studio progresses.

Last week a majestic gentleman came to Z to discuss a commission and see the work of others who strive here. Signore Vendramin is a great noble; how imposing he was in fine velvet robes. He is a not only a patron but a friend; Z visits his grand house. I am anxious to know what he wishes my master to depict. Like all he was astonished to find me at work amongst the others. I tire of that as well. I no longer regard myself as a novelty, although strangers may continue to do so. The great man came to my easel and expressed wonderment that a child, as he addressed me, could demonstrate such skill. Your preeminent apprentice, he remarked to *Z,* smiling broadly, as if such a thing were preposterous. Indeed, she is a miracle, my master replied.

The gentleman then offered me a commission of my own, suggesting a subject for me to attempt, the myth of Persephone, suited, I suppose, to my girlish perceptions. He must know it is a dark story. I shall attempt to make a mystery and a poem of it, as my master makes of all themes; it shall not be a pretty girl gathering hyacinths. Zorzi will counsel me; he is never far off. He jests with the others, speaking of our marriage as if it had taken place many years ago, and all laugh. To marry him would be an admission to heaven. Vincenzo would approve such a outcome, I believe. Zorzi is not a gentleman in the customary sense but is in every way superior to most young men. There remains the immovable obstruction. Nucca would run mad and accuse me—and Vincenzo if he supported me—of defaming the family reputation, blighting the prospects of her children, promoting scandal and dragging ourselves into the mire. Respectable people would shun us. The fiction of my father as a stern moralist would be brought to bear and she would lapse into one of her frenzies. She will not betray his trust! Not while she breathes!

She is preparing such a scene, I believe. The other night at supper she inquired of Vincenzo, as if in passing, as if of no matter, how the Jewish lute player was faring. Did Vincenzo think he would hire him again? It was odd to have a Jew in the house, she had to say, although his playing was tolerable. She is suspicious and seeks an occasion. I affected indifference. Vincenzo remarked calmly that the Jewish lute player happens not only to be a Christian but also the finest young painter in Venice. Is that so? replied Nucca. One would never know. Looks like a Jew. God forgive me, I wish her dead.

Yet what is to become of us? It is painful beyond measure to meet only in public places. *Z* suffers accordingly. He has said to me that we must have solitude; it is torture to live in the pretense of happy friendship. A moment, Clara, he said. We must have a moment. I was standing near to his table with no one about. I replied that I will think; I will find a way.

And so I do think. I thought first of the house and wondered if Donna Tomassa could be brought to understand. Men come to Le Vergini. I can think of nowhere else. I shall open my heart to her. If I were to paint another portrait, I could spend some days there. Perhaps she will allow me to receive him in the public room. She knows what Nucca is. I am nearly sixteen years with friends already married. I will speak to her. How Zorzi will laugh that I have indeed made arrangements. We are to meet in a convent!

APRIL 10

He came last night.

Donna Tomassa perceived the nature of my plight and agreed to confer her protection. She is a mother to many; for me she is the only such one in my life. I begged her to allow me to make her portrait but she will have me paint Buona, who is not at all pretty but the best musician among them. She believes a careful rendering will bestow confidence upon Buona—this said with a meaningful smile and raised brow. I shall someday paint that lovely, witty face.

He arrived after the girls had gone to their places. Donna Tomassa herself received him. She regarded his face when she brought him to me in the public room. He looked so hand-some and, most moving to me, uncharacteristically youthful and shy. We spoke for some moments. She left us then, saying she would return in one hour.

There we two stood in that place I know so well. So unlikely was the proximity and so mislocated did he seem that I could not refrain from laughter. Shaking his head, he said to me, Oh, Clara, what I am made to do for you! This man who frequents splendid salons stranded in the sparse comfort of a convent girl's public room.

A fire had been laid at least, and I led him to the seat before it. We sat speechless at this new liberty until he drew me into his arms and kissed me with an ardor I could not but return, we having been so long deprived. He held me close and pressed my breast until I feared I would be annihilated. Thus we were for I know not how long; I lost awareness of any actuality but the enthrallment of his nearness. At last I recalled our circum-stances and gathered myself to remind him. We calmed and sat near together, his arms about me still, each gazing into the fire, flushed by what had come upon us. What are we to do, Clara? he said at last. We must marry. I told him then of all my life: my lost mother, Papa's death, Nucca, the little sisters; that without Vincenzo I would have been undone; my childhood aspiration to be a painter; how astonished I felt when first I saw him, even my dream. What an exceptional man he is, a genius, so beautiful that even now I cannot believe that he can care for me; that I would give my life for him and would love him alone until the day that I died.

He sat silent. She will prevent us? he asked softly. She will try, I replied; nothing shall prevent me. Clara, he said, taking my face into his hands, say that you will marry me and we shall find a way. I will marry you, Zorzi, I said; I will die for you.

Once again he held me, and I felt his tears upon my face. We will tell Vincenzo, he said. No one must take this from us. But Clara, he then said, we must be together, and—laughing— will you trust me to find a place for us that is not a convent? I will trust you with my life, I said, but, Zorzi, the convent you mock has graciously enabled this singular and auspicious interview and cannot be disparaged. Indeed, Clarissima, he replied, smiling. And so we sat talking, until the hour was up, of our life to come, our work, our children, and could neither of us then cease from smiling.

MAY I

The world has become beautiful with the spring upon us. Gardens bloom, the air is warm and sweet, the lagoon sparkles, and every person looks renewed by the freshness of the season. No one, I think, could be so happy as I. My eye is enraptured by all it falls upon; each leaf, every flower, reflects back to my delighted senses the goodness of the world. The windows are left open in the studio all the day to soft breezes. *Persephone* proceeds. I have depicted her as Nencia, a betrayed and preoccupied child; she stands small before a great cave carrying a faded garland; it is autumn and sunset. I mean to represent the first return from yearly redemption. In the distance her goddess mother weeps. The cave must feel fraught with ambiguous expectation, a sad subject in the glory of these days. *Z* works as well on his picture for Signore Vendramin, his canvas a marvel and himself possessed.

His patron is enthralled by a recently published text accompanied by remarkable drawings that tells of a young man's dream of ancient times. In this dream he encounters the goddess herself. This last is the subject *Z* has taken. The story is placed in Treviso, so near his home in Castelfranco, that inspires him as well, but my master makes all things his own; each theme must pass through the transforming flame of his imagination.

The young man in attendance to one side of the canvas wears the costume of the society of theatrics to which both Z and his patron belong, but the goddess herself, who sits upon a bank nursing her child, appears the embodiment of divine fecundity, and in her abstraction insinuates a sacred realm. A vast turbulent landscape unfolds behind. I have never seen so splendid and impassioned a picture. It has become my most cherished of his masterworks. In my heart, I imagine that it speaks to me.

We have told Vincenzo of our betrothal. He kissed us both and affirmed that there are no two people upon the earth he loves so well. We wept. We spoke then of the certain dangers that face us. Vincenzo says that for our own safety we must keep this news secret until some way can be found for us; he will exercise everything in his power to facilitate our union, but the opposition will be formidable and unpredictable, as we must know. This is the first time I have heard Vincenzo speak in so unconstrained a manner of the menace that Nucca presents. I believe it gives him great sorrow, good man that he is, to accommodate so deformed an element into the dignity of our inheritance.

We managed a celebration nonetheless. We three removed to Zorzi's rooms, which I had never before seen. They are large, airy, and situated in a high corner of an old palazzo remote upon a small *rio,* spacious and all but empty. Z says he does not paint here; he thinks and reads. Supper was brought in from a neighboring house where a good woman prepares his food, and Vincenzo provided excellent wine. How pleasant life could be.

A happy meal we had then. At its conclusion, Zorzi rose to

speak. I wish to express my love and gratitude to you, Vincenzo, he said, for being the best of friends, a fine and admirable artist, and so handsome a Venetian! Whereupon we laughed until my master grew serious and continued, And to express most profoundly my everlasting debt for enabling me to discover the treasure who sits here between us, she whose remedies might never otherwise have arrived to redeem the singular and disarranged existence which has been mine. She is the sun of my soul, my muse, my contentment and delight—my brilliant, beloved, most unanticipated Clara. Upon these tender words he presented to me a small box in which I uncovered a golden band onto whose curve had been inset a sparkling sapphire, the color of Venus and the heavens. Too overcome to speak or look into his face, I sat undone; he took my hand and raised me, embraced me then, and bent his head to mine with so gentle a solicitude as cannot be expressed. If through misfortune or malice we be prevented our happiness, and I pray with all my heart it be not so, this night shall endure forever as the consummation of hope.

Vincenzo and I made our way home, he speaking quietly to me all the while. I must not let the ring be seen; it would arouse inquisitiveness and outrage. I replied that if I must wear it on a ribbon I will not be parted from it. He softened then and said, I rejoice for you, Clara, you have won the love of a good and gifted man, a man worthy of your fineness and devotion. I stopped him where we stood and kissed him. Looking into my face, my brother smiled. God help us, he said.

MAY 10

I have told Taddea in confidence of my betrothal. She rejoiced, although she has never met Zorzi. I assured her that she will rejoice the more when that happy event takes place. Her generous nature prompts her to offer us a gift. I expressed my gratitude and embraced her but repeated that no one must know of these tidings, since Nucca will have ears placed all about. If you are asked, Taddea, if I have been here, I said, you must say that I have. She assured me she would do this, but became as severe as I have ever known her, warning me to be wise, to be sensible, to be *sane,* she said at last.

I have been alone to Z's rooms. I have done this before speaking with Taddea. It frightens me to be so bold but what are we to do? We have not been abandoned. It would be ingenuous to deny that temptation exists.

MAY 13

How swift and gracious is Taddea. Her gift is to be my portrait, which Zorzi will make. Her brother Giacomo is to be the patron. Z has asked Vincenzo if he may paint me in his rooms and not in the studio, where we will be made to feel foolish, with everyone about making jests. Vincenzo was reluctant but so delighted at the prospect of the portrait that he will allow it. He is incapable of prying thoughts. So many days alone!

JUNE 3

This time has been pleasure of a new order, to sit before him and contemplate my master in profound immersion, to watch patterns of concentration and inspiration cross his face like swift clouds above a lovely valley and know that it is myself he studies and struggles to realize. He brought me a handsome red coat lined with soft fur, such a one as the northern masters might employ, he said, to bring forward my skin, this one being a man's coat but appropriate for me because I am a true artist, better than most men, he said, then wrapped around my neck a white scarf that is the symbol of our marriage. He will paint me as Laura, he said, just such an ideal as Petrarch's but not so unattainable, rather as the true and present beauty of the world, which is in itself as divine, mysterious, and resplendent as any man's dream. Think of your work, Clara, he said, and—smiling—think of me. As if it might be possible for my mind to wander elsewhere in his presence.

For two weeks we worked thus daily. He looked and looked at me but seemed rather to regard something beyond me; rarely did our eyes meet in the way I love so well. He is sudden and swift in his application, ever changing and modifying, consumed, his body poised and focused, his eyes seemingly on fire.

Three days ago he stopped. He sat for some moments regarding the picture, then came to me. Clara, he said, will you be brave? His smile was tender, nearly rueful; I saw that he was in some necessity regarding his conception. He wished, I somehow apprehended, to carry this picture into the realm which has opened for him with the storm painting, a vision of the earthly divine, and that this was an expression of his love for me. Without hesitation I removed the coat, untied my shift, and drew it to my waist. He rearranged the coat about me and returned to his easel, nor did he speak; his face, I saw, was most deeply moved.

For three days I sat then in this manner. On the afternoon of the third day, he stood away from his easel and quietly said, It is finished. I wrapped the coat about me and went to him. We stood in silence gazing at what he had made. Such a thing has never been done, Clara, he said. Will it do? Shall I change it? So poignantly was I affected by the restraint and mastery expressed in this, my own true image, that I went to him, laid my arms about his neck, and held him with all the adoration that I feel in my heart.

That afternoon we knew each other completely for the first time. Before God, if not the church, we are joined now forever. If there be so fine a thing as sacred ecstasy, I affirm it has been revealed to us.

JUNE 9

It is my birthday. I languish in this hated house. Vincenzo wished to have a grand party for this my sixteenth birthday, but Nucca said she is unwell and cannot bear the confusion of such an event. We had therefore a small occasion at the studio, which was cheerful enough but much like our usual day. Nucca has taken a new tack and speaks now incessantly to Vincenzo and myself of an elderly gentleman in Padua who has expressed an interest in marrying me. She believes it an excellent opportunity and the best of my prospects. She has for the moment dropped her ambition of the convent as my most congenial alternative; no Venice, no painting, a miserable life with an old man in Padua would suit me as well. She has an inkling that a notion of marriage is raised, how I cannot imagine, and wishes to ensure that her candidate will prevail since, in spite of his years, his wealth is abundant, his lineage excellent, and she is able to control him, whoever he may be. Most important, he is not a lute-playing Jew. What demonstrable delight she takes in these machinations. *Evil sow.* Heaven forgive me.

I may say that my portrait has produced a sensation, although only Vincenzo has seen it. Dear man, he was shocked, I know, but could not but grasp what a masterwork it is. He and Zorzi signed it together on the reverse, named Giacomo as well, and then embraced. Colleagues, Maestro! Vincenzo exclaimed. He loves my master and accepts with courage the troublesome aspects of this exploit. The picture may not be widely viewed. Not until we are out of the land of Egypt, my Jew and I.

A U G U S T I

Sweet Gemma is ill. She is running a strong fever and has been weak for many days. Nucca will not accompany Vincenzo and me to Riposa, although she wishes us gone. I cannot rejoice that good fortune is given me through a beloved child's suffering. Her boys, alas, go with us. I cannot care for them; they are devious and spiteful. Also, they are spies and malignant in their instincts. Still, we shall have a kind of freedom. Z will visit and we three plan a journey to Castelfranco to see his altarpiece. I pray for the restoration of the innocent.

S E P T E M B E R I 5

A glorious time in the countryside. We dined in the fresh air and had splendid walks through verdant fields. Nico fell upon us, barking with joy, and Viola must surely have exhausted herself with such pleasing, abundant preparations.

Vincenzo and I ranged far each day and painted into the evening while the boys went off to their ponies and games. I could not but notice how alert and watchful those two appeared each time Zorzi came to us. Tonio in particular, the twelve-year-old, is a malevolent boy. We offered no opportunity to his scrutiny. While Z was there, we walked miles until we were certain of solitude before expressing candor of any kind.

Upon our return we found Gemma not yet recovered. I can hardly recognize the hearty child I knew in this pale face. Nucca is in terrible distress; my own heart is moved in pity. Although she wished us away, she seems now strangely to blame us, as if by our absence we have further damaged her child. Vincenzo does not attempt to reason with her.

Madness has befallen us.

Tonio was indeed assigned to spy upon us. He has told Nucca dreadful stories, fabrications of a perverse and precocious imagination. Perhaps he has manufactured these appalling tales at his mother's prompting. Whatever the fact, she has gone demented. It may be her grief that drives her but Nucca has determined to believe that it is having me in the house—a slut who whores with a Jew, she called me—that has corrupted the health of her daughter. I was unable to remain calm in the face of this accusation and cried out, How dare you! How dare you! I began to sob without restraint and could not prevent myself. Vincenzo took me in his arms and said, That is enough, Nucca, you are not yourself. Still she would not cease and raved that I bring contagion to all her children; I am unclean and deceitful, not a decent girl but one who must consort with Jews in the gross indulgence of my pretensions and vanity, more and more until she appeared in truth to foam at her mouth and Vincenzo was required to shake her to restore her to sense. Rest, Nucca, he said. You are overwrought and exhausted; you are saying words you cannot mean. She did then say no more but cast at me an evil glance and took herself away. Vincenzo held and comforted me; I wept in the fury of my despair. When at last I was able to regain composure, we two shared a quiet supper passed in silence, so great was our shock and distress. Vincenzo assures me that we will find a way, but he himself has been shaken by this episode.

Gemma died this morning. Merciful Mother of God, embrace this innocent soul.

I have been ill. For many weeks, it appears. I am not able to recollect much of this passage of time. Vincenzo has told me that the day we laid Gemma to rest was a chill, wet day and that upon our return to the house, I became warm and shivered violently. I had taken a fever, which persisted in spite of remedy, and was unable to sustain consciousness, or briefly, for many days. The doctors believe it is the same infection that took our baby Gemma; she was too young and heavily assaulted to rebound from so violent a strain of contagion. Contagion, that is what Nucca said that I engendered. Perhaps I have turned my contamination upon myself. Does that prove her right or wrong?

I am weak and must be careful, my brother says. He has nursed me assiduously. At those moments when I felt myself rise struggling from the shadow of delirium, with wild, near-blinded eyes, I would see his face before me and sometimes imagined I saw Zorzi as well, whispering to me and holding my hands. I cried out to him, but ever and always he faded and I sank once more to an infernal place where Nucca's voice shrieked and Gemma's little arms reached out; again and again she fell away into blackness while my leaden limbs strained piteously to pursue her. Even now vapors of that horror recur.

Vincenzo has said that we are alone here with Zuane and Lorenzo. Nucca has taken her children to Padua and will not return until she is assured that the house is safe from poison. Is that myself? I inquired. He laughed, No, he replied, the poison has gone to Padua. Is it true, I asked, that Zorzi was here? Yes, he answered me, he was here as soon as she left and has been in torment. I may see him? This evening, he replied, but you must rest so that we may all have a little supper to celebrate your deliverance. I was weary and fell again into sleep. Later I attempted to rise to comb out my hair but my legs gave way.

In the evening Z came, and Zuane and Lorenzo; what a boon to my soul was the sight of my master. Lucia kindly prepared for me a thin soup which I managed to swallow, as well as a glass of wine, which Vincenzo said would return roses to my cheeks. I do not wish to contemplate what my appearance must be. My two young brothers appeared shocked to regard me. I am thin and wonder if I am ugly as well.

I grew weary, so the others left. Z came to me, laid his head near mine, and brushed my hair with his lips. Am I the same? I asked. You are my Clara, he softly said, his mouth at my ear, alive; dear God, how frightened I was. I have brought something! he exclaimed, sitting up and finding a box in the pocket of his jacket. I took and opened it and found a large and gleaming pearl, golden and rosy at once, a drop of palpable light, it seemed. In my weakness, I began to weep. No, my darling, he said, this is what you are, what you have ever been to me. He took me into his arms and I was, in a moment, again insensible.

JANUARY 9, 1507

A sad holiday it was with sweet Gemma gone forever. God keep my darling. Nucca too is gone still, busy at whatever she is devising. Perhaps she herself will marry the old man in Padua. A boon too gratifying to be granted.

Z dines here in the luxury of our freedom. I am well enough

to dress and come down but not sufficiently strong to return to the studio. Vincenzo will paint a Madonna for his confraternity, and Z has begun to experiment with a vision that emerges, I think, from the storm picture. He spoke of drawings of majestic muses and virtues that he wishes me to see.

Last evening we came at last to the inevitable subject, the return of Nucca to our now-peaceful home. Zorzi has heretofore regarded Nucca as a foolish impediment to our happiness but loathes her now because he believes it was her cruelty that precipitated my illness. Vincenzo said we must give thanks that by the grace of God I am alive, and our course must be reasoned and practical. Can you stay here, Clara? he asked me. Where might I go? I replied. Would you be happier at the house? You would place me in a convent? I cried. Of course not, he answered, but it is a place where you could live; it was Donna Tomassa's thought. She was here? She spoke to me, Vincenzo said. I looked at Z. Can we not marry now? he asked. No, Vincenzo replied, more time is necessary. Nucca will be full of schemes when she returns; there are the civic authorities to consider. She would accuse us to the authorities? I exclaimed. She may attempt to incriminate Zorzi, he returned; she is not without resources. The lion's mouth if nothing else, he quietly remarked. We sat silent and sobered. She would destroy his reputation and his life on the false witness of a twelve-year-old boy? I asked, dread filling my heart. Who can say what she knows, Vincenzo replied. She has agents. Our best course is to stay out of her path and see what time brings. Of course he is right.

Z and I sat long by the fire. I am recovered sufficiently to desire him.

· · ·

A faint scrabbling at the door distracted my attention. Not a moment to be interrupted by a rat. I opened the door to find Leo himself standing at the threshold; he rushed into the room. What are you doing here? I asked.

I sent him, Lucy called, from the bottom of the stairs. I thought you might enjoy some company. Where are you?

Recovering from contagion, I replied.

Ah, she said. I'll be thinking of you. Tell him to lie down and he will.

Thank you, I called. Is Matteo waiting for this?

Lydia wants to go next. He said okay.

Lydia can come and read what I've finished. Tell her. I'd like her to.

All right. Nel?

Lucy.

I heard her walk away.

FEBRUARY 5, 1507

I am here with my friends. Donna Tomassa came to me in January when I felt myself stronger; she had sensed in her conversations with Vincenzo that I could not thrive in the climate of my old home. She said we must not condemn but rather pray for the souls of the tormented. She has allowed that I may meet with Z from time to time in the public room.

In spite of the happiness I have known here, I confess that I am feelingly aware of the restriction imposed by this manner of life. Nor am I the dutiful, striving girl I was. I am returned to my old room. Tonso appears pleased and had his first glimpse of a cat in several years, one who strode along the path by the rio; he shrieked with delight. He has knowledge only of the affections of gentle Bini. I wonder with painful regret what was the fate of my good cat, carried away suddenly and without my knowledge.

Vincenzo has told me that Nucca is returned. Her time in Padua has not calmed her, he said; there is tension in the house. I intuit from his careful locutions that he has come to believe she may be declining to mania. She is hard with Angela, as has never before been the case. Angela is but seven years old and a gentle girl.

My own life is simple. I spend mornings helping with the instruction of the younger girls and teaching those of all ages to draw and paint. Nencia is a clever artist; it rejoices me to think that she may have an engrossing vocation. I shall stand by her as I can.

A woman has been coming to the studio. She is fabulously attired and escorted by decorated attendants, men and women. She is pale, wonderfully beautiful, and asks always if Maestro Zorzi of Castelfranco is at work here. At her first appearance, Z looked up suddenly with apparent alarm and left the studio by a back stair before she was able to perceive him. We all sat astonished. She has returned several times, asking always the same question and laughing. Tell him he is a naughty boy! she addressed to no one in particular as her entourage passed out the door in an uproar. Each time the noise and chatter approaches, Z is risen and gone.

Today the event occurred yet again. When he returned I regarded him with bewilderment. He attempted to smile and continue his work but could not but be aware that I was disturbed, so he came to me, took my hand, and we left the studio and walked to the embankment. Who is that? I inquired at last. Clearly gathering himself, he replied, It is a woman I have known since soon after I came to Venice. I said nothing and so he went on. I made a painted piece of furniture for her, a cabinet door, while I attended Messer Bellini's workshop. Who is she? I reiterated. She is a famous courtesan, he replied, with a distracted manner. You know her well? I asked. Yes, I know her, he answered. What is her name? I inquired. Her name is Cecilia. Cecilia, I said. She is certainly very beautiful. Many think so, he responded. Zorzi, I said, what is this that you are saying? Clara, my darling, he replied, it is a life which should never have touched yours, but since we have come to it I will tell you that this is a woman who will accommodate none but her own wishes, and I am therefore at a loss.

He then revealed to me the story of Cecilia.

At sixteen, when he came first to work with Messer Bellini, she appeared in the workshop one day to place a commission and saw him there. She required that he himself make and deliver the work. He was at the time flattered and did his best to make an impressive show of his skills, which piece he then carried to her home, a rich and ornate house. I was new to Venice, Z said, and had little in the way of a refined life here. She welcomed me and asked me of my work and expectations. Soon she invited me to play my lute at her entertainments. I was praised and admired; I met important, interesting people, and finally one night she took me to her bedroom. It was overwhelming to me then, Clara, like a fantasy. It was indeed a fantasy.

She doted upon me and, in truth, did all she could to advance my work. She was good to me, I cannot deny it, but her way of life became intolerable; the nonsense and trivia bored me; I was more and more engaged in new and congenial friendships and associations. I could not remain, but she was determined not to let me go. I have visited her now and again because she adamantly demands it and because she has, in truth, been a friend to me. She is not in any way an evil person; she is, rather, a good person caught up in a meaningless life, a life you are unable to imagine.

And have you seen her since I have known you? I asked, unable to turn to him. No, he replied, not since we have been betrothed. But before? I asked. Yes, before. She loves me, Clara; I do not wish to aggrandize myself but that is the case. I wish it were not so; I wish I could walk from her with indifference but I cannot. For all her folly she is a heartfelt woman who suffers a painful loneliness, but I have never been once intimate with her since you and I have made this vow. Clara, he entreated, you cannot imagine that I have not known women. I have known women, too many; there are women for the taking. For all of that there are lovers of every sort about, watchful and eager for opportunity, but none, none since I have found you. I have told Cecilia that we are to be married. I have expressed emphatically to her my devotion to you. She is chagrined and angry; she also will conspire to block our path, but none can succeed; we are of another order. Clara, dearest, I would rather perish in your preservation than lose this bond. I had not seen his face so anguished.

How may I describe my emotion at this confession? That he has been familiar with women, that his life has been heretofore nearly reckless, I have heard these things; they are known to me. But that there is a single woman of importance who seeks him out with persistence, that she has a claim upon him, that he might someday return to her when he has wearied of the blandishments of a distracting child, set my soul to turmoil. When I was able to speak, I said to him, Zorzi, you must think through these things most seriously. Is it not possible that you are not utterly candid in your remonstrance? Are you beyond certain that you do not retain some lingering inclination in your own heart? This is, after all, an alluring and cultivated woman of great beauty and some renown. I wonder if you are not merely amused and diverted for the little while by an art-less curiosity such as you have not so far encountered in your large experience. I may not at last, you must realize, embody the inducements necessary to retain your regard. Clara, he exclaimed, I am a man now. I know my soul. I have been starved and wanting, I have sought in all places and found nothing to answer my necessity. I will flog Cecilia if I must to drive her from me, but you cannot leave me, you cannot leave me alone!

Each distraught and trembling, he took my hand and we walked. We walked, as I knew we must, to his rooms. With a candor never yet expressed, we reclaimed ourselves.

JUNE 10

Z has undertaken a most magnificent new work, unprece-dented to my mind. It pictures a majestic sleeping Venus and a small cupid before another of his atmospheric landscapes. None before has imagined such a subject. The work has been commissioned to celebrate the marriage of one of his patrons, Girolamo Marcello. Z tells me that Messer Marcello asserts that Venus is the traditional patroness of his family; his lineage is ancient and Roman; they claim to be descended from the goddess herself. How one may assert such a thing I cannot tell.

Z has portrayed her reclined in sleep amidst pale draperies upon a grassy hill; the very countryside seems to resonate about her entranced figure. He has of late become engaged with the rendering of heroic bodies in sundry postures. Draw-ings of such abound upon his tables; indeed, this goddess seems to float nearly free of the scene that contains her recumbent person. The plump cupid sits more firmly upon the ground. A divine dream of love and a daring innovation that only he could conceive. It will be energetically imitated.

There is no one to equal my master in genius. He himself asserts that Messer da Vinci is his own master. He met the great man when he visited Venice. *Z* was able to regard drawings brought with him from Milan that astonished and aroused him. *Z* was struck as well by the boldness of his personality, his strength of opinion. He maintains that Leonardo is a wizard. And yet, he says, even so great an artist as da Vinci cannot apprehend the marriage of color and light as a Venetian is able by simply opening his eyes. *Z*'s colors have always been complex; of late he has simplified. He is under the spell of vermilion in these new drawings.

My own work, modest and dim in contrast, proceeds. Signore Vendramin protested his delight with *Persephone,* declared the picture haunting and unexpected, and congratulated my poetic insight. He has offered me another opportunity. He would prefer me to search among classical themes. It recurs to me to paint *Z* as Orpheus, but I would not wish to risk disappointment. I might render Venus herself as a child, a budding girl, perplexed, abashed even, at the reflection of her burgeoning grace in a pastoral pool or fountain. Girls and women have a dissimilar awareness of their own being to that which is apprehended by men.

Yesterday was my birthday. I am seventeen years. It is strange to have been away from home for so long a time. Nucca has become more placid in my absence, Vincenzo tells me, although she continues the inexplicable and subtle persecution of her own daughter, who, he says, is each day losing her brightness. I regret that I am unable to comfort and hearten sweet Angela and dread the toll that loneliness and dismay could take upon her. I am not a stranger to her dilemma.

We had a small and convivial celebration at the studio and a festive dinner in the public room here. Vincenzo and Zorzi were in attendance, as were Taddea and Giacomo. Donna Tomassa herself came in. This is the first that Taddea has seen of Z and I believe she was awed; she sees only her brothers and the brothers of others and has never encountered a man of his allurement. Z played and Taddea sang. She is truly exceptional, a near perfect voice. It was Z's turn to be amazed. At last all departed. We could not manage a time alone. I feel marooned. I am neither a nun nor am I a wife. I do not wish to be the one, and though I yearn to be the other, it cannot be. She would somehow contrive to drive us from Venice it is generally agreed. Where else could Zorzi's work be done except in this city where he is loved so well? And so we wait. For what we are waiting is not clear.

JULY 30

Wonderful news! It is widely rumored and nearly certain, we are told, that Z is to be offered an exceptional commission to make a large painting for the Palazzo Ducale. Signore Aurelio, one of the Council of Ten, is an admirer from his close acquaintance with Signore Vendramin. This will be an occasion of great good fortune and handsomely recompensed. All at the studio are in a state of rejoicing that Z may have this opportunity to demonstrate his genius on so grand a scale. A celebration was declared to take place in his rooms in the evening. Vincenzo and I went along. How disconcerting it was to see so many persons reveling in what has been always and only our exclusive sanctuary. Zorzi was jubilant; he played and sang; all joined and danced. I myself danced with Pietro who stretches canvas and mixes pigment for us. Pietro is a vigorous, ancient bald person who swung me about. Z laughed with delight, ever increasing the pace of his music to keep Pietro lively. A happy, hopeful evening. I am full of expectation to see what a masterwork awaits us.

OCTOBER 20

The worst has happened. I pray for release which does not come.

NOVEMBER 12

Full of dread and shame, I confessed my disquiet to Zorzi. To my astonishment he was in no way alarmed but seized me in his arms. We are free! he exclaimed, then spoke most earnestly of the gratification this news affords him. He has chafed at our prohibition and does not fear Nucca as Vincenzo and I do. I have been afraid that an occurrence such as this might encumber and vex him at a time when his work evolves so strongly, but in the warmth of his happiness I began timidly to experience my own so far unacknowledged joy. We shall take council with Vincenzo, an inevitability I anticipate with dread, to compromise and shame one who has been forever faithful and generous. There is Donna Tomassa as well. I must assemble my courage. Merciful God, I give thanks that my master is steadfast.

NOVEMBER 20

Zorzi has spared me the distress of so difficult an encounter and taken it upon himself to speak first to Vincenzo. When they came to me, my brother had endured whatever chagrin this news must surely have caused him. He, in turn, has spoken with Donna Tomassa. All has been softened and made as reassuring for me as such a situation may allow. Vincenzo says I must leave Venice at the earliest moment. He will undertake to go to Riposa and alert Viola of my arrival, so that the place may be prepared and welcoming. He knows as I do that Viola will provide a sympathetic refuge; she has known us since childhood, was devoted to my father, and has ever found Nucca and her children, sparing the girls, a burdensome intrusion on what she regards as her domain. We shall prepare for this journey quickly and quietly and set out as soon as we are able. Arrangements will be made for Zorzi and me to marry in Castelfranco on the way and we shall then have Christmas together in our old home. Vincenzo will devise a pretext for his absence and tell Nucca nothing. There is little likelihood of her journeying to the countryside in this chill season. Z is joyful. I am frightened.

Someone on the stairs. A soft knock and Lydia came into the room. I heard I was invited, she said, and couldn't wait. This came for you—she handed me a phone message in Lucy's handwriting—Lucy thought it odd; it was a woman who spoke perfect Italian, very crisp, she said, businesslike. I have to admit she was laughing when she gave it to me to bring to you.

I took the paper and read it. *Please be in touch with Antony on Monday. He will be away for the weekend and not available at the hotel number. Many thanks.* And then, in Lucy's parentheses: *Just how many thanks do you think?*

Well, well, how amazing, I said. She seems to have organized an ad hoc management office. Moving swiftly. Opening the games. He let her do it? I'm surprised. We must be in a new phase. This is bold.

Who?

Nicola. The facilitator, girl of all trades, the contender. Her name came up when we spoke. He called her relentless. I was to disregard publicity. I think you understand.

Very well. Won't that make it easier?

Easier? What is that? Thinking about their conversations makes my hair stand on end. I hate this. If only I could turn around three times, spit, and have it over with. Make everyone happy. I'd tear this thing to shreds if it weren't in Lucy's hand-writing. Well. Oh, well. I don't know. A chilling juxtaposition, at any rate. I dropped the paper on the floor and handed her the pages I had read.

Lydia laughed. So how is this? she asked. Lucy won't speak.

You'll see.

My God, Nel, she said, her eyes running down the page, the personal story of a fifteen-year-old in 1505? Just amazing.

That ceases very soon to be the amazing part.

Why? How does it make you feel?

As if I'm sitting in front of a blazing fire when I've been try-ing to stay warm with matches and twigs.

The phantom genius? He's there?

Yes. You'll wish he were here, at least so far. I think I trust him.

You of all people.

Thank you. We'll discuss that later. Now, if you'll for-give me, I really must get back to my work. Lydia smiled and we sat down at opposite ends of the bed. Leo, between us, looked at each of us, made his decision, crossed to me, plopped down, and went back to sleep. Comforting to be chosen.

DECEMBER 16

On this sacred day, my beloved master and I were joined as one soul. The sacrament took place in the chapel of the gentle Madonna of his fine altarpiece. I sought and beseeched the Holy Mother to look upon us with mercy. Only Vincenzo was present and Zorzi's good mother, an old and kindly woman of dignified simplicity to whom my husband is devoted. He is her youngest child.

No one who may speak of this occasion must be made aware, so we were quiet in enacting the holy rite and the good priest assured us of his discretion. We went then to an inn where we three had been happy upon our summer journey. Our family— how it gladdens me to name it thus—enjoyed there a simple heartfelt celebration. Zorzi has made for me and carried with him a small painted chest. It is very nearly like his storm picture, to which he knows I am devoted and which for him represents the divinity of this our earthly life; thus he blesses our union, signed here with the name that now is ours to share.

I write these reflections several days past the event but am required by my heart to honor the time.

JANUARY 3, 1508

Viola has been indeed a gracious benefactor, happy to have us and sparing no effort. She approved at once of my excellent husband and dotes upon him with some display of preference. Nico is an older, more gentlemanly dog; he too extends cordiality. Vincenzo has regaled us with accounts of poor Tonso's perilous journey. Although his cage was wrapped in blankets he made known his indignation with furious shrieks. He has since settled and enjoys Viola's indulgence with overt demonstrations of favoritism that strike me as treasonous and unkind. I am often uncomfortable, although content in a way I have not known. *Z* must soon return to the city to complete his painting for the palazzo. Vincenzo will stay with me until a few weeks more. How strange it is to occupy this house in winter.

My husband is joyful and doting. Since meeting his mother, I believe I comprehend his spirit more discerningly than heretofore. He venerates the traditions and devotion in which she holds and sustains him howsoever God has blessed him with gifts. He is the child of these fertile hills and valleys. For me, the earth itself.

FEBRUARY 7

Nearly unable to raise my pen, so heavy and enervated have I become in this strange body. Viola plies me with teas and soups. I will soon be very well, she assures me. Nico and I spend our afternoons before the fire. I wish to sew or draw but find myself napping before I am able to organize an activity. Vincenzo was here. All is quiet in Venice. *Z*'s painting is magnificent, he says, populated with massive heroic figures. I long to see it.

FEBRUARY 17

Z returned. I wept with joy. He has brought a cradle, which he himself assembled and painted, tender lambs and flowers. His mother wishes to visit, he has said. I welcome her.

MARCH 30

Yesterday Zorzi's mother came upon her visit. Viola went to a great trouble to prepare a meal which we partook in timid mutual regard. She is not outspoken but expressed concern for my condition. I assured her that in spite of my lethargy I am robust. She is called Grana. She was made uncomfortable, I think, being entertained in such a manner, but brought fine things she has sewn for the child, embroidered clothing and knitted blankets of pale soft wool. She would not remain the night but said as she departed that I am her daughter and no man is so good as Z. We embraced and looked long at each other with comprehensive understanding. Outside an old man waited in his cart.

APRIL II

What a time we have had of it.

But days after Grana came, Viola awoke me before dawn in frantic haste. A villager had come, pounding upon the door; he reported that Nucca was on her way. Word had passed down through the towns as Viola had required of her friends that it might, should such a mischance befall. We were in extremity at this news.

She dressed me as well as she was able, wrapped me in a blanket, and we rushed out into the chill morning. I was to be taken to her cottage but a mile or so from there. We hurried as best we could—I was cumbersome and far from swift, although we managed to run some of the distance in our distress. Later in the afternoon, she returned to report that Nucca plans now to remain a month or two in the house in order to fortify her health, which she feels has flagged in Venice because of memories of Gemma that haunt her there. Of this there had been not a word of forewarning. She has brought Tonio and Giano, Angela, a tutor, maidservants, and many trunks. This plan has been long hatched and most subtly if Vincenzo was not alerted by open preparations. Viola is certain Nucca knows I have been there and was disappointed not to surprise me. She went through the rooms searching, but Viola in her prudence had returned earlier and, with the help of all who work there, gathered my things and delivered them to me at her home in time to avoid detection. Tonso arrived in a state of fresh outrage and to my relief the cradle was not forgotten. I would not wish that woman to cast her wicked eyes upon it. I am comfortable here in Viola's pleasant cottage and begin to regain my composure. I have sent for Vincenzo and Z.

APRIL 14

It is over.

Last evening a most acute pain came upon me. Viola was not at home, but her young daughter, a girl of eleven, was attentive, laid cool towels upon my head and spoke kindly to me. Viola was sent for, but my suffering became terrible until I believed myself certain that I must die. Viola appeared at last and saw me through the long ordeal. All now is over, all. The torment of last night seems mild to that I now endure, more laborious to my body than the piteous trial which engendered it. I grope half mad, sunk in blackest misery.

Z and Vincenzo have come to me. Z came resolved to murder Nucca in his fury and brought with him a knife, but Vincenzo restrained him. We have wept until we can weep no more. Our precious daughter, who never drew a breath, lies in a small coffin prepared for her. Tomorrow we shall take her to Castelfranco and return her to her Maker.

JULY 7

I am here with Grana. I am a little recovered but know that I shall never cease to grieve for my child. I do not wish to be in Venice. Z must be there to execute a new commission to make frescoes on the canal face of the new German customs house; it is a great honor for him to have been chosen, and I would not have him decline for my sake although he was prepared to do so. The truth is I am better alone in my sorrow. I am soothed by the peace of the countryside and cannot find it in myself to engage with any in the customary way. I am better alone with only Grana, who asks nothing and cares for me. I am better alone. Of late we have had workers here each day, good men of the village who disturb us little. Z wishes to make additions of his own devising to the cottage in order to enhance our comfort. Grana and I prepare a meal for them daily; the occupation is consoling. I do not allow myself to think of Nucca.

OCTOBER 18

The days have gone by, I see. Three days past, Z and Vincenzo arrived with a wagon filled with furniture and decorations. The additions are completed. We have spent the time adorning each room, and all now seems delightful to our eyes. We were nearly gay.

Z is tired, I think, but exhilarated by his work on the frescoes, which I understand to be monumental and vermilion. I am reminded of another time when I observed him in early preoccupation with heroic figures and with red. How long ago it seems; what I was then I cannot recall. Titian and others are helping him, and he has at last established a workshop of his own. These colossal nude figures that he has devised interest him immensely, men and women in heroic attitudes, each marked with an arcane symbol.

Vincenzo says that they entirely approximate genuine statues in their mass and depth and yet are flat upon the wall. Zorzi has ever wished to prove that painting is the most capable of the arts, encompassing the potentialities of all other mediums. He believes he has now demonstrated the irrefutable truth of his conviction.

We have a bedroom of our own and can be together tenderly

at last. He has brought painting materials on the wagon and wishes me to attempt to work once more. Vincenzo encourages me as well. My impulse is not strong. I have done nothing since *Persephone,* and that picture seems sadly prescient to me, as if it were my own lost child held entranced before compelling darkness, soon to be snatched away. But my daughter will not return with the springtime. Nor am I a goddess with powers to call her back.

DECEMBER 27

We celebrated as merrily as we were able. Late in the evening Vincenzo mentioned Nucca for the first time in as many months; it is a subject no one is able to contemplate without an excess of emotion and is thus avoided. *Z* is yet murderous in his inclinations. Vincenzo engaged us in so disturbing a matter because, he confessed, he has come near to desperation. He is the only one of us who must encounter her. He believes she is now entirely mad. Her unprovoked persecutions of Angela have become appalling to him; she calls her by my name and rains accusations upon her which the poor child cannot understand and which terrify her. He would like to get the girl away but can find no pretext. He says also that Nucca is manifestly unwell in her body; she has become thin and yellow and suffers pain in her stomach and head. Bring Angela to me, I said.

FEBRUARY 15, 1509

It is cold and quiet. The fields that stretch about our home are beautiful to me even in so bleak a season. Viola has brought Nico; he pined, she told me, but I know it was my own loneliness she sought to comfort. We two have walks each day but do not go far, his legs begin to trouble him. Vincenzo has given

me books, Petrarch for my edification and an *Aeneid* for entertainment. He is concerned that I do not wish to return to
Venice and am too much, he thinks, alone. It is my solitude
that heals me.

Z comes often in spite of his pressing work. He has painted
a portrait of himself as David the giant killer and brought it
for me to approve. To make such an allegorical depiction of
oneself is yet again a daring innovation. The picture is a wonder, like him in beauty and vigor, yet he has conveyed the
restraint that is ever within his regard, whatsoever high spirits
he may exhibit. I felt tempted, as all will be, to kiss his painted
lips.

APRIL 5

The world is abloom; infant leaves emerge on every withered
branch. I took, for the first time, a small canvas and a few
paints, went off some distance with Nico, and made there a
landscape with our home to one side. How stiff and unaccus-
tomed my fingers felt, but concentration seized me and I experienced once more the enthrallment of such efforts. The very
pleasure of the enterprise reawakened my sorrow. I wept in the
fields for my soft-haired daughter.

APRIL 29

Vincenzo and Z have rushed here to tell us that Pope Julius
has excommunicated Venice from the Church and that warfare
is expected. This upon the previous awful news of a terrible
explosion at the Arsenal only last month. The city, they report,
is in turmoil. It is hard to conceive of such terrible events in
the beauty that surrounds us. We had heard nothing of these
developments and were amazed. We determined to remain;
both Vincenzo and Zorzi believe it to be the best course. Z

assures us that the men of Treviso will never surrender to foreign influence.

MAY 19

A great battle has taken place at the town of Agnadello on the Adda River to the west, and most astonishingly the forces of Venice are reported overcome by the French and Milanese. Threats of attack and rumors of invasion have always plagued the terra firma, and confrontations have sometimes occurred, but never before has there been an outcome so catastrophic for the Republic. The city itself was not assaulted, although Vincenzo says that all there are in confusion and mourning, the people full of suspicion, the piazza before the Ducal Palace swarming with disturbance. He is certain that Venice will prevail at last. Nothing has changed here. Treviso, as *Z* predicted, remained defiant, although other regions have succumbed to the authority of the foreigners without resistance. Our daily life goes on as ever; each day dawns in loveliness. How remote these clashes of powers seem, yet at any time we may find ourselves overrun and crushed. I believe firmly with Vincenzo that Venice is eternal and all will be restored to us.

MAY 31

Nucca is dead. I heard at once the voice of Donna Tomassa in my heart entreating forgiveness, but I cannot forgive. Vincenzo says she was in great pain at the end, her body terribly wasted, nor did she speak of repentance herself in her extremity but went to her grave angry and indignant. A desolating and desolate life. Somewhere in my heart I will find the charity to pray that God in his mercy will purify and transform her soul. It is madness, I know, but I do pray fervently that she never encounter my innocent daughter in paradise. Vincenzo has seen to her interment; she shall not share a grave with our dear parents, for which discretion my heart is grateful. The boys will be returned to her family in Padua as she wished. No provision was made for Angela; Vincenzo will bring her to me. May I be safeguarded from madness that could devise such cruelty.

Talk of the war has subsided and life in the valley has resumed its usual course; still, for each, and always, our individual destinies seem ever to transform in unanticipated and deep-felt ways.

JUNE 12

Angela has come to us. I cannot recognize the gentle girl I knew in this haunted face. She is but eight years old yet seems a weary unfortunate of long experience. She will not be kissed nor touched and replies to inquiries with expressionless utterances. She has brought with her a cloth doll given her long ago by my father; she clings with ardor to the bedraggled toy. I have attempted to speak of Papa, but she regards me with a blank face. She seems nearly effaced. How shocking to see the effects of malice and neglect. Once more I praise God for my devoted brother, without whom I myself might have become an abandoned sufferer.

JUNE 26

I have taken Angela with me into the fields while I paint. She sits a little away from me, braiding flowers as Grana taught her. She has begun to speak a bit more, most often to Nico, who listens indulgently. She alludes to Gemma as if to an angel of her acquaintance. She does not trust the memory of happiness. Nucca is not mentioned. Vincenzo is real to her; she refers with confidence to him. Each night she wakes crying out from her dreams but has of late allowed Grana to lull her back to rest.

How curious is Angela's response to Zorzi when he is with us. Something in his vitality and warmth compels her. She does not approach him nor respond much when he attempts to engage her, yet her eyes seem never to leave him. He often catches her in this and makes a silly gesture which I have seen bring her nearly to a smile which she represses at once. Today he worked in the vegetable garden that Grana cultivates and waved a carrot in her direction; it is certain that a laugh issued from her delighted face before she ran off as if in fright. She is more sturdy and rosy and digs about in the garden when Grana is with her. Perhaps Z reminds her of Papa's genial good humor, or perhaps she is unable to resist his attractions, as no one can.

Z is engaged upon a new commission; it will be Christ bearing the cross and will be installed in the church of San Rocco. He has told me it will be a tribute to his master, da Vinci. I expect a miracle.

An extraordinary day, one that must never be forgotten.

Vincenzo came with a carriage to carry Angela and me to the hills of Asolo to escape the heat and to offer we two painters a new prospect. We had a pleasant progress to that village and brought with us a meal that Grana prepared for us. Once we had achieved a considerable altitude we left the carriage and walked yet farther into the heights where we enjoyed our repast in a pretty shaded grove. We then set out to find a point of interest at which to set our easels. I came upon a rocky meadow which lay before the opening of a deep cave, ever an incitement to me, and Vincenzo went on to higher ground to have a more comprehensive vista. We promised to meet again in the meadow when he had accomplished his work.

I sat down to my drawing and was soon absorbed. Angela was nearby, singing softly to herself while she gathered flowers to make a garland for Vincenzo. Some time passed as I worked, oblivious to all but my design. I seemed then suddenly to start from my preoccupation with the realization that Angela's voice was no longer in my ear. I glanced about the meadow but she was nowhere to be seen. Angela! Angela! I cried, and at no response from the child and with growing concern I began to run about the meadow calling. I looked into the woods nearby and down the slopes that surrounded the place but found no trace of her.

I turned back to behold the cave entrance, and my heart dropped within me. My pulse began to race—it was indeed a deep and terrifying cave—but I gathered myself in growing terror, ran to the dark opening and cautiously crept in. Clinging to the damp walls as sunlight receded behind me, I inched farther into the increasing gloom, calling her name. The walls were mossy now, and indeed I could hear water dripping into what must have been a pool somewhere before me, the sound echoing in an uncanny way within the enormous vault. I heard another sound, a panting as of some animal come to drink, alarmed, perhaps, and angered by my intrusion. Fear then threatened to overwhelm me, but I struggled with all my courage to stay sensible and alert. My eyes had grown more accustomed and were able to detect something white in the dimness before me. I presumed with dread that it was her dress and imagined in my horror that she had been assaulted by whatever beast might lurk there, but soon I could make out

fair hair and at last her form. She lay half-concealed and clinging to a pointed rock at the edge of black water. It was she who
panted. I surmised that she had grasped the rock as she lost
footing and was now too terrified to call out. The smell of the
place was dank and metallic, my senses reeled, but I cried out
to her, Angela, dear baby, I am here! I dropped to my knees and
crawled to the verge of the pool, my clothes heavy now with
the pervasive wet, my hands sliding in deep mud. I reached her
at last in what seemed an eternity of time and grasped her dress
at the back. Once I had determined that my grip upon her was
sufficiently strong, I began with my other hand to pry her own
hands from the rock until she became sentient enough to
throw her arms about my neck, when, with a firm tug, I pulled
her from the slippery bank and lifted her into my arms. I rose
awkwardly and, moving with the greatest care, bent over and
clasping the trembling body, I cautiously made my way to the
cave entrance, following the light.

In the next moment we were returned to the meadow; the
sun blazed down upon us like the warm grace of salvation
itself. We sobbed and clung to each other, filthy and soaking
but saved. I kissed and kissed her drenched face; she wept in
my embrace. Exhausted then, we lay down at last upon the
grass. In the heat and rapturous brilliance of the summer afternoon, we felt our lives return to us.

I stared up into the sun, the very eye of redemption, letting
it burn away my tears with its life-giving immensity and
strength, but then, quite suddenly, all seemed to shift. I was in
an instant levitated from my body by the grace and power of
the light itself, lifted up, so it seemed, by a strong invisible
hand, and in that entrancement I somehow apprehended,
spontaneously and certainly, that I had been cleansed and
transformed—I was risen and free. How may I express so

incomprehensible an event? By whatever miracle, the pain of myself and my life dropped away from me and I entered—how it may be I cannot say—the light of life itself, light without boundaries, divine light. My spirit was suffused and transported. I have heard of revelations such as these in the stories of the saints, but there was no voice of God calling to me; if a god did speak, it was the god of my eyes, the god within my body, the god of the world to which my body belongs and before whose power, the very sun above me, I fell back in wonder and gratitude.

Shaken and exalted, I began to laugh and cry once more, but now with joy. I held Angela to me and she, good child, laughed happily as well with as free an animation as I had not yet witnessed.

Vincenzo arrived to find us in this state. To say that he was astonished would not approximate his response. We related the event as best we could, Angela spoke of monsters and black pits and I of salvation. Vincenzo, bewildered and anxious, gathered our things and hurried us to the carriage, in which shortly we two adventurers fell into an exhausted sleep until we were returned at last to Castelfranco. Grana received us as she would any two bedraggled pilgrims. God bless these valleys and hills.

SEPTEMBER 30

Z has been teaching me of late the techniques of fresco which have so engaged him. I am concerned at times with his long sojourns amongst us and wonder if he should not be at work; he is so happy here and I so happy in his company that days pass in pleasant disregard. He does not lack for opportunity but has ever refused proposals that do not engage him.

We practiced this method on an outdoor wall upon which *Z* made a most beautiful and voluptuous angel to protect our house and to demonstrate technique. He recruited two boys from town and has shown them how to lay plaster and mix pigment in lime water so they will be available to me in my attempt. He became taken with his experiment and we have now a wall of muscular angels watching over us, one of whom incongruously bears Angela's face. She is our domestic muse. I shall attempt a picture of the meadow and cave, Angela coming forward, with the face, if I am able to render it, of one delivered.

NOVEMBER 5

The fresco is completed. *Z* most congratulatory. He tells me he regrets it was not I but rather the truculent Titian who assisted him on the customs house. Angela is delighted to encounter herself at every turn.

DECEMBER 25

A great feast, all of us together and Angela a joyful girl at last. Our only sorrow is that good Nico has left us, quietly and before the fire just two weeks past. Grana and Angela and I were made so disconsolate by his loss that I have made a fresco of his slumbering form. Tonso whistles for him still. *Z* has promised Angela that she shall have a puppy in the spring. Vincenzo has also brought to me a letter from Donna Tomassa. He has told her of my work, and she requests me to return to Venice to make a fresco on the wall of the workroom. *Z* encourages me. I am reluctant to leave my rural life but confess to temptation. We can surely return here often and someday forever.

JANUARY 20, 1510

We are installed in our old rooms. Z has endeavored to make them comfortable and pleasant, but they are for me replete with memories of other times. I have been to see Donna Tomassa and Taddea. They did not speak of my loss, but my heart was moved by the tender warmth of their welcome. Donna Tomassa declared herself delighted with my drawings for the fresco. The subject will be myself, I am nearly chagrined to confess, but in the persona of the antique figure of courage. I need not remark upon my inspiration. I chose this apparent self-praise not to enhance myself but to affirm that a girl such as I myself was in this very workshop, and thus those who may regard my picture, might be inspired to endure all obstacles, and through the grace of God and the beneficence of divine nature be strengthened to comprehend the everlasting goodness of the world in renewed faith and hope.

FEBRUARY 17

How daunting is this scale! I have attempted chalk sketches on the wall but — having learned from my master to revise and reconsider — these have been reimagined more than once. Fortezza herself will stand upon a rise and encounter her viewer with urgent inclination, behind her the fields of Castelfranco, brooks and glades. Our home will be depicted and beyond, in the far distance, cloaked in mist, the hills of Asolo, where, unseen, will be the cave of blessings. Her lion companion will stand by her. I cannot but be reminded of Nico, who had indeed the heart of a kind lion. Wild spring flowers dear to memory will surround her, and in her face will be the radiance of one who has achieved hope. Hope, I now believe, is not a thing heedlessly given to be crushed by the vicissitudes of experience; rather it is the unanticipated reward of struggle endured, a gift of grace. I have in my life found this to be so. I believe as well that innocence itself is won through patience and endurance, nor is it the infantile luxury so often remarked. One must gaze long and with fortitude to begin to see clear. I cannot with my own experience imagine that the world is kind in all things, but I am certain in my soul that rich and mysterious gifts are concealed in the dark folds of pain. It is this intuition that I wish to impart, and in the profound and inspirited manner of my master, who does not so much apprehend truth in appearances but rather unites with it and expresses an exalted union. Nevertheless I am hesitating and must soon surrender to plaster and paint.

APRIL 10

Never before have I been required to climb ladders to approach my work. A scaffold has been constructed for my use; the girls are amused and delighted to see me crawling about above them. They sing while sewing and drawing; it is a pleasure to be accompanied at my task by an angelic choir. The boys who assist me are abashed to discover themselves amongst this gleeful company. Color begins to emerge. I am pleased with the diverse greens of the valley counterposed to the violet of faraway hills, from which the glory of the sun will eventually arise.

MAY 1

I have been reluctant to acknowledge the signs that have come to me but am encouraged to believe. It is true, I think. I had not spoken of this to Z until today. As I confessed my suspicion, we two began to weep, so reticent have we been and careful not to hope. Now we are mad with joy. May dearest Grana keep alive to bless this most welcome child.

JUNE 9

Never has there been so auspicious a birthday, I am sure. Vincenzo arranged a large and festive celebration in our old home, friends I have not seen for so long a time. All windows were opened and the evening sweet with fragrance. Such gaiety, song and delight. I am twenty years now and feel that I have stepped across an unseen border into what opens before me like a promised land. I am strong in my heart; my work is inspiring, and my love a divine benediction. I gather myself to receive this grace. Z has given me a most beautiful picture of a young shepherd with a flute, his face a paragon of tender warmth and beauty. May we see such a boy!

AUGUST 8

We have been to Castelfranco where Grana and Angela are installed for the season. How lovely it looked. Angela's puppy has been delivered to her; she is in the full throes of maternal zeal. His name is Zorzon. Z and I shall remain for this time in Venice, since I must complete my fresco before I am physically unable, and Z is engaged in a most arresting picture of musicians in the countryside in the company of yet two more of his monumental nude women. It occupies him intensely. I continue well and not compromised in my strength. Z asserts that he will not look at my work until the final moment, which is nearly upon us. Another month. We are happy in spite of the heat.

AUGUST 26

There is plague in the city. I will go to Grana. Z will not come in spite of my protest. He is near to completion of his picture. I have made him swear to come should it become more terrible here. The outbreak is not yet rampant. Donna Tomassa has prepared the hospital. Pray God she will be safe, and also my dearest Taddea, who will remain to assist her. The younger girls will be returned to the island where they will be more removed from the threat of contagion.

SEPTEMBER 20

I am well but heavy as a cow. Vincenzo has been with us and Z also for extended days. Much expectation surrounds this great stomach of mine. The distant hills are lovely in the autumn mists; I laugh to think how nearly I resemble them. The outbreak in the city is abating, for which all offer thanksgiving. Grana dotes and is more impatient than I to meet this already vigorous child.

OCTOBER 12

Vincenzo believes it is safe to return to the city, but the journey seems daunting to me. I shall remain here until I am delivered. So heavy. Heavy also with anticipation.

OCTOBER 15

Vincenzo has arrived again to take me back. My husband is ill. Grana begged me to stay but I will go to him.

OCTOBER 17

He is sorely ill. To my despair and fury, he has told me that Cecilia, herself ill, feared that death approached and sent for him. He, the fool, the fool—the finest, vast-hearted, most necessary fool—went to her in the generosity of his heart. She has destroyed him. If she be not dead, I shall murder her a thousand times and then a thousand times more. May she suffer the torments of hell through all eternity for the agony she has brought to us.

OCTOBER 19

We will take him to Tomassa. Dear Heavenly Father, let her work a miracle. Mother of God, pity us.

OCTOBER 24

cannot

NOVEMBER 15, 1510

My beloved friend Clara Catena, wife of Zorzi of Castelfranco, charges me, her devoted sister, Taddea Fabriani, to record here that she has been delivered of a son who shall be called Zorzi Vincenzo. She begs leave to importune Our Merciful Lord through the indulgence of His Eternal Charity and Grace, that the strong and everlasting spirit of his excellent father may carry this boy safely through the world. She requires me to assure to this her only son that no child was ever so longed for and beloved. She desires of this her child and son to be forever proud and honored by such a father.

Gracious Lord, I fear for her. Protect her, Beloved Jesus.

CHAPTER EIGHT

I spoke to no one, left the house and walked on the most remote embankment I could find, reliving every sorrow I had known and feeling the appalling helplessness that other people's pain inflicts.

What could this possibly have been like for her? The most beloved person on earth gone in a swift and horrifying plunge to death, plague in the air, the child within her alive, innocent, part of him, waiting to be born into a shattered world. Grief, unanticipated grief, hurts; it hurts the body, I mean, as well as the heart, the mind, the soul, everything. It doubles you over, tortures and exhausts you with its thousand serpents' teeth. And there was that child tucked inside the agony, wanting and needing to live. Twenty-two days she endured. In what incomprehensible extremity? It must have been for the child that she prayed, willing herself to live. And she painted? I thought she did; holding a brush must have been like touching him, touch-

ing what they were, what they had, losing herself in concentration, turning her face away from the world, released briefly
from hell. What else could she do?

When I came back, I couldn't bring myself to go to my
room. I lay on the couch in the empty salon, the same couch on
which my eyes had opened weeks before. I felt, as then, that
everything had veered into a new perspective, only this time it
was the brevity and horror of life that stunned me, not its
latent charms. How quickly and catastrophically the world can
change. In my own crisis, I had been too frantic to take the lesson in. The lesson being, I supposed, that anything can happen
at any time. We're not protected by a dependable reality no
matter how we struggle and suffer and prevail and do or do not
find happiness at last. I thought of Clara's joyful birthday when
she felt she'd crossed a border into a promised land. There is no
promised land. But there are borders. Was the message futility? Futility seemed the least of it. It's finding the courage to
face the truth of utter precariousness and still risk the immense
chance that being alive, being conscious, however briefly,
offers. Easy to miss it. The challenge must be to come unstuck,
resist habit—the same things over and over, as Lucy said—to
wake up, pay attention, try to face how strange, miraculous
and fearful it is, every life, every day. That hurts too, waking
up, finding oneself so small and vulnerable, knowing nothing.
But suffering holds gifts, rich and mysterious gifts concealed
in the dark folds of pain, Clara said. Hope and innocence, she
said. I couldn't think of her life as tragic in spite of her sorrowful fate. Being alive is inexplicable, a maze of terror
and desire. The lion that courage tames—no, never tames,
that was the point—the lion that courage befriends. Best
approached awake. And with respect and gratitude. Things
Clara came to understand. Twenty years old.

Are you ill? Matteo said, as he came into the room.

No. Just devastated. Have you read it?

Yes.

And?

Well, it's all there. The answers. And everything else. My God, what a document. Their lives. It's staggering to find out what he was like, to hear him speak, this completely unknown person, to feel almost that I know him.

And her.

Yes, impossible to think of him without her. He sat down on the edge of the couch and smoothed my forehead and hair.

Matteo, it happened in this house. Those people were here, *are* here—Taddea, Tomassa, all of them. Giorgione. Clara. Which was the public room do you think? Which fireplace? And then here we were, thrown together, the three of us, five of us, so unsuspecting. Are there only coincidences?

I think I'd prefer to think not.

I think I'd prefer to be an Italian of the sixteenth century, I said, sitting up, a Neoplatonist. I think I'd prefer to be a genius.

There's more left than we think, he said. It's still the world.

The others began to arrive. Lucy first, Leo, then Lydia and Ronald. It was evening by then. Annunziata brought glasses and a bottle of wine. We took our places around the low table where Lucy had once more placed the box. It looked now like a miraculous apparition.

No one spoke until Lydia said softly, perfidious fate.

Indeed, Lucy replied. It broke my heart.

I still cannot take in that such a document exists, Ronald declared. Not only every major painting documented, new dates, but a man, a personality, where there was nothing. Unimaginable, really.

I was shocked to discover that I expected betrayal, said Lucy quietly, such a man as this one must have been. It made me feel jaded and foolish. A nonbeliever.

He wasn't a spoiled noble, Lydia responded; he came from that valley, but came with spectacular gifts and a great appetite for life.

It was a moment when there were such people, Ronald observed. Michaelangelo, da Vinci, Titian, Tintoretto, so many. Shakespeare and Cervantes a few decades later.

And Clara, I said.

She was certainly something, he replied. I wonder what became of her work? I'd love to see the *Persephone* that delighted Vendramin. Not to mention Zorzi. Hard to call him anything but that now. It probably exists somewhere; I doubt we'll ever find it.

I'd love to see her portrait of Taddea, Lydia said.

But we've seen her masterwork, Matteo replied. And we've seen her.

Yes, Lucy agreed, we've seen her. Only a child, she was born with something. Vincenzo saw it and Giorgione recognized it at once, a soul mate. Dreadful phrase. He might have had anything but he wanted that connection.

There's something mythic about it, I said, or Shakespearean. Was there such a man as this I dreamed?

Or like Dante and Plutarch, suggested Ronald, with a rather nice sex life thrown in. He did, after all, crown her with laurels.

And this house! Lydia exclaimed.

Yes, I suppose the rooms should be cordoned off at once to

keep the public out. You're a museum now, Signora, Matteo observed, smiling.

Not I, she replied. This is our home.

So she made the fresco while she was expecting the child, Lydia commented.

And not in despair, declared Lucy, but full of joy. All of that radiance is fresh hope, the plains of Castelfranco behind her, emerging from his world, healed, I suppose.

Well, one might say that nature is in many ways the protagonist of Giorgione's work, Ronald mused, the bliss and beauty of Arcadia. For him, I think, it was essentially allegorical, although I liked him in the garden with the carrot.

She didn't really have a world of her own, I said, except for Vincenzo. I suppose Nucca went mad. She must have had cancer as well. Did they have painkillers? Pretty awful.

Well, as Clara understood, Lydia replied, it was all about the dowries. Catena was rich and she wanted that for her own daughters; she had pretensions to the nobility, Clara says, buying her way in. I think that was beginning to happen, but paranoia got the best of her, imagining Jews everywhere. Without Vincenzo, Clara would have been put away. Going to Riposa was another attempt to get rid of her. Scare her to death when she was vulnerable. Expose her as a whore.

Did she know they were married, I wonder? Lucy asked. Even if she did, she couldn't help herself. That's a fairy-tale quality, isn't it? The wicked witch is destroyed and the spell is broken.

But Clara had a will to live, I said. Look at Laura's face. Also she had that sort of Neoplatonist revelation, being transformed by the powers of the universe. And a cave! She actually emerged from darkness into the light.

Mythopoetic, Ronald said, laughing. Giorgione must have enjoyed that. With Persephone in her arms as well. In the fresco Z becomes Apollo, the sun god, not Hades, ruler of darkness, but the light that illuminates her, the light of Castelfranco, the genius.

Oh, very nice, said Lydia, smiling. But remember she paints herself as Fortezza; she gets some of the credit.

She gets all the credit for the fresco, Matteo said. What did you say, Ronald, how many out of ten might give it to Giorgione? Second prize was early Titian? Not too bad.

One wonders what became of the child, Lucy murmured. And Taddea and Vincenzo.

Catena lived on until 1531, Ronald replied. I looked again at the wills; it's all about his brothers, stepchildren — unnamed — and his religious brotherhood. He was touchy, kept changing the executors. Maybe Clara's son was considered a stepchild. He appears to have remained a bachelor, although a mysterious woman named Domenica got a few things. He became pretty well known as a painter; Bembo mentions him. Taddea, I suppose, we'll never know.

Unless we do, Lydia remarked.

Vincenzo loved his sister, Lucy said, and he loved Z; he must have missed them very much. One cannot imagine that he forgot. I personally hope that Domenica or whoever brought him some joy; he certainly deserved it. And the old mother? What about her?

Col tempo, I said.

Indeed.

Gather ye rosebuds, said Matteo. They did manage that.

Do you have the inscription yet, Matteo? Lydia asked.

Yes, come and see.

Up the stairs once more to the fresco room, drinks in hand. Clara's face now had the resonance of someone known and loved; all her life was in it.

Lydia went to the wall and looked closely at the scroll. Is it what it looks like, Matteo?

Yes, I believe so, although my Latin isn't entirely up to it.

What is it? Lucy asked.

I told you I recognized the *Aeneid* in those manuscripts in the armoire? This is it, this is from the *Aeneid;* obviously they knew it here; didn't Vincenzo bring her a copy as well? This is the tribute Aeneas makes to Dido, the queen of Carthage who welcomed the defeated Trojans to her shores. Of course she fell madly in love with him. Why this? Maybe Clara was offering the tribute to Z. Odd.

What does it say? I asked.

It's famous; I know it, more or less, Lydia said, reading: *So long as rivers flow to the sea, so long as clouds move over the mountains, so long as the sky tends the stars*—this part is concealed in the scroll—*so long shall survive honor to you, your good name, and praises of you.* Probably the best-known quotation in the poem.

She seems to be referring to his paintings, Ronald said. Rivers, mountains, clouds. All the elements of his landscape.

That and everything else, Matteo said. She's referring to that and everything else.

Evening was falling swiftly; we stood in semidarkness; her face held its radiance.

The moment of discovery, of rescue, Lydia speculated, perhaps that's it? It disregards the fate of Dido.

Strangely prescient. She was, after all, abandoned by his death and could never recover, I said. The visit to Cecilia was something of a betrayal.

Fate is not all there is to it, Lucy remarked; there is also the life. She stood erect and still, her own face solemn and preoccupied.

Matteo and Ronald were devising a strategy about how to proceed. I hoped it would belong to the two of them and make them famous collaborators, like Giorgione and Catena. Renzo would have to be brought in, but too late for his little talk to spoil anything. He might confuse Clara with a nun so his early prediction could be confirmed, but he would not be able to deny the beauty of the work. He would defer to Ronald on the box; Ronald was, after all, a protégé. He would offer his benediction and be thanked. Renzo would remain the authority, Renzo would be satisfied.

And what would become of Clara's wedding chest? It would transform into a cult object, the unbelievable Giorgione find. It would travel the world, long lines, then be displayed at the Accademia next to *Tempesta,* a climate-controlled case, a room of their own. Special tickets.

Someone must have brought it to her here after he died. Were the paintbrushes his or hers? The tribute to his father— did the boy ever hear it? Taddea would have told him, but Taddea was locked up by then. Vincenzo perhaps. But Taddea kept the diary, kept it to keep Clara. All of her things were left. Everything now would be displayed.

One sees these objects in museums—clothing, jewelry— and tries to imagine the life that permeated them before they went cold, to imagine the first time they were placed on warm bodies and for what occasions. I had stared into portraits and miniatures, trying to conjure a living person. I remember being so taken with Holbein's portrait of Kristina of Denmark in the National Gallery, made as a marital audition piece for Henry VIII, a luminous picture, painted in just three hours, I'd read. What were her thoughts, how did her life feel to her when she looked at it, and later his in London appraising her pretty pale face? She said if she had two heads she might have considered his offer, witty girl. And there the picture remained, essentially stripped of purpose, another Holbein, a lovely one. That was the fate of objects, I supposed; they endured long after the events that produced them had been lost to memory, the flesh that warmed them, the lives they served. Casanova's bathtub. Kristina's audition. Nils's red jacket. They persist because there's nothing else for them to do. Renzo said that in Neoplatonism the material world is an emanation of the mind, so these surviving artifacts may be nothing more than long memories, displaced bearers of someone else's dreams. Hieroglyphics, cave paintings, nuns' portraits, photographs. Reality itself.

After Nils died, again and again I held his clothes to my face and breathed the smell of his body, his body that was no longer there. All that was left between me and his famous red jacket was emptiness. I couldn't resist; it was the only remaining way to be with him. I still had the jacket. Like a strict guru, it insisted on the void. His old familiar smell was gone.

But I was not. I opened the window and breathed the night air. I could see another crescent moon and one star. Venus? The cold air on my skin made me feel warm and alive. Lucy said it is not fate but the life that matters. I thought I would take that to heart, surrender to living, however that's done. Jump into the river even if I jumped alone. Oh, Clara, I feel so glad and sad for you, I thought. I feel as Taddea must have, devotion to your brave gifted spirit and the hollowing sense of losing you too soon. But if on this side we were led by fate to rediscover you, if this reunion began the moment I stepped off the train, you were coming toward me as well with your brilliant scattered clues, something of a timeless rescue mission for both of us. Uncanny, but I believed it was true; it felt that way. You, my dear friend, four hundred years gone. But I should tell you, I envy you that man.

Signorina, telefono, Annunziata called up to me.

Lydia and I had just returned from visiting the tarot reader; she had gone back to perusing the armoire after our enlightening adventure. *Grazie,* Annunziata, I said, running down the stairs.

Hello?

Nel, it's Antony.

The very one Signora Marchioni mentioned, the reversed King of Swords.

Hi. How's Paris?

Paris is great. Using my French. Doing fine.

Antony learned French at a summer camp to which his mother sent him since he was destined to be the Sun King.

You're enjoying that?

Well, you know, we got this offer, since we were already over here, to do a benefit in Paris for AIDS in Africa, so we came, and now we've decided to cut a live session at a concert hall with great acoustics. Nicola does PR for a lot of these major classical venues; she set it up.

Nicola?

She was in Italy with us. She's been helping out and asked if she could arrange this.

That was nice of her. You must have told her how much you love France.

She's European, speaks a lot of languages, has to, for her work.

Good. How long are you staying?

We may go to London for a Save the Earth benefit. The usual crowd, Albert Hall; I don't have to be back for a month. Nicola has to go to New York and offered to bring Liddie back; you and I can take her home. She'll miss some school, but that's okay.

I'm glad you're having a good time, I really am. So am I.

Silence.

How long will you be in Paris? I asked.

Another week or so. Until Liddie gets here.

Shall I run up there to see you? Would that be okay?

Sure. Be nice to see you. Will you come to London?

We should talk about it. You sound great.

This has been a great tour. You're still having fun?

It's been amazing. I've learned a lot.

You like that.

Yes. So give me the Paris information and I'll let you know when I'm coming. He did. I hope I'll see Boris and everyone. Will you tell Boris I'm coming? I think I'll take the train. My French isn't any good, but I can probably make myself understood, don't you think?

They're used to Americans. Next week is good. Paris is great. I'm glad I reached you, I wanted to tell you that plans have changed. We're doing the London benefit in New York later in the fall. I'll be on the road but I can get back.

I was tempted to ask if Nicola was among the organizers but realized I didn't have to.

Antony, I had a tarot card reading today.

No kidding. Are you enlightened?

It was interesting. It was about change. Things change; it's important to pay attention, she said. It's not about judgment, it's just about change. How people change.

Have you changed?

Haven't you?

I don't know. I feel pretty good.

Silence.

I guess I do too.

Good. Okay, Nellie, I gotta go, sound check. Great to talk to you. Love you.

Antony?

Yes?

It's okay, everything's okay.

I'm glad to hear it. Gotta go, Nel. Take care.

Okay.

Bye.

Bye.

Antony?

He was gone.

Sometimes when I would go through a door, Antony would stand aside and make a courteous little bow. It looked attractive and humble, but as I passed by I felt a cold shiver of hostility that made me want to hit him. I think he loved me more honestly when he slammed doors in my face. I would go to Paris. First Paris and then the river. Maybe the river first.

Well, Lydia was saying to Lucy when I came into the salon, the Fortezza image was much earlier, Signora Marchioni said. She knew the *Tarocchi* prints; those were specifically Cardinal Virtues, more traditional. The symbol then was about classical attitudes toward pain and danger, not seeking them out but not avoiding them either. Later the tarot card meant discipline and enlightenment, understanding rather than subduing.

What I found most fascinating, she went on, is that on the tarot card itself there's a valley behind the figure, like Clara's valley; it wasn't there until much later decks; it's as if Clara intuited it as the appropriate context for strength. This woman was so interesting and articulate.

Fascinating, Lucy replied, and those two seemed to grasp these arcane ideas so personally. What did the signora say to you two?

Lydia is the Queen of Pentacles, I said, sitting down next to Lucy. Things will go swimmingly for her. She also got the World card, all things guaranteed; we won't have to worry about her anymore, a great relief.

Lydia was laughing. No, really, it was very heartening. Nel got the Star and the Lovers and the Hanged Man.

I knew I would get the Hanged Man.

Hanged Man? What does it mean? Lucy asked. It sounds awful.

Surrender, living in the present. Fairly obvious. On the other hand, he's upside down and dangling by a foot.

Lydia smiled. It was more profound when she said it, I assure you.

What did she look like? Lucy asked.

Like a university professor, I replied. We were disappointed; we wanted a druidess.

Fascinating. Is there an ancient person card?

You are undoubtedly the Empress, I said. She told us we are both under the influence of the Empress; we each had the card. The Empress is beautiful, close to nature, given to extravagance, nourishes life, offers pleasure. Who else could it be? The cards, in fact, were pretty remarkable.

It's not the cards; it's the cards one chooses; we chose the cards, said Lydia.

Matteo tells me we're going to Castelfranco tomorrow to see Zorzi's altarpiece? Lucy inquired.

Really?

He wants us all to come. A nice trip on a pretty day, which I hope it will be.

At that moment Matteo came into the room.

Castelfranco? I asked.

Will you come? I want to look at the landscape on the altarpiece to see if there's any congruence with the fresco. They were married there, so she had seen it. One night. Lydia, come. All are welcome. Lucy?

I have the armoire, Lydia replied.

Perhaps, Lucy said. I miss the country. I'll decide tomorrow. An outing would be nice.

Lucy decided, after all, not to come. It turned out to be a rainy day, so it was me and Matteo setting out with overnight bags and umbrellas. I was unusually chic in one of Lucy's old raincoats. Really, I remarked, this doesn't feel like a day-in-the-country sort of a day to me, as the wind blew sheets of rain into our faces. Matteo was having the same thought and suggested we postpone, go see some Catenas, and have lunch somewhere. He looked at his watch and said it might be open but often wasn't.

We headed off into the deluge and arrived finally, quite damp, at a little *campo* full of Gothic buildings. We crossed to the entrance of a small church in a narrow adjacent alley. He tried the door and it opened.

Miracle, he said. Venice in Peril restored this place but you can never get in.

Inside, the church was small and plain, not a tourist attraction. What's here? I asked.

This, Matteo said, leading me to a side altar above which hung a glowing painting of a female saint surrounded by enchanting boy angels, with Christ and another angel on luminous clouds above. It's the *Martyrdom of Santa Cristina,* he said; they tried to drown her with that millstone but the little angels intervened. Later she managed to get herself shot to death with arrows. These martyrs can never really get enough. This is Catena at his best. What do you think?

I like the angels. She's pretty grim-looking, but the boys are nice.

He's under the influence of Titian here, but don't you find something of Giorgione in the angels? The softness, the sense of individual presence?

We gazed at the picture for some minutes, and then I saw it.

Matteo, I exclaimed, look at that little angel on the left, the one with the millstone, pointing to the smallest boy. That face. Does it remind you of anything? The eyes, the nose, the mouth, the hair? Do you see it? The three-quarter profile, everything?

Matteo looked. My God, he said, I think I do see it. It's as if he painted her as a child.

Or painted her child. What year was this?

Around 1520, I think. He would be ten years old.

It's the most moving face in the picture. It comes out of the darkness like hers does; the shape above his head really does suggest laurels. How could it not be a reference? And the angel behind him, isn't he very like the shepherd in the painting he gave her for her last birthday? The blond hair, the pretty face, when she says "May we see such a boy"? I had found the reproduction in my monograph.

The Hampton Court shepherd, Matteo said. Yes, yes, the likeness is there—strong, in fact.

So in Cristina's salvation there may be an acknowledgment of some more personal redemption? The little boy who takes away the millstone? These two angel faces are so tender, the rest is pretty abstract. The boy must have been with him. Ronald said that Catena didn't show Giorgione's influence until later, didn't he? Are we making this up?

Clever girl, Matteo said, leaning closer to look at the angel. I think it's actually there. Ronald will be proud. I'm impressed myself. You may have a future.

Very kind, Matteo, thank you. If it is him, I feel enormously reassured that this child is accounted for. It makes me want to rush home and tell Clara. What century are we in, do you think?

Hard to say. We'll bring the cabal to have a look. Zorzi Vincenzo. The lost boy. So strange. Do you ever feel a bit dragged along? This whole thing has been so surreal. Coming here today? I suppose the rain was a special effect. Cunning. All very cunning.

We left the church. The real rain had slowed to a mist so we walked around the *campo* looking at the crumbling Gothic palaces. One was particularly decorated. Ruskin admired it, Matteo said, but most of the carvings were looted. Half of Venice was stolen from somewhere.

We went to a charming restaurant, full of locals, better than anything I could think of in New York, unless it was the wet, soft afternoon that made it so agreeable. We sat for a few hours, drinking, talking, eating, the joys one imagines. Matteo made me laugh, not with Nils's incisive wit or Antony's clever self-referencing performances, but with an almost weary, old-world humor that I found pleasing. This was the first day we'd spent alone together. I was sorry to see it end, but the afternoon was getting late so we gathered our things to head home. We headed instead in the opposite direction, toward the lagoon.

Where are we going? I asked.

To see the water in this light, he replied. The light was extraordinary, a smeared wet palette of pink, fuchsia, lavender and aquamarine. We came to the canal and walked along admiring the iridescent reflections, then turned into San Marco, crossed the spot where we had met, came out again, and finally turned into a byway I knew very well, the little *campo* outside the Gritti Palace Hotel. We went in. Matteo paused at the desk and we crossed to the elevators. A door opened, we entered, it closed and Matteo pressed a button.

What are we doing?

Lucy said you're leaving. Are you leaving?

Yes. No. For a bit. Oh, Matteo, who knows?

I wanted you to know something before you leave.

Here?

We exited the elevator and proceeded down a familiar hall. Matteo pushed a tasseled key into the door and we entered a room, the last room I had seen in this place, Leo's room, my room.

Matteo, I said, laughing, what is this?

The room of the lonely art student, he replied.

How did you do it?

A phone call. And good luck. Did they remember Ms. Everett. She'd like her room.

When?

About an hour ago. It occurred to me it was a good idea.

A good idea?

Why not? We're in Castelfranco, aren't we? Do you mind? Mind?

The windows were open. A tray sat on the desk, glasses and a bottle in an ice bucket.

This is very cavalier of you.

We deserve it, he said, crossing to the desk and pouring two glasses. After what we've been through? Art, life, death, plague? We deserve something. A moment on the small *canale* you liked so much? A little of Zorzi's peace and light? The pale sun was indeed filtering through thin curtains with blissful softness.

You're surprising, I said.

And you, he replied.

We lifted our glasses, drank them down and dropped them on the floor. Speechless, watching each other, we began to take our clothes off until we stood naked in the dim light of the room.

Beautiful Nel, Matteo said. Beautiful Matteo. He opened his arms and I stepped into his embrace.

I was awake; the windows were dark. I felt him beside me breathing quietly, his lovely shoulder pressed against me, his arm around my waist. I tried to think about what had happened but was transported. The room, the unanticipated event, the cool night air from the open windows drifting over our bodies. I remembered the sensation of my hands on his strong, smooth back, his warm skin, his hands on me, his mouth, being carried into a sweetness and intensity that was staggering, as if we were inside a breaking wave. How could Matteo be such a lover?

Poor Nel, you've been out in the cold too long, this is the river, warmer than you remembered, but Matteo, so tender and present—so able, let's say—what an inspiring reinitiation. We fell asleep and woke again; he rolled me onto him and brushed the hair out of my face. Are all Italian men like this, Matteo? I inquired, kissing him. No, he said, laughing, only me. Me and great George. No wonder she threw caution to the winds, I murmured, sliding down his chest. This is for you from Clara then. Later he said, Yes, and this is for you, *cara,* from Zorzi. And for everyone who brought us here, I said— Taddea, Lucy, Renzo—I began to laugh. Please, he said, covered my mouth with his and we were gone.

Light was beginning to appear. Lying there I felt calm and released, as if a burden had dropped away, not dropped, evaporated, vanished. It was more like something I'd been struggling to remember, something puzzling that had finally recurred to me. Impossible to say what it was, but it had arrived, an essential piece. I wished for nothing more than to be in that moment. I felt that I myself was the river, deep and still and flowing. Flowing. Was that what I had forgotten?

I crossed to the window and stared into the rising sun hoping to shock myself again, but it was too early. Streaks of pink, rosy fingers, were spreading across the sky; the rooftops and canal glimmered in the silent morning. Happiness felt to me like a lotus unfolding, pressing out to every extremity; the pleasure was nearly painful. The lotus in the river. Daybreak, a pink sky, the world. All me, all mine.

Venus greeting the dawn? said the voice from the bed.

I turned and smiled. He was sitting up, and there was that body again.

Oh, Matteo, I'm glad you're awake. Remember last night when we thanked everyone? We forgot Leo!

Oh, no, our hero! We can't have that. You'd better come over here, he said, opening his arms.

How was Castelfranco in the rain? Lucy inquired. I felt myself begin to blush.

Worth the trip, Matteo said. We must go back.

Perhaps next week, Lucy replied, giving me a sidelong glance. Lydia has discovered something very interesting.

So has Nel, Matteo said. We saw the Catena at Santa Maria Mater Domini on the way home.

We were at luncheon. This was our first public appearance. Leo greeted us enthusiastically. Matteo kissed him and said, You're very welcome.

What did Lydia discover? I found it difficult to appear normal.

She said that most of what's left up there are institutional documents but she found a house record, Donna Tomassa's. Not a diary, nothing particularly personal, brief reflections on the girls' progress, projects she was planning, that sort of thing. There were entries regarding Clara. Let me get them, Lydia wrote them down. She left the room.

Matteo smiled and gave me his hand. *You're very welcome*—I laughed.

Lucy came back, put on her glasses, and read. This is 1510, she said.

DECEMBER 31. My beloved child will come to us.

FEBRUARY 10. Praise God, she is herself.

APRIL 11. *C* astonishes me, how sure she is in this work.

JUNE 9. Clara's birthday. She expects a child. I bless my joyful daughter.

AUGUST 30. Wall a wonder. One dreams of such a student. Ladder worrisome.

SEPTEMBER 9. Prepared the beds. Who to keep? Mella and Taddea insist. Clara must go.

OCTOBER 10. Worst is over. Praise to you, Mother of Sorrow, my girls are safe.

OCTOBER 17. V and C say that he is ill. Insist they bring him.

OCTOBER 20. Too late. Will not leave him. Dread her seeing this. Insist on herbs in her clothing. She is in extremity.

OCTOBER 24. My poor child.

NOVEMBER 1. Distraught and suffering, not ill, thank God. Asked for painting material. I beg for rest, she is frantic.

NOVEMBER 6. Too thin, eyes hollow. Beg her to eat for the child's sake; she tries, unstrung. Has made an appeal to the Holy Mother.

NOVEMBER 10. Quieter. Pale. Cleared the hospital.

NOVEMBER 13. Pangs have begun. Taddea with her.

NOVEMBER 14. Too much suffering. Too long. Vincenzo here, weeping.

NOVEMBER 15. A son born at dawn. Child is safe. My child feverish, joyful, distraught. Son beautiful.

NOVEMBER 17. She asks me to complete her painting. Assured her she will be able but insists. Too ill to nurse. We have a woman. C watches and weeps.

NOVEMBER 19. Delirious. I am in despair. She is gone beyond us. Taddea with her. Vincenzo comes. She calls out for her husband.

NOVEMBER 21. Quiet for two days, very cold. God protect her.

NOVEMBER 24. My child is gone. At nearly midnight.

She endured a month. Into your arms, Beloved Jesus, I surrender my peerless daughter. My heart goes with her. May her soul rise in glory.

NOVEMBER 26. Poor, kind Vincenzo has laid her to rest. We will keep the boy until certain of his health. The grandmother will be with him and the other girl. My poor Taddea loves the child. We are a sorrowful house.

DECEMBER 2. I have written as my child asked me. I wept.

Matteo poured us another glass of wine and we sat in silence.

The boy lived, Matteo said. He told Lucy what we had discovered yesterday.

You feel sure? Lucy asked.

You'll see, he replied.

How cruel it is that life goes on, she remarked. How many untold heart-wrenching lives go by and life goes on. How helpless we are.

What did Lydia say? I asked.

She was moved. She also wondered if our theorizing about the *Aeneid* text was to the point. She thinks Donna Tomassa chose it. Apparently one of the abbesses used those words in an oration before the doge. It doesn't matter; the sentiment is the same.

She'd already expressed all that she intended, I said.

I like to think of Donna Tomassa writing it, Lucy replied. That we see her hand in it. I believe she meant to praise Clara.

Not a house of betrayal, after all, Signora, Matteo said softly. Just the usual agonies of life.

Yes, Lucy murmured. Only that. Well, what will we do now?

We will give Clara to the world, he answered. We will show

her work to Renzo and then find the proper way to announce her. The box will detonate like a bomb and we'll watch the art world blow up. That will be our gift to Ronald. And yours to me, my dear friend. One of many.

The day was beautifully cool and clear, a perfect early autumn day. I spent the morning shopping for warmer clothes. I wanted to look Italian. Lucy ransacked her closet and gave me piles of her glorious wardrobe; they would hugely enhance my usual black rags and make me feel loved. We had a charming time going through them all and trying things on; we decided against hats. I asked her what she wore when she was married. It's long gone, she said. Made for her by Fortuny; she wished she had saved it and dyed it red. What a different world it must have been when people looked the way she must have looked. She was still beautiful and chic but said she gave up caring about such things long ago. Gardeners don't dress, she remarked.

I thought Lucy knew what had happened to Matteo and me; I sensed a protective edge in her dealings with us. I told her I would go to Paris in two days. And come back? she asked. Ah, that was the question. Part of me was afraid that when I left the magic kingdom it would vanish like a dream; grim gravity would draw me down. It would help to wear her clothes. All efforts in the past to assert my concerns with Antony had disappeared into the chaos that whirled around him. I thought he would have to hear me this time, but I would be breathing another atmosphere, would be there by myself, and he was unnerving. My best hope was Nicola. He may have meant to keep that on the side, but if he were angry enough with me he might take the plunge, get there first. Up until now he had been protected from the Nicolas of the world by my presence, the cartoon wife; he could have it both ways with no requirement. Bringing Liddie back from New York meant she saw a viable opportunity. I wished her luck, I truly did.

And I would do what? Everything familiar would be gone. Antony would solidify a new safety zone in another relationship, but another relationship wasn't what I wanted, not all I wanted. Did I imagine that this would be easy? This would not be easy. I wondered if I was about to maroon myself. The Hanged Man was smiling. I asked Signora Marchioni why in his predicament he was smiling. He smiles because he has hung himself upside down himself, she said. He could get free, but he is looking at things from another angle, you might say, and enjoying it. He is not unhappy, she said. He did it to himself. He was not unhappy. Unhappy was too obvious. I wasn't doing that anymore.

And Matteo? Thinking of him gave me a little thrill. So unexpected a man, realer than I was used to. Whatever became of us, this was the magic zone and did not bear examination. And there was Lydia waving from a table on the quayside of the obscure *rio* at which I had miraculously arrived.

Buona sera, Signorina, I called.

Buona sera to you, she said, as I sat down. *Come vanno le cose?*

The things go pretty well, I replied. Some of the things.

Castelfranco was nice? Smiling the smile. Lucy thought you enjoyed it.

Is that what we're calling it, Castelfranco? Everyone knows? It's fairly obvious.

Well, I recommend Castelfranco. Not to be missed. We were laughing.

Two days? she said.

Yes.

Lucy has invited us for the night before. Scared?

Cornelia enters free fall.

It will be breezy, anyway, she replied. We ordered food and the inevitable bottle of wine. You're worried about what you'll do? You're not supposed to, Signora Marchioni was very firm about that. Would you like me to go with you to Paris?

No, I'd like you to be here when I come back.

And when will that be?

Sooner rather than later, I hope. I don't mean to dwell on what I'll do, but I wonder what I'll do. I want to do something I care about.

You care about Clara. Take these things and do something with Clara.

Something like?

I don't know. Figure it out. Hang upside down for a while. It's your fate. She laughed.

You're very cold, I said.

Very. She smiled. I think you just hang there for however long it takes and all will be revealed. Is this not the best risotto in Venice?

Walking home, I had the impulse to revisit every place I had been on the enchanted island: the Casanova show, Florian's, Enrico's shop, the Accademia, the Arsenal, the gardens, the hallowed Gritti. These foolish things. Try to understand what this month had meant—was that what it had been, a month? Shakespeare famously sends his helpless characters to these places, these islands, to be transformed, and I understood why. No escape. Water, water everywhere. And only wine to drink.

I passed through the Frari *campo* and thought of the translator. Not tempted to revisit Titian's memorial, I headed

toward what I hoped would be the Grand Canal. Water is consoling, forever transforming and always the same. Someday
Titian's massive tribute would crack and tumble into its arms;
water would reclaim it all. Venice couldn't last forever, nothing could. It was all a dream. Was there such a man as this I
dreamed?

We dream it all. My Antony is not Nicola's Antony, not yet
anyway. Clara's Z. Nils, who must by now be a myth, the personal saint through whose mercy I consoled myself. He did not
seem so perfect once. He would like the paradox. *Things are
not as they seem, nor are they otherwise,* he used to quote from an
obscure sutra in a guru voice. He felt nearby, circling close in
his cosmic orbit, a drop of pure light. Gone for ten years.

Perhaps it took ten years to recover from a shock. Life is
short, yet everything seems to require so much time. I hoped I
wouldn't spend another ten years recovering. Antony and I
were both in a state of collapse when we met. Maybe it had
been an extended recuperation. We had protected each other,
but it was no longer necessary or interesting. We could go back
to being whoever we were—a no-fault statute of therapeutic
limitation. I was sick of feeling rejected and blaming him. If I
bored myself, how much did I bore him? He may not have
been wonderful for me, but it wasn't his fault that we didn't
care about the same things. He needed someone to care about
his public life, someone useful and decorative. I was neither,
not in the way he wanted, not ambitious; it didn't interest me.
Nicola was probably the girl for the job. Still, we had been so
happy once, so connected, so sure. It was sorrowful to see that
wash away, tumble into the flood and dissolve to nothing.

I had arrived at San Marco. There were the tourists, a few, as
usual, appearing to be devoured by pigeons. I felt a tenderness
toward them, the pigeons as well. Crossing the piazza I re-

membered the four of us in the darkness making our way to Renzo's, the dream of midnight debauchery, the enlightening afternoon, my history here. I felt nearly Venetian. And here was the turn for the Accademia Bridge; why not have a last moment alone with *Z*?

Back up the little staircase to the dim room and there it was, looking not at all like a disconnected artifact, looking instead and still like a profound and sacred dream. Clara's favorite. Was this Cecilia? It hardly mattered. Even if it was, it wasn't. This wasn't a picture about love and loss or time; this was the apprehension of essential, eternal beauty, archetypal, abundant. This was the heart of the dream that is life. To see that, Matteo said. To paint it. His eyes were on fire, Clara said. So, apparently, was his soul. He loved music and poetry; this picture was both, irreducible. He saw through things. How wonderful it would be to enter that scene, fly through the stirring sky like Clara's white dove. But who could bear it.

Ronald said Titian was fond of saying that Giorgione was jealous of him. Critics tried to deny his existence. Of course they would want to claim him, the heart of the lion. That was the way of the world. He was a lord of life; no one can tolerate that. But no one could deny him now either.

I turned to leave and encountered the face of *La Vecchia,* so enigmatic and unforgiving a portrait, everything *Tempesta* was not, the ravages of time. This was a face he loved as well; he hadn't attempted to make it anything other than what it was, ancient and collapsed. She was unnerving for that, but *Laura* wasn't idealized either. He wasn't ashamed of his mother. He didn't love a disembodied beauty. The light was shining everywhere for him. Maybe that's what *col tempo* really meant, to be immersed in time, the present moment containing all things. What a bright world he inhabited. Well, the Renaissance, nothing so fresh and revelatory for us. That's not what he was doing, it occurred to me, suggesting that he could see what we could not. It's always there. That's what he understood, what he saw in these women, these skies, these landscapes, himself. It's always there, inextinguishable, glowing, just behind the veil. You see, you see. He was generous to Clara; he was generous in all things and left these gifts, these insights that would never come loose from his meaning. Light is all—pay attention. Perhaps I was truly becoming a Neoplatonist. I had seen his light and for a brief moment my own. You had to start somewhere.

Outside, the day was still brilliant. I decided to go on walking and turned again toward the water. The Zattere quayside was expansive and nearly empty, a few people lingering over coffee outside cafés and seagulls shrieking, circling above looking for handouts. Then I saw it—on the façade of a church, oddly enough—the first one I'd seen, a *bocca di leone,* the lion's mouth. These menacing receptacles, by location, were designated for different sorts of offenses, everything from tardy garbage collection to treason. Which complaint did this one serve? Whatever it was, it would do.

I tore a page out of my red notebook and sat over a cup of coffee. I lit my last cigarette and tossed pieces of bread to the screeching gulls. Various declarations occurred to me, the furious to the apologetic. These for once would have to be my own feelings. For years my feelings had orbited around him. I felt his feelings, took them on as an act of devotion, his insecurities, his resentments, was fervent in justifying him; I thought it was expected of me, that he would love me for it. I gradually became aware that he was keeping the happy triumphant feelings for himself, not sharing those. I had become a sort of repository for his dark side, no longer Nel but the anti-Antony. Ready, willing, and disabled. The opposite of Clara. Was that the secret? The thing I had never understood? While I had taken up citizenship and pledged to die for a country whose map I had never seen, I was not a soldier after all; I was the national bank, perhaps the *bocca di leone,* a vault in which he could deposit everything not suitably enhancing. And that was intimacy. He could shine as I grew dark and dim and difficult.

It began to dawn on me, sitting there by the sparkling water, gulls crying, how simple it really was. Why do that? Why not do this instead? I didn't have to follow him around carrying resentment like a sherpa, awash in loneliness and disappointment. I could take myself away and become something else. Could it be that simple? Step off the juggernaut and watch it sail away or sink? We build a world on a moment of connection and cannot begin to imagine what that world will become. It always begins as love. Love and the unknown. Lucy said she expected betrayal in the diary; how much had her own betrayal cost her, beautiful and kind and good as she was? I did not want to live my life expecting betrayal. I would be stranded in a strange new place, but it would be somewhere; it would be mine, and a life that knew it was living whatever might befall. There would be time later to be a ghost. It was blasphemy to live like that.

Antony's face appeared to me suddenly from the very old days, a face I had loved, a face from an old photograph. Had he heard me? I conjured him? Could it be that he wanted that too? He had seemed to once. There was a time when I would have given everything for a private life with him; now I couldn't even think of him as a willing person, someone trying his best, a friend, a partner. 'Tis bitter cold, and I am sick at heart. But perhaps he did have hopes. I wasn't the one to ask. If he did, I wished him luck. I truly did wish him luck. Why not? Good luck to everyone.

But we were married. Changing that was no minor event. Marriage for Antony had been like a tax he had to pay; it martyred him; it made him angry and bored him. It always would, I thought; it didn't suit him. He probably shouldn't do it. But who could know? He didn't believe in change, but I did. I would always love something of what we had been, I thought, but I would never be his pearl, his blessing, his gift. Nice as that might have been. Nice as that might be. Well, I did my best, *caro,* I gave it my everything. Now let a thousand flowers bloom. I put out the cigarette.

Antony Casson might have done better. So might we all. His former wife, Cornelia, wishes him well and hopes that he will learn to pay attention. No charges sought.

I finished my coffee, dried my eyes, left the correct change, and crossed to the scowling letter box. Go, little book, I said. I folded the paper and dropped it into the grimacing jaws. Under a shining Venetian sky, I began the long walk home.

CHAPTER NINE

Lucy, it seems almost criminal.

Why is that? When have people not privately owned fabulous things? It does, after all, belong to us; the art police cannot come and accuse. No one knows it exists.

Clara's ring.

She would not want it to go out of the family, Lucy said, I'm sure of that.

We were in her room before the guests arrived for my farewell party—not farewell, bon voyage. Clara and I must be your daughters, Lucy, we must have been together at some point. China, I imagine, or India.

There has certainly been—what would one call it?—a kind of gravity, a force drawing us here, even the great Giorgione. We should feel grateful, not ask too many questions. It is this house! Alvise thought nothing of it, regarded it as third prize, but what a wellspring it turns out to be! You know, my dear, I lived quietly here for many years, just me, Annunziata, my dear dog, Bella, and then the wonderful Leo. I was perfectly happy with my work and the peacefulness, I had no idea. When Clara's wall began to peel, in swept Matteo, followed by you, then Lydia and Ronald; now I am spoiled. You have been a great blessing to me, Nel. In this short time you have indeed become like a daughter, something I never knew I wanted. And what a splendid one I got! Just at the last moment!

Do you regret not having children? I asked.

You know, I never thought so. Now I wonder. I might have loved all sorts of things I was unwilling to imagine. Perhaps with Alvise and the war I became a little afraid. Perhaps I lacked *fortezza*. I've always thought that there are mothers and there are daughters and that I was an eternal daughter. Or perhaps a sort of nun. I can see now that they were attractive. How can we know what other lives might have been? But look at the gifts we have been given! I am immensely grateful just to have survived to receive them. Very mysterious. But I don't want you to be afraid, my dear, I would like you to have everything you want, everything to make you happy. I want you to be as brave as can be. Imagine everything. Isn't that what mothers say?

Mine didn't, I said.

No, nor did mine. But I am saying it. And remember that whatever our relation may be, you are loved and I will be here for you as long as I am able.

I could not speak to reply.

Oh, and there's something else, she said, dabbing her eyes. Should you be interested. I think I would like to share the history of this house. If the old countess knew what we have found here, she would feel the same way; it would be a credit to the da Isola name, which meant so much to her. She laughed. How absurdly forgiving life can be, such eleventh-hour largesse. At any rate, I will make a grant available from the foundation if the project interests you, a comfortable grant. It will be a nice preliminary to your work with Clara.

Oh, yes, my work with Clara.

Now, now. Lydia believes you will do something with Clara, and we can never doubt Lydia. But you must learn Italian, you know. *Tu devi imparare italiano.* That won't take long. And you must come back. Leo has told me you must. Now, we can't keep them waiting. We have a special evening.

She took my hand and we walked together down the stairs and into the salon.

There were gifts from everyone. Lydia gave me an Italian grammar and an embroidered Indian shawl, Ronald a charming old reproduction of Gafurio announcing *Harmonia est discordia concors,* and Matteo a tiny antique mosaic pendant with a view of a town on a gold chain.

Is it Castelfranco? Lydia inquired, laughing.

It's Arcadia, Matteo replied. I had it authenticated.

We were well into the second bottle of champagne when Annunziata brought in the first of six courses, seafood antipasto, followed by risotto, a roasted chicken with grilled radicchio, salad, cheese, and finally tiramisu. It was an unexpectedly warm evening; the windows were open, the candles flickering. Leo seemed to know I was going and had not left my side. We'd all been toasting each other.

I would like to raise a toast to this young man—I said, turning to Leo—without whose enterprising spirit none of this happiness would have been possible. He took great risks and I believe he knew what he was doing, since he now knows how to order room service, has been invited out, and is surrounded with devotees. Lucy insists that we must listen to what dogs say. What Leo is saying is, I think, in the deathless words of William Blake, *Enough or too much!* To Leo the wise, to Leo the hero, to Leo the poet!

To Leo! everyone shouted. Leo, his name proclaimed, went leaping about among us.

The evening grew late, we became quiet but no one could leave the table. Everything would change now; we would no longer be a cabal. Perhaps when this enchantment faded it would be followed by something even sweeter and more enduring. It could happen.

My dear friends, Lucy said, poor celebrated Leo must rest. One last toast to the most extraordinary September in memory! Good night, my darlings, until we meet again. She regarded each of us with a smile and left the room, Leo at her heels, looking back, smiling his own familiar smile.

Soon after, Lydia and Ronald took their leave. It was impossible to imagine that by this time tomorrow night I would be in another country. Matteo closed the door and we stood again in the courtyard.

I found this place frightening, Matteo, the first time I saw it. I was afraid of Annunziata. I didn't think much of you.

I was sorry to see you arrive, he replied, I hoped you'd go away.

He took my hand and we went into the house. It was late.

His room was larger than mine. The ceiling was frescoed, the bed big and four-postered, a grass-green silk duvet, an ancient chest against the wall, pale pink plaster. I guess you weren't a nun, I remarked. No, never have been, he replied. It doesn't matter, I said, I have Clara. Well, yes, he replied, but I have you. We fell onto the bed.

This is nicer than the Gritti, I murmured into his neck, this is home.

I think so, he said, pulling off my sweater and kissing my shoulder. Soon he had pulled off everything and we were back to the obliterating place so recently discovered. It would be hard to leave this man.

You'll come to the airport? I asked.

The airport, whatever. You'll be back?

Wild horses, Matteo.

Wild horses?

I don't know what it means. It means I'll be back.

I woke at dawn and watched the morning assemble in my window. There was a quiet knock at the door and Annunziata appeared with a tray, coffee and rolls. This was unprecedented, her goodbye.

Grazie, Annunziata, e che bella cena ieri sera, I struggled to say, congratulating her on last evening's meal. I was on shaky ground, but she understood and wrapped me in a great hug. With an effort equal to mine she said, Come here! Come here! Then, pleased with her success, she backed out the door.

I had packed my things. Although it seemed appropriate and symmetrical, I would not be taking the train. I would fly. The train was overnight and I didn't wish to arrive a sleepless, rumpled mess. I put on Lucy's sweater, Matteo's necklace, and Clara's ring.

It was time to go downstairs. Goodbye, Clarissima, I said. I love you. Wish me luck.

Annunziata carried my bag to the courtyard. Matteo and Lucy were having coffee. Lucy poured a third cup and buttered toast for me. A good day for travel, she said, not a cloud; I don't know why anyone would look so desolate.

I'm covered with talismans, I replied. Energy overload. Come here, Leo. I gave him a piece of toast. I know it's forbidden, I said to Lucy, but I want him to long for my return. He never had a proper breakfast at the Gritti because we were apprehended.

Seized and detained, Matteo said. We must leave.

Leave.

We walked to the courtyard and stood at the door. I picked Leo up. Don't forget me, I said. He gave me the single solemn kiss reserved for Lucy, the kiss of true love.

You will call? Lucy said. You will tell me how you are?

I will call. I will tell you. I couldn't continue.

Arrivederci, cara, God bless. She took my hand and then embraced me; Leo squeezed between us. Remember that we are not a dream.

Or that we are, Matteo remarked, lifting my suitcase and opening the door. We will be here in any case.

Lucy waved with Leo in her arms until we turned the corner and headed for our water taxi.

These are both deities. This one is a goddess who destroys illusion, and this little elephant-headed one hands out candy and protects joy. I'm giving you Ganesh and I'll take Durga with me. Does that seem right?

My suitcase was gone. We were sitting in a lounge having, believe it or not, a glass of wine. Matteo regarded the gods. I think it's better if you leave me in charge of illusions and you take the happiness protector. I'm probably the one given to fantasy. He smiled.

You think I would forget? That this has been a lark? I didn't come here because I was happy, Matteo. I didn't know why I came. I never expected a Neoplatonist conversion, but who would. I'm spoiled. Lucy said that too. I may be back sooner than anyone cares to see me, such tender good-byes and I'm at the door in time for luncheon.

In the way of Italians, Matteo leaned across the table and kissed me at length.

My plane was boarding, a disembodied voice announced. I had to go through security. We rushed to the passport check and I was on the other side. We regarded each other across the barrier, people pushing past me. We blew a kiss and turned away.

How strange airports are, how quickly they neutralize life. Everyone falls into a zombielike trance animated by a diffuse subliminal tension. People don't often laugh or cry here. Children withstand being damped down because they're not in charge of anything. Children and drunks.

The plane lifted into a brilliant sky, the magical island spiraling away beneath us. Matteo was probably home by now. Home. Where was I going? Antony would send a car for me. I would be deposited in a hotel room. Did I have a book? No, I didn't want to go dormant waiting for him. If it was a nice day in Paris, I would walk. Even if it wasn't a nice day. Leave a note, go to the Louvre and look at sixteenth-century paintings, stroll in the Tuileries. It was Antony who loved Paris, but he would no longer be a free man. Nicola was by now in New York, collecting Liddie. I wondered how Natalie would respond to that. She would very deliberately treat her like an au pair. The old nonsense was rushing back and having the same effect as the airport; the chill was rising.

I tried to concentrate on Matteo leaning across the table and kissing me. I could feel some residual warmth but time and place are implacable. I was helplessly elsewhere already.

Outside the window, the fields were green and lush. I wondered if we had passed over Castelfranco. The house protected by angels, was it still there? Looking down on the countryside drenched in golden light, I saw it, *La Tempesta,* everything I felt seeing it for the first time, Zorzi and Clara, Lucy, Ca da Isola, Matteo, my darling Leo. It was mine. It would not let me go.

Are you all right? asked the Italian businessman seated next to me. Quite kindly.

Yes, fine. Thank you. Sorry.

And how did you enjoy Venice? he inquired.

ACKNOWLEDGMENTS

The author would like to thank her early readers for their insight and patience: Gillian Walker, Marguerite Whitney, Faith Stewart-Gordon, Clare and Eugene Thaw, Agnes Gund, Maeve Kinkead, Susanna Moore, Mary Porter, Louisa Sarofim and Tim Curry. Thanks to Sally Walker for preliminary brainstorming. Greatest thanks to Victoria Wilson for taking the chance and for her brilliant, and very firm, editorial guidance. My gratitude to K. J. P. Lowe for the indispensable *Nun's Chronicles and Convent Culture,* Mary Laven for *Virgins of Venice,* and, most of all, Jaynie Anderson for the definitive *Giorgione, The Painter of "Poetic Brevity."* Helen Brann, for imagining this.